Carly Reagon is the author of three novels: *The Toll House*, which was a Waterstones Welsh Book of the Month, *Hear Him Calling* and *The Infirmary*. In 2019 she was shortlisted for the Lucy Cavendish Prize for fiction. Her writing is inspired by her love of the Welsh countryside, where she lives with her husband and three children. She works as a senior lecturer at Cardiff University, is a keen runner and singer, and has an interest in anything historic.

THE
Infirmary

CARLY
REAGON

SPHERE

SPHERE

First published in Great Britain in 2025 by Sphere

1 3 5 7 9 10 8 6 4 2

A CIP catalogue record for this book
is available from the British Library.

ISBN 978-1-4087-3337-0

Typeset in Garamond Three by M Rules
Printed and bound in Great Britain by Clays Ltd, Elcograf S.p.A.

Papers used by Sphere are from well-managed forests
and other responsible sources.

Sphere	The authorised representative
An imprint of	in the EEA is
Little, Brown Book Group	Hachette Ireland
Carmelite House	8 Castlecourt Centre
50 Victoria Embankment	Dublin 15, D15 XTP3, Ireland
London EC4Y 0DZ	(email: info@hbgi.ie)

An Hachette UK Company
www.hachette.co.uk

www.littlebrown.co.uk

For Wilfred, Ebah and Taliesin

One holds the knife as one holds the bow of a cello or a tulip—by the stem. Not palmed nor gripped nor grasped, but lightly, with the tips of the fingers. The knife is not for pressing. It is for drawing across the field of skin. Like a slender fish, it waits, at the ready, then, go! It darts, followed by a fine wake of red. The flesh parts, falling away to yellow globules of fat. Even now, after so many times, I still marvel at its power—cold, gleaming, silent.

RICHARD SELZER,
Mortal Lessons: Notes on the Art of Surgery, 1974

REGULATIONS FOR THE OPERATING THEATRE

Spectators are only permitted by invitation of the surgeon. Only the surgeon, dressers, and surgeon's assistant may stand close to the table. Visitors must remain silent throughout.

CHARLES KELLER, 1848

1

AUGUST 2023

Liam

I lean over the steering wheel, my chin almost touching it, trying to make out what lies beyond the immediate shaft of light. It's dark, way darker than it ever is in the city. There's a sense of space, or rather emptiness, on either side beyond the hedgerow, and the air is sweet through the open window. I reach down, lift the paper cup from between my thighs, swallow a mouthful of coffee. It's two hours since we stopped at the services, ate over-priced pasties and pored over the route on Google Maps. The coffee is decidedly cold and everyone else is asleep: Jessica next to me in the passenger seat, Summer and Xanthe wedged between carrier bags in the back.

I pinch my forehead in an attempt to stay awake, buzz the window lower.

The house is amazing. Huge. A place to get lost in. You won't be disappointed.

The words from Callum's email circle my mind as I stare across at my sleeping wife, resisting the urge to reach out and touch her. She looks so perfect like that, her skin porcelain, her natural ringlets disappearing into the darkness. This year's been tough – the move and Jess's new job, Summer's new school, all the stuff that happened with Xanthe and that girl, Mia Williams, in our old town. Jess deserves a decent holiday, more so than she realises. I hope the house is going to be everything Callum promised and more.

At the thought of Callum, I peer into the rearview mirror, but there's not a car or person in sight. No headlights, no fleeting shadows. I breathe more easily, reminding myself it's just a holiday. A space to relax. Despite my reservations, Callum's doing us a favour.

I turn my attention back to the road ahead, weave the car around a bend, the headlights picking out a vast block of white, making me start. But the thing ahead of me is just a church in white stone, probably the church with the same name as the house: St Cross. I laugh at myself, wiping spilled coffee from my shorts. I'm nervous, that's all, and it's not surprising. I've never been to Suffolk before, and this is the holiday where I'm going to tell Jess everything. No more secrets. No more lies.

I wedge the paper cup back between my thighs.

The road darkens, deepens. Trees again. The sense of things closing in around me. I reach for my phone and jab in my password, illuminating Callum's instructions. After the church, there should be a gate. I concentrate hard through the windscreen, turning up the heater fan to clear the condensation. The atmosphere's changed, the heatwave that's plagued us for weeks has finally broken and we've driven through a couple of showers to get here. Typical for the weather to turn, just when we're getting away.

Another tight bend. I grip the steering wheel harder, thrusting the gears into second. A tall metal gate with elaborate ironwork leers back at me in the headlights, huge metal snakes weaving lifelike around the pickets.

I park in the middle of the road and get out. An immediate whip of sea wind throws me backwards, wrestling hair from my forehead, rippling my T-shirt. I grab the gate to steady myself; grab hold of one of the snakes. It's bloody cold. The snake. The wind. Goosebumps rise along my arms. It's like the depths of winter out here. I push against the gate, panicking that it's locked, that we'll have to spend the night huddled in the car. Looking behind me, I see how precarious the car is on the bend of the road. The lane is so narrow, there's no room to manoeuvre around it. I'm so stupid, parking like that; someone could easily come whizzing around the corner. I push harder, desperate, my mind running through worst-case scenarios: headlights, screeching tyres, the smell of burning rubber. The gate groans. It's stiff, that's all, requiring all my strength to ram it open, to slide each half against the tangles of ivy.

Back inside the car, I wipe my hands down my face as Jess straightens up and peers through the windscreen. 'Are we there?'

'Uh-huh.'

I nudge the car down the driveway. A rabbit bolts from the undergrowth, disorientated, zigzagging down the track. I follow it, enjoying the pursuit, the driveway bending one way and then the other, finally opening up into a larger area with a central turning circle and an austere stone fountain. But there's something in our path, blocking the way. The engine stalls as I focus. A silver snake like the ones on the gate, only this one's alive, twisting on the gravel. Not twisting, I think, watching it flicking itself up and down, but *writhing*. I'm about to point it out, ask Jess if she knows what the hell it is, when it disappears. I blink. There's nothing there. Just the empty drive and the fountain and the house: St Cross. The place Callum described as a quintessential English manor house. Picture perfect. Only it's not that at all. From what I can see in the headlights, it's a monster of grey stone, the chimneys and the domed roof stark against the moonlit sky.

'Here we are,' I say, trying my best to sound upbeat. But really, I'm still thinking about that snake.

I open the car door and wrap my arms around myself for warmth. Jess follows, and I can feel her hunched at my shoulder, taking it all in, silently passing judgement.

In front of us is a stone porch. An unlit metal lantern swings in the wind, creaking back and forth. I find myself whistling as I walk beneath it to the front door, a crisscross of iron rivets. Whistling to prove I'm brave. That this is all as expected. I lift the knocker – another snake – and send it clattering down on the old wood, knowing no one's going to answer. It's a stupid thing to do, because I've got the keys in my pocket.

Jess looks at me quizzically as if so say, *What did you do that for?*, and I shrug. I can't explain it. I've been told there's no one here, that we'll have the place to ourselves, but I can't shake the feeling someone's waiting for us inside.

Invitation card, dated 27 July 1840:

St Cross Infirmary, Grand Opening

Built to honour the twenty-first birthday of the son of Lord and Lady Massingham of Blythe Manor, and to support the care of the sick poor, St Cross Infirmary will open formally on the third day of August 1840 for public inspection. The building has been built to a modern design, mimicking those institutions of a penitentiary nature, the purpose being to optimise care and surveillance of those most in need. At his lordship's invitation, visitors are welcome to take a tour of the house followed by tea in the garden.

2

SUMMER

———⊸⊷⊶⊷⊷⊶———

It takes a moment to remember where I am, stretching beneath the stiff bedsheets and the faded patchwork quilt: not home but St Cross, the building that was only a shadowy outline of chimneys and windows last night in the dark. The bedroom is lit by slanting sunlight – Mum doesn't believe in closing curtains unless it's winter – dappled by the fingers of ivy that brush the window in the breeze. I breathe in the smell of the room, dust and old linen, a smell I should have got used to over the course of the night but which irritates me still.

I reach beneath my pillow, pull out my phone, groan at the practically non-existent signal. There's no way I can survive without Wi-Fi out here. Throwing off the quilt, I search for the slippers I dragged from our case last night. On the opposite side of the room, Xanthe sighs in her sleep, tossing in the cot bed that's way too small for a kid of seven.

Last year had been different. A million worlds away from this. Dad had written a bestseller and we'd spent the summer holidays in the south of France, hanging out at the pool, Mum and Dad in the bar, Xanthe on the sun lounger. And then there was the boy from the chalet next door, the boy I'd got friendly with. *Harry.* Two years older than me, doing his A levels, light-brown freckles, a fringe that flopped over his eyes, a grin that made me melt inside. While Mum and Dad were at the bar, we'd made the most of our freedom, inventing cocktails from his parents' minibar and walking hand in hand on the beach. Afterwards, we'd kept in touch, swapping text messages, making plans to hang out in the holidays again, the same block of chalets, the same pool, the same lethal drinks.

But, this year, Dad hasn't managed to sell anything more than a couple of short stories, and Mum's always moaning about the rent. So we're here, in the Suffolk countryside rather than the French Riviera, house-sitting some old lady's mansion whilst she visits her son in Scotland.

Country pile, Dad had tried to sell it to us, but judging from what I've already seen, more like a pile of shit. For a start, the place is caked in dust, which means Mum will spend the whole holiday cleaning, flexing her OCD muscles to the full.

Slippers on, I tiptoe towards the door, trying to guess where the creaky floorboards lie and the best route to avoid them. No point waking Xanthe, she'll only be grumpy. Worse still, she'll insist I climb into the cot and play vets. Too late. The floorboard wheezes beneath me and Xanthe shifts. Shifts but, thank God, doesn't wake. There are plenty of bedrooms Xanthe could have chosen, bedrooms with proper beds.

Instead, she'd decided to squeeze herself into the ridiculously small cot.

'Why?' I'd asked her last night, too tired to argue properly.

Xanthe had shrugged. 'This place is really creepy.'

I'd given her a hug. Fair point. The house *is* creepy, not the place Dad had painted at all. When we'd arrived, I'd sensed the house before I'd seen it, like a stranger watching me in the dark. Immediately, I'd not wanted to go in. Even in the moonlight, the building was ugly. *Openings*, I'd thought without knowing why, hating the way the word had crept inside me. *Openings*.

I open the bedroom door as quietly as I can and make my way on to the gallery landing. From here the entire house seems to be visible. I see the hall where we entered last night, the piles of magazines on the table, the dust, the cobwebs. The whole place reeks of cat shit, reminding me of the other job Dad had tried to impress on us as a perk: looking after the old lady's three house cats. The entrance hall reaches all the way to the domed roof, capped by a circular window that casts a dappled, uneven light. What looks like a couple of seagulls pad about on top, distorting the light through the dirty panes. Just below the roof, to the right of where I'm standing, there's a window on the inside wall that's been blocked up. A blotch in the plaster, the outline of the window still visible. It must be an attic room.

I lower my gaze. On the ground and first floors, doors lead off in every direction. No corridors, just the massive hallway with its earth-coloured tiles. The thought strikes me that there's nowhere to hide. Or rather, there are plenty of places to hide, but no way to really escape. There are no corridors, only the space I'm looking at now and the doors. The only way out, unless I'm mistaken, is through the entrance hall. The landing is like some weird surveillance platform. But I'm being silly. Why would I need to escape? It might not be France, but it's hardly Alcatraz either. There must be a back door somewhere. *Openings.*

I creep downstairs, past the room directly over the porch – the room Mum and Dad have claimed as theirs – then down the staircase with its deep red runner, into the hall. The staircase is freestanding and sweeps to the right as it descends. The banisters are worn oak and the posts at the end are crowned by a pair of dusty statutes.

I try a door on the left, looking for the router – a study that smells of old books; then a door on my right – a lounge with gross, flower-patterned furniture and an ancient TV. No luck. Next, I try the door directly opposite the front one, and find myself in a large, old-fashioned kitchen, painted in peeling brown and cream, the walls divided into two by a waist-high panel. There's a wooden table which presumably we're meant to sit around to eat but is jammed with papers and crockery and empty jars. My eyes are drawn to the servant bells near the ceiling, supported by coiled loops of metal swathed in cobwebs; the sort of bells you see in the stately homes Mum likes to take us to. Only some of the labels on the bell board are legible.

FRONT DOOR || DINING ROOM || PARLOUR

The rest are too faded with age to read. I wonder briefly if they still work, if they're still rigged up. Then I carry on my search for the router, desperate now, scanning the workstations, hefty wooden units that look like they've stood here for ever, moving stuff aside: empty jam jars, pill packets, newspapers, cookery books, bags of cereal. There's an ancient first-aid kit that spills when I lift it, the lid coming away freely. A roll of yellowing bandage runs away from me across the floor. Rusty safety pins scatter at my feet. There's a smell of antiseptic and the sharpness of old metal. I bend down, bundle the whole lot back inside the box, set it on the worksurface, then sift through the rest of the junk on the table.

Something shrieks at me from the side.

I press a hand to my chest, *God*, and drop what I'm holding – an open bag of Alpen, the contents spilling all over the tiles – my gaze landing on the back door, partly hidden behind a floor-length curtain. So there is another opening after all. A matted ball of black fluff is scratching through it to get out. One of Mrs Clarence's cats.

'Hey, little one.' Ignoring the mess, I bend down and nervously reach out a hand, expecting at any moment to be attacked. 'You're meant to be a house cat.'

The cat stops its scratching and purrs loudly, rubbing its back against my outstretched hand. Its fur is stuck out at angles, flecked with loose skin, a cobweb tangled over one ear.

'Poor thing.' I try unsticking the cobweb but it's welded to its fur. The cat presses harder against my hand. 'You're hungry, right?'

I look around for food. There are three feeding bowls on the floor beside the range stuck with dirt, a bowl of water, a litter tray that stinks and doesn't seem to have been changed in ages. Mum's going to have her work cut out. Eventually, I locate a half-bag of kibble and some tins of sardines in one of the cupboards, but the cat's scratching again through the curtain, desperate to get out.

'Okay,' I relent. 'As long as you promise to come back or else I'm in deep trouble.' I draw the curtain back fully, then turn the key in the lock. 'Promise me, you'll come back, little cat?' I hunt for a name but there's no collar. 'I'll call you Alpen, okay?'

I say, glancing at the split bag of Alpen as I lower the handle and open the door.

The key slides from the lock, landing with a tinkle on the tiles. I bend to retrieve it, and the door swings wide, letting in a breeze. Straightening up again, I let out a small scream. A woman is standing on the terrace, staring right at me.

'The doctor's here,' the woman says.

I blink, trying to unscramble my thoughts.

'The doctor's here,' she says again as if I haven't quite heard her. 'I saw him from the path.' She's wearing a dressing gown patterned with tiny blue flowers. Her cheeks and forehead are lined with wrinkles. Her greasy white hair is scraped back from her face into a low ponytail, pinned with a crisscross of kirby grips.

'I'm sorry?' I say, my mind still racing. Is this the owner, Mrs Clarence, not gone to visit her son after all, but checking up on us? Checking how well we're looking after her mangy cats? Instinctively, I survey the garden, looking for Alpen. To my relief, I spot him on the stone wall that divides the upper garden from the lower one, arching his back in a stretch. He seems to be having a stand-off with a Jack Russell who's growling up at him from the foot of the wall.

'Angel and I saw him from the path,' the woman repeats, turning in the direction of the wall, at the path that leads through a gap to the side of it, and the wood beyond. 'And I thought you should know.'

'Mrs Clarence? You are Mrs Clarence, right?'

'Marianne Clarence is away. She's gone to Scotland.'

I nod. *Right.* I don't know what to do, whether to invite the woman in, whether to ask what she's doing on Mrs Clarence's property. If she isn't Mrs Clarence, who the hell is she?

The woman reaches out and rests a hand on the door frame. 'We saw him in the dining room, Angel and I.' She points along the length of the back wall to an out-of-sight window.

'I don't think I get you,' I say, still trying to get a grasp on the situation. 'There isn't a doctor here.'

'And I'm telling you, there is.'

I force a smile. 'Okay. I'll look out for him. Is there anything else?'

The woman hesitates as if to say something more, as if there's something playing on her mind, then she flashes a thin smile. 'Take care, that's all.' She turns away without saying goodbye, calling the dog to follow her. I wait until they've vanished into the wood, then scan the lawn for Alpen, my gaze flitting to the wall, the garden shed, the remains of what looks like an old greenhouse. But the only movement is the wind in the trees, and the ripple of pink and purple flowers. Alpen's disappeared from sight.

3

Liam

I awake with a start, my heart pounding, my forehead covered in a fine film of sweat. Sitting upright, I run my hands through my hair. My scalp is clammy and my back is cool against the iron headboard. There was something in my dream, something deeply disturbing, something that makes my stomach twist even now. But it darts away from me before I have a chance to catch it. The only thing I can remember is light through a window and the sound of tapping.

Tap . . . tap . . . tap . . .

I swing my head, wondering if I'm still dreaming, but the sound immediately disappears. I smooth my fringe from my eyes, pressing my back harder against the bedstead. I need a shower, a shave, a complete freshen up.

The night before comes back to me, the long drive, the iron

gates, the snake, the swinging lantern. St Cross – the place I'd told Jess and the girls I'd found on the internet. House-sitting for the summer. A country mansion in Suffolk. The lap of luxury. *God.*

I run my hands down my face, ashamed of my lies, then reach along the cool width of the bed, searching for Jess. She's not there. First day of our holiday and she's probably organising the house or fixing breakfast. Problem with having a near-perfect wife is I feel constantly inadequate. I turn my gaze towards the ceiling, the black mould spores spreading through the cream, permeating the air. Fleetingly, I wonder if it's safe, breathing it in. I remember the peeling paintwork in the hallway, the general mustiness, the cracked linoleum in the bathroom where I cut my foot last night.

I turn in the opposite direction, towards the window. In the summer, Jess always sleeps with the curtains open, insisting she likes to wake up with the dawn. But the window unsettles me. A sash window like the window in my dream, crowned with a glass arch. I have the uncanny impression I've been staring at it all night.

I close my eyes, listening to the pulse in my ear pressed against the pillow, but the window's still there in my mind, and another fragment of my dream comes back to me. I was lying in an almost-bare room, staring at the window, watching the snow fall outside, rigid with fear. *Fear.* That's the part that doesn't make any sense. Why on earth was I fearful? I have a boyish delight in snow; I prefer winter to summer, cosy evenings in, watching films with the girls while the weather rages outside.

I hurl myself out of bed and instinctively look out through the window – the real window this time. The driveway is empty except for our car. There's no sign of anyone else about. No cars. No people. We're safe here, I remind myself. Flecking sleep from my eyes, I make a fuller inspection of the room we only glanced at last night: the antique chest of drawers, the wardrobe set in the wall with ornate brass doorknobs, the red Turkish carpet and the green chaise longue. If you don't look too closely, if you ignore the moth holes in the rug and the ripped silk on the chaise longue and the bedsheets that are so old they're practically translucent, it's almost passable. I yank open the chest of drawers beneath the window. There's a pile of folded lace-edged handkerchiefs and old-fashioned knickers, brushes with ebony handles, a handheld mirror. Shoving it closed again, shutting out the smell of mothballs, I wonder whose bedroom this is. *Or was.* The instructions Callum gave me are clear: Mrs Clarence's bedroom is locked, but the rest of the house is ours for the duration; we can use whatever we want, there are no other inhabitants, and yet this room . . . This room is clearly lived in.

I open the wardrobe door nearest to the window, the smell of old clothes making me gag. A deep fusty scent of wool and stale body odour. One hand over my mouth, I run the other over rough tweed coats. A sandy-coloured stole, draped over what seems to be an opera coat, looks convincingly like real fur, and when I pull it out, I see the glassy eyes of a fox's head. On closer investigation, it's not just the fox. There's a weasel and another, lighter-furred animal, both turned into hats.

I push the whole lot back into the wardrobe and close the door, then drag the chest of drawers away from the window so it's rammed against it. It would freak Jess out if she found all this, and a freaked-out wife is the last thing I need. I need this holiday to work. I need Jess to relax.

The door swings open and Xanthe screeches into the room, throwing me backwards on to the bed.

'Hello, Little Bear,' I say as Xanthe clambers on top of me.

'Hello, Daddy.'

'What do you think about the house?'

She rolls away from me and sits upright. 'I've drawn a picture of our room.' She shows me the diary in her hand, then unlocks the little padlock, and turns to today's date. The room she's drawn is depicted through the bars of the cot. She'd insisted last night she didn't want to sleep anywhere else and for reasons I couldn't fathom – I still can't fathom – it had made me uneasy. The drawing shows the wooden bars, the old-fashioned teddy sat at the end of it, Summer's bed on the other side of the room, Summer fast asleep, one arm trailing down, brushing the floor, the sleeve of a frilly nightdress.

'It's brilliant,' I say, searching for something constructive to say. We've been told Xanthe's artwork is exceptional for her age. 'You've captured the light, and the furniture, and Mrs Clarence's old clutter. But you should have drawn pyjamas. Summer was wearing pyjamas last night.'

Xanthe frowns. 'No, she wasn't. I drew her this morning, when I woke up. It was exactly what she was wearing.'

I laugh and ruffle her hair. 'You know best, Little Bear. After all, you're the one who's going to be a famous artist one day. We'll have to call you Leonardo.'

Xanthe jumps off the bed. 'I prefer Picasso. Come on, let's find Mum and Summer. I think I smell croissants.'

I laugh again at her wishful thinking and follow her out the door to the landing. But while Xanthe happily patters downstairs, I find myself strangely immobile. It's the space that strikes me, the cupola, the view down to the ground floor, the doors barring the view of the rooms around the entrance hall. The hall is lined with shadowy paintings, variations on the same religious theme. The fact I'm not remotely religious makes them all the more sinister; it's like they're passing judgement, scowling at the nonbeliever. As I stare, I've a weird impression the doors in the hallway are gently opening and closing, as if waiting for something to happen. Something to escape. But nothing else moves. Not even one of the mythical cats. Only specks of silver dust, hovering in the murky light from the roof, and Xanthe running into the kitchen.

'Hurry up, Daddy,' she calls over her shoulder.

I'm suddenly aware of my vulnerability, standing there in my boxers and T-shirt. I know it's stupid. Normally, at home, I'd think nothing of padding downstairs in my underwear, helping myself to whatever cereal the girls haven't eaten, drifting through the morning with a cup of coffee and my phone, then getting dressed fully about eleven. But somehow, here, I feel naked. Really naked.

I turn back into the bedroom to throw on a pair of shorts, catching sight of my phone beside the bed, blinking into life. I pick it up. There are a couple of WhatsApp messages and a notification from my broker. I scan the messages quickly before switching the whole lot to mute, then I grab my shorts from the chaise longue, inadvertently ripping the green silk with my fingernails. I stare at the ripped silk in silent horror, another detail from my dream spiralling through my mind.

The room was green. The room I was lying in, watching the snow fall, was plastered in light-green wallpaper.

4

───⊗⊗⊗───

Jess

The kitchen is already causing me a headache. The jars, the newspapers, the dirty floor. How can anyone live like this? I step around what looks like spilled cereal, heading in the direction of my eldest daughter. She's standing at the window, engrossed in her phone, and jumps when I touch her. I hold my hands up. 'Sorry, I didn't mean to scare you. Have you seen the cats?' I glance at the empty basket on the floor. 'I've seen the white one and the tabby, but there should be three. I've looked everywhere.'

Summer shakes her head. 'Is there any coffee around here?' She opens a cupboard and grimaces.

I rub my forehead. I know exactly what Summer thinks about this holiday without even asking. This year's been difficult in more ways than one. I also know there was a boy at the chalets last year in France, Summer's first love, a boy she was hoping to meet again this year. I lean over her shoulder, examining the rows of Kilner jars: dried beans, dried lentils, brown rice. No labels, so it's impossible to know how old this stuff is, whether there's anything actually edible. According to Liam, we can help ourselves to anything in the house, but the crusted jar tops don't fill me with confidence.

'I brought coffee with us,' I say. 'It's in one of the bags.' I rummage through the plastic carriers on the workstation, find the jar and hand it over. Then I make a decision: I'm going for a walk. Before I tidy this place up, I need some fresh air.

Leaving Summer to her coffee, I step outside. The mustiness of the kitchen is immediately replaced by a tingling sea breeze. The sea is two miles away, and I'm determined to make my way there. It's exactly what I need after a stressful year, losing my job, finding a new one, trying to make ends meet. I tell myself St Cross might not be perfect by a long stretch, but at least it's a break, a chance to spend time together as a family. A chance to relax. A chance to spend quality time with Liam. I windmill my arms, then reach behind and massage my shoulders.

From what I've seen on the internet, googling in my lunch breaks, the Suffolk coastline is amazing. Maybe Liam will be inspired here? Maybe he'll let me read his new book? The last one, a fantasy, had sold in the thousands, made the *Sunday Times* bestseller list, and we'd celebrated with champagne before treating ourselves to a fortnight in France. But since then, there's been nothing of note – Liam still hasn't delivered his second manuscript – and in hindsight, last summer seems decidedly reckless.

I breathe deeply, filling my lungs with fresh air, still smoothing the knots in my shoulders. The garden is huge but simple:

a two-tiered lawn with a wall dividing the levels, a terrace and a couple of flowerbeds. I decide I'll spend time out here rather than in the house. There must be deckchairs somewhere, I'll go rooting for them later.

I walk along the terrace to the left edge of the garden until I locate a broken part of the hedge. I straddle it easily, then walk along the side of a rough-grassed field to a dirt track that follows the perimeter of the wood. Eventually, the dirt track meets the road and a small, red-bricked cottage. It takes me by surprise. I'd not anticipated any other residence for miles. Last night, the place had seemed desolate. I admire the neat red brick, the tidy flowerbeds, the path lined with plastic windmills that fly around merrily in the breeze. There's a homeliness to the house that is missing from St Cross and, not for the first time in the last twelve hours, it makes me wish we'd found somewhere else to spend the summer. A cottage within easy walking distance of the beach. A static caravan. A tent in a field.

It takes me a moment to realise I'm being watched, stared at by a teenager standing beneath the porch.

'Hi,' I say, feeling embarrassed. 'Do you live here?'

He rolls his eyes at my question and lifts a vape to his lips.

I cough awkwardly into my fist. 'Do you know how I can get to the beach?'

'Yes.'

I wait for instructions before realising I'm not going to get any. He's answered my question literally. 'Down that road, then. Right?'

'Right.' He turns indoors.

I push aside my irritation and continue along the road, passing another cottage, this one smaller and single storey, reminiscent of the gatehouses I've seen at stately homes. I wonder if it was once connected to St Cross. Perhaps the original driveway ran through the wood? But the styles are different. The cottage is rectangular and plain, whereas the house is all arches and decorative stonework. Compared to the other cottage, the gatehouse is unkempt. The net curtains at the windows are stained yellow, the garden is a tangle of long grass and weeds, the washing line is spotted with rust. But there are signs of life: pillow cases billow on the line, and a dog yaps as I pass, jumping at the gate, then following my progress along the road until it reaches the far edge of the garden. I can still hear it yapping as I leave it behind, stretching my legs along the tarmac, feeling the fresh breeze against my skin, my eyes watering. The weather's changed. A week ago, it was too hot to exercise other than first thing in the morning, but today the wind is cutting.

The road bends to the left as I near the sea. I take the way-marked footpath through the field ahead, keeping a straight line towards my destination. I hear the waves before I see them, smashing against the rocks below, the smell of salt and seaweed drawing me down. But reaching the coastal path, I realise there's no direct way down to the beach from here.

Reluctantly, I turn back the way I've come, retracing my steps past the gatehouse and the cottage. This time, I take a direct path through the wood to the house. The wood is deeper than I'd thought, and I'm careful to stick to the wider path, ignoring the myriad smaller openings on my right.

Soon, I'm back in the garden, taking the ascent towards the house. There's a man in the middle of the upper lawn, fiddling with the starter string on his mower. He tips his cap at me as I near. 'Morning.'

'Morning,' I say, slowing to a halt. 'I'm Jess. We're staying here. I'm sorry, we weren't expecting anyone . . .'

'Harrison,' he says, wiping an oil-smudged hand down his overalls. 'Peter Harrison. I keep the gardens for Marianne Clarence.'

'Nice to meet you.'

'Nice to meet you too.' He shakes my hand. 'I'm here most days. How are you getting on in the infirmary?'

'The infirmary?' A breeze whispers against my neck, lifting my ponytail. I look up at the dark house, the place that until now, I'd presumed was the local stately home.

Peter Harrison follows my gaze. 'St Cross.'

'We only arrived last night. We're still getting used to it. Why did you call it the infirmary?'

He rests his arms on the handle of the mower. 'That's what it used to be in the old days.'

'I thought it was the local manor.'

He shakes his head. 'The manor house was pulled down yonks ago. It was back there in the fields. There's only a gatehouse standing now. It was the lord of the manor who had the infirmary built.'

I glance back the way I've come, remembering the little house and the yapping dog, but I can't see the road from here. 'I'm afraid I don't know anything about the history of the place. My husband found the house advertised on the internet. We're looking after the cats while Mrs Clarence is in Scotland.'

Peter smiles sadly. 'It'll be the last long trip she makes.'

'The last trip?'

He picks a callus on his thumb. 'She had a stroke last year. My wife, Susan, found her on the terrace. We were surprised when Marianne said she was going to Scotland. She's very unsteady on her feet, poor thing. There's only so much time before she's housebound. But she's proud. Stubborn.

She doesn't want any help, not from the services, not from anyone.'

'I see. I'm sorry. That must be hard on her son.'

He snorts and chews the callus. 'Money-thieving bastard. Probably can't wait to see her pop her clogs. The only time we've seen him around here is when he wants something. Is that one of yours?' He nods again at the house, and I turn to see Xanthe on the terrace, holding her diary.

'My youngest. Xanthe.'

'You have more?'

'We've two. Summer is sixteen.'

Peter digs in his overalls, pulls out a packet of cigarettes and lights one. 'I'm surprised.'

'Surprised?

'Marianne isn't one for children. Never seen children at the house before.'

I look back at the terrace, waving at Xanthe before she disappears inside. 'What about her son?'

'Stepson by her second marriage. He was an adult by the time she married Mr Clarence.'

'And this was originally Mr Clarence's house?'

'No.' He takes a drag on his cigarette and blows out smoke. 'Marianne inherited the property when her first husband, Mr Laurence, died. Now she's there all alone.'

I remember the feeling I'd had last night when Liam had flicked on the light switches, the slow blink of electricity illuminating the gloomy paintings in the hall. I can't imagine why anyone would want to live in a place like that on their own, but then I remember the cats. Mrs Clarence isn't alone, is she? I mention this to Peter and he scowls.

'You don't like cats?' I say.

'I'm allergic.'

'So that's why she advertised for someone else to look after the place.'

He snorts again. 'I don't know anything about that. That'll be that meddling stepson of hers. Mr Clarence died twenty years ago. She should have cut ties with her stepson there and then. Should have sold St Cross and bought something more manageable. But she's something of an eccentric. A fact you've probably gathered from the state of the house.' He grinds his barely smoked cigarette into the lawn, straightens the rim of his cap. 'Well, it's been nice meeting you. Look after your daughters. If you want anything, we're down at the cottage.'

'The cottage? I think I met someone there earlier. A boy——'

'Our grandson. He's a handful. Staying with us for the summer.' He chuckles to himself. 'Think they know everything at that age, don't they?'

I smile politely, thinking about the monosyllabic youth, then say my goodbyes before running up the final slope of the lawn. I open the back door to a flurry of activity. The tabby cat skitters across the floor, chasing a tennis ball, followed by Xanthe. Summer is sitting on top of the workstation, scrolling through her phone. Water boils fiercely in a pan on the old range, billowing steam. Liam has cleared a space on the table and is using a knife to prise open a plastic wrap of fish. There's a smell of cats and coffee and decay.

'Morning,' he beams, the knife flashing. 'I found kippers in the freezer. I'm microwaving them for breakfast and poaching eggs.'

I raise my eyebrows. Liam's cooking is infamous. 'I think I'll have porridge.'

I search through the plastic carrier bags we brought with us from home, find a box of oats, then look for a saucepan, my eyes drawn momentarily to the servant bells.

FRONT DOOR ‖ DINING ROOM ‖ PARLOUR

I take a step forwards, reading another label in the altered light:

WOMEN'S WARD

'Did you know this place used to be a hospital?' I say then immediately regret it. Liam hates hospitals. He's got a phobia, something to do with a botched-up appendix operation as a kid. It's a white snake of memory on his lower abdomen and one he never talks about. I haven't pressed him either – it's the one subject that's out of bounds. As a result, I'm in charge of all things medical. Whenever the kids get ill, it's my job to oversee doctor's appointments, or buy painkillers and cough syrups from the pharmacy. It's exhausting carrying the weight of it all, but I know I have to. Someone has to.

Liam pierces the knife through the wrap of kippers, stabbing the table. 'Shit.'

I look at him pointedly and mouth the word 'language'. From the workstation, Summer rolls her eyes.

'It hasn't been a hospital for years,' I say, trying to play down what I've just said. 'Not according to the gardener. I met him in the garden.'

'Right.' Liam sounds relieved but he doesn't look it, still stabbing the fish through the plastic wrap.

*

I unpack the suitcases, starting in the girls' room, finding a space in the wardrobe among the heaps of yellowed linen. I make the bed, smooth the blanket in the cot, plump dust from the old-fashioned teddy bear. *Marianne isn't one for children.* I wonder who the cot belonged to. It's an old style, white wood, a painted Mickey Mouse at the head end, a lumpy mattress. I'll try persuading Xanthe into one of the other rooms, though she'd seemed determined last night; she wanted to sleep near Summer.

I retrace my steps to the room next door, the bedroom overlooking the porch. Despite sleeping here all night, it's the first time I've really looked at it: the huge iron bedstead, the tatty furniture. The wardrobe is much smaller than the one in the girls' room, and the chest of drawers is rammed against the doors at the far end. I lay our clothes in piles on the chaise longue, counting the clothes in threes – *one, two, three; one, two, three* – an old habit, but one which makes me instantly calm. As I'm counting, something catches my eye beneath the window. I walk towards it and bend down. It's a slim notebook wedged behind the exposed pipework, in the space – judging by the marks on the floor – where the chest of drawers had once stood. Intrigued, I pull it out, wipe away the film of dust and cobwebs. I open the faded red cover and realise it's old. Very old. The pages are water damaged and scrawled with spidery brown ink that's almost illegible. I turn to the front of the book, and trace the lettering on the inner page, larger than the rest and easier to read: *Charles Keller 1847.*

There's something about the writing that pulls me in, that invites me to read further, or rather, spend hours deciphering what's written there. It's written, I think, with *passion*. But not now. Not until I've finished tidying. So I put the notebook on the chest of drawers for looking at later.

In the bathroom, I arrange our toothbrushes in a pot and make a mental note to scrub the huge freestanding bath before I take a dip. There's no shower, and the linoleum floor is so cracked and dirty, I'm afraid for the girls walking on it in bare feet. I leave the door open to allow the air to circulate and explore the other rooms on the first floor: four more rooms filled with junk. Beds are heaped with boxes of books, knickknacks, damp-smelling linen, old scraps of lace, ancient electrical items – radios, cassette players, vacuum cleaners, toasters. Despite my earlier enthusiasm, I decide there's no point even starting on these rooms; unless Xanthe really wants a bedroom of her own, I'll leave them as they are. Mrs Clarence is obviously a hoarder and the air is stale; a fusty, rotten smell. I open the windows in each room, just a crack, as far as they'll go, then close the doors.

There's only one other room to explore, on the other side of the girls' room, but it's locked. Mrs Clarence's bedroom. I pause outside the door, almost as if I expect to hear someone moving about inside. The smell is stronger here. The foetid smell of the house I'd put down to the cats last night. But, now that I think about it, how can three cats make a building of this size smell so bad? Besides, it's not just the smell of a festering litter tray. It's worse than that. It's rotten and sweet; a smell that creeps beneath my skin. I bend down and press my eye against the keyhole. I can't see much, but what I do see confuses me. Bare floorboards, a simple chair, a window like the one in the room Liam and I have taken, only narrower and without curtains. There must be a bed, but it's hidden from sight, and it doesn't seem exactly homely. There are none of the trinkets adorning the other rooms. None of the soft furnishings as far as I can see.

I look again, pressing my eye harder against the keyhole, but immediately, the space inside turns black as if someone's thrown a cloth over the doorknob, or someone's standing right behind the door, purposely blocking my view.

Cold tingles down my spine. 'Summer? Xanthe? You know you're not supposed to be in there.' But even as I say it, I know the girls are downstairs.

I stand upright, testing the doorknob one last time, feeling something brush my legs. I look down startled: the tabby cat is circling my feet. The room is firmly locked and, as far as I'm aware, there's no other way in. My mind whirls. It's probably just a cover for the keyhole on the other side, swinging free with the pressure of my hands. But, still I can't shake the sense there's someone in there. Someone who doesn't want me prying.

I'm impressed by a sudden feeling it's not just the room. I'm being watched from somewhere else in the house. Somewhere along the landing. I spin around just as a scream cuts the air, followed by a deathly silence. The tabby cat slinks away, reaching the top of the stairs and then descending. Do cats scream like that? I must have stood on its tail by mistake.

I watch it make its way down the stairs, into the entrance hall, settling in one of the chairs by the front door. The light through the glass roof changes as a cloud passes the sun. The cat flicks its tail up and down as if it senses something. And I sense it too, or rather, I *see* it: the doors on the ground floor gently, ever so gently, swaying.

ST CROSS INFIRMARY
RULES FOR PATIENTS

- Upon admittance to the infirmary, all
  patients must bathe immediately.
- Not more than two visitors will be permitted
  for each patient and only with express
  prior permission of the matron.
- Patients must keep their beds neat and tidy and,
  where able, assist in the general tidiness of the
  house, keeping their person scrupulously clean.
- Indecent language or conduct will not be
  tolerated. Any such misconduct will, if not
  immediately corrected, result in dismissal.
- No male patient must enter the ward of the female
  patients. No female patient must enter the ward
  of the male patients. No patients must enter the
  children's ward without express prior permission.
- Where admitted together, mothers must obtain
  permission from the matron before visiting their
  child to avoid unnecessary circulation of miasma.
- Loud talking is forbidden. Only minimal noise is
  permitted in the wards, landing and hallway.
- Windows must be kept open two inches
  to aid healing and to freshen the air.
  Patients must not force the windows beyond
  this measure to prevent draughts.
- Patients must <u>at all times</u> adhere to the Christian
  ethos of the house, understanding that disease
  is in nature both physical and spiritual.

5

⎯⎯∞∞∞⎯⎯

Liam

I stare at my reflection in the art deco glass above the bathroom sink. It's cracked at the corners, splitting from the rusty nails that hold it in place. I give myself the usual appraisal: skin far too pale, cheekbones too sharp, hair too grey. I pull down my lower eyelids, inspect the whites of my eyes and the size of my pupils, count the tiny blood vessels. Then I work methodically downwards, measuring my pulse, inspecting my arms and chest for unusual marks or lumps, fingering the white scar from my appendix operation, pulling down my boxers, checking my balls. A routine so familiar, I don't even question it. I feel a wash of relief when I don't find anything untoward. It takes the edge off my anxiety, though it never goes away. It's always there, at the back of my mind. Even now, I can't shake the haunting whisper: *There's something wrong with me.*

But then I remember what Jess told me earlier and everything seems a whole lot worse: the place I'd been made to believe was an idyllic country mansion is actually a hospital, or *was* a hospital at some point in its past. Callum didn't mention the history of the house and the thought of what I've let myself in for makes me feel sick. I can't even start on how much I hate hospitals – the uniforms, the sterility, the cool metal smell. It's kind of ironic for a hypochondriac, but I never go to the doctor's. I can barely bring myself to step inside a pharmacy. It's a fear I just can't face.

I close my eyes, my heart skipping a beat, which has me grabbing my wrist again and measuring my pulse.

Thud. Thud. Thud.

For a moment, I'm back in the treatment room at school, the room where kids are given plasters and wait for their parents to collect them if they're ill. I can smell the TCP and disinfectant; see plastic chairs and antiseptic wipes and mounds of paper on a desk; hear the sound of the school counsellor clicking and unclicking her pen, waiting for me to answer her question.

So tell me, Liam, how many times has this happened?

Sweat slips down my forehead. I swallow hard, not finding the words to answer. Even if I *did* find the words, I know I wouldn't use them. Because I've been told not to make a fuss. *We're tired, Liam. We're tired of it all.*

I open my eyes into the bathroom at St Cross, and wipe the sweat from my forehead. I need to get a grip. This place has clearly been a domestic residence for decades. I'm not going to allow myself to get spooked by its past. By *my* past. I can hardly tell Jess and the girls we're not going to stay here another night, that there'll be no holiday after all, just because I'm scared, because this place has a history.

I make a conscious effort to slow my heart rate, resting my

hand on my chest, breathing deeply. Maybe this holiday will be the difference I need to turn over a new leaf, to finish the book. The book my fans have been nagging me about for months: *Jake's Return*. The last book finished on too much of a downer. Readers loved it, but not the bit where Jake, the flawed inventor – the hero I based on a better if crazier version of myself – ended up in the underworld. They didn't quite get the point I was trying to make about the hubris of technology. That everything turns to rot in the end. And so, I've been persuaded to write a part two.

I glance at the bath, wondering whether it would help to wash, to at least try to relax. It's a deep, freestanding tub, stained black where the water has run against the enamel, resting on lion's paws made out of iron. The sort of thing I'd always imagined for myself, but now strikes me as impractical. There's no place for the soap and the chances of lowering yourself in and not being able to get out again are way too high for comfort. I lean over and twist the taps, hearing the water gurgle in the pipes before spluttering out, flecked with what looks like bits of metal. I shudder at the thought of Jess using it earlier after her walk. She'd moaned that the water was tepid but she hadn't mentioned the dirt, which means it's probably just me. *The water's running dirty just for me.*

I turn the taps off again, and pick up my phone, tempted, so tempted, to look at my notifications. But I know it's a slippery slope, and one which Jess knows nothing about. So, I just check my messages. Nothing from Callum, not even a text asking if we've arrived. I close my eyes, remembering the visitors who'd called when Jess was at work, the elbow thrust into my throat, the knee in my groin, the heart-thumping fear. Jess knows nothing about that either, and I have to remind myself that, out here, we're safe.

6

Jess

The dining room runs the width of the house, with windows on three sides. I wonder, briefly, if it had once been a ward. I imagine beds standing side by side, nurses moving softly between them. The image is comforting, the white sheets, the stiff grey blankets, the swept floors. A world away from the house I actually see before me.

I peer beneath the table, calling for Xanthe. I haven't set eyes on her since breakfast and I'm starting to panic. The room is as cluttered as everywhere else and obviously not used as a dining room at all. I look beneath the armchairs, behind the curtains.

'Xanthe, please come out.' The desperation in my voice is palpable even to me. 'Please stop hiding.'

It's been over two hours since breakfast. All this time, I'd presumed Xanthe was with Summer, until I'd realised Summer was outside on the lawn, sunbathing. Not that there's been much sun. It's a dull, mizzly day, and the dining room feels cold and dark, a cave rather than a room. I feel guilty about Xanthe; she's forever making dens, finding secret places to play make believe. I should have kept a closer eye.

I step back into the entrance hall, gaze up at the circular glass roof. The sun doesn't penetrate it as well as it should, and the window looks like it's never been cleaned. The panes are splattered with bird shit, making the shadows uneven.

If I was a seven-year-old child, where would I hide?

It strikes me that the building is as exposed as it is cluttered. So many places to hide, and at the same time, nowhere to hide at all. Because the only way out is through the central hallway. Even the windows only open so far – not far enough to squeeze through. It's a quirk of the house: someone's actually stuck nails into the frames to stop the windows from opening completely. It should be comforting, the lack of escape routes, but it's not. It makes me feel claustrophobic, like I can't quite breathe.

'Xanthe,' I call, hearing my voice echo up to the roof. I feel as if I'm playing a game of hide and seek. Hide and seek without counting to ten, without setting any ground rules first. My gaze alights on the locked door next to the girls' bedroom, and I shudder at the memory of being able to see through the keyhole one minute, and not the next. The memory of the cat screeching.

'Please.' My voice is softer now, desperate. 'Please, Xanthe, come out. I promise you I won't be mad.' I picture myself standing in front of the locked door, turning the doorknob, finding it open after all, Xanthe jumping out and saying boo. 'I'm on my way,' I say, playing along with it, hand on the banister. One stair and then the next, watching my shadow creep ahead of me up the wall. I'm certain now; that's where Xanthe is. 'I'm coming to find you.'

Footsteps sound beneath me on the tiles, mirroring my own. I spin around, grabbing hold of the banister. Xanthe is standing in the middle of the hallway, her hair messed up, her knees muddied. For a moment, in the silky light from the roof, it feels like I'm dreaming.

'Xanthe!' I run back down again, taking the stairs two at a time, my feet gliding off the deep red runner. I draw Xanthe into a hug. 'Where were you? I've looked everywhere. Are you all right?'

'I was playing.' Xanthe gabbles her words. 'Outside in the wood. I met the gardener.'

'The gardener? Mr Harrison?'

'He told me not to run off. He said it was naughty. But I didn't mean to.' She starts to cry and my anger melts. 'I went the wrong way. I got lost, that's all. And then I found something in the wood. A little house, just like this one, but made out of wood. But I didn't go in. I promise, I didn't go in.'

'It's okay.' I don't know what she's talking about, but she's trembling against me, properly trembling. 'He frightened you, that's all. Did the gardener frighten you?'

'Not him. Not Mr Harrison.' Xanthe shakes her head and wipes snot from her nose with the back of her hand. 'It was the funny feeling in my head. The tingling feeling. And the wood. And the cold. I didn't like the cold.'

I reach down and press lightly on Xanthe's scalp. Please God, not this again. I'd thought Xanthe was over all this after the trouble with Mia. The GP had put it down to stress, a psychological reaction, a *natural* reaction. I force a smile. Xanthe's T-shirt is encrusted with mud and there are twigs in her hair.

'How about I run you a bath? A bath always makes things better. You've had a shock, that's all. Getting lost in the wood.' But, even as I say it, I guess there's more to it than that.

It takes all my effort to loosen the taps in the bathroom, filling the ancient tub for the second time that day. The water is even colder than before, and I feel a flush of guilt; inadvertently, I must have used most of the heat after my walk.

'Ready,' I call when I've filled the tub halfway.

No response, so I knock on the girls' room and enter. Xanthe is sitting on Summer's bed, wrapped in her fluffy bathrobe, diary on her lap, writing. I sit down beside her, hoping she'll show me, let me in, but immediately she closes the book.

'I'm sorry,' I say. 'I wasn't going to pry, not if you didn't want me to see. Were you writing about the wood?'

'I wasn't writing. I was drawing. But it's not ready yet. It's going to be a surprise.'

'Oh, I see. I love surprises.' I try to sound upbeat. Really, I want to talk about Mia. I want to talk about the tingling feeling in Xanthe's head. Or rather, I know I *should* be talking about these things.

Xanthe smiles. 'Can I have my bath now?'

'Sure. All ready for you.' I pull a leaf out of Xanthe's hair, grateful for the distraction. 'Just mind you don't slip when you get in.' I survey Xanthe's dirty clothes on the floor, the muddy T-shirt crowning the pile. 'I'll tidy up here.'

Xanthe leans in for a hug, then pads off to the bathroom, leaving me alone. My gaze flits to the abandoned diary, the key resting in the tiny padlock. Then, I stand abruptly, shaking off the impulse to peek, and walk to the window, pushing the sash as high as it will go. Like all the other windows in the house, it jams after only a few inches, nails rammed into the channels on either side. I turn around. The fustiness in the room seems suddenly stronger, as if the house is laughing at my efforts to freshen it up.

Out on the landing, I know something's wrong. I run towards the bathroom door and twist the knob. The door is locked but steam is drifting steadily from the gap at the top.

'Xanthe,' I shout, banging my fist on the wood. 'Open the door.'

Panic rings in my ears. I try the doorknob again, my hand slippery on the brass – the brass indented with a miniature twisting snake. I place one hand on top of the other, grip and turn. Abruptly, the door flies open. Not locked at all, just incredibly stiff.

Everything is a blank, a fog filling the space between the door and the bath. I wave a hand to clear it and see Xanthe standing naked on the mat.

'Wait,' I call. 'Be careful—'

Xanthe steps into the bath and screams.

ST CROSS INFIRMARY
RULES FOR STAFF

- All staff must abide by the rules
  laid down by the governors
- All staff must be neat and clean in appearance
- No fraternising with patients must occur whatsoever
- All staff, including groundsmen, are required
  to attend the morning service on Sundays
  and, in all matters, act in a Christian manner
  reflecting the Godliness of this house

7

SUMMER

⸺◦∞◦⸺

My dreams make no sense. Mumbled words I can't make out, the sound of a young child crying, something clunking, wheels spinning. I know I need to wake up but I can't. I'm sleeping too deeply. It's like a drugged sleep, like the time last year when I had the flu bang in the middle of my mock GCSEs. My legs and arms feel heavy. My back sinks into the lumpy mattress as if it's trying to become part of the bed. As if I have no control over it. I breathe deeper, aware of a different feeling, but I can't make it out. Something is pushed against my mouth and nose. Gently at first, like a kiss, then harder, forcibly. I splutter, choking in the stench of old cotton, fighting for breath. No longer asleep, but awake, alert.

I shoot upright into the moonlit room at St Cross, grabbing the quilt and the bedsheet, wrapping them tightly around me.

THE INFIRMARY ‖ 43

In the darkness, everything feels magnified: my heartbeat, my breathing, my fears – the things I've been determined to push to the back of my mind now that it's the holidays.

The last twelve months flip through my mind. Our landlord selling up and throwing us out; Mum being made redundant and getting a job in a different town; the brand-new school for my GCSEs; the brand-new set of classmates. *Form 11b.* I grab the quilt. God, I hate those words. Hate the images that flood my mind whenever I think about school, the girls who laugh at me behind my back. I've tried to disappear, but it's impossible. I'm the tallest in my year. My thick, almost black hair doesn't want to hide away, and my skin is too pale despite the make-up I wear. But it's not just that; it's not *even* that. It's all the other stuff – the stuff I did in the first week of term. The stuff I try not to think about.

I lean forwards, burying my head in the quilt, catching my tears in the old wool. This year, I'd hoped we'd go back to France again, hoped I'd see Harry, then everything that has happened since would seem inconsequential. But, I'm not in France, am I? I'm in Suffolk. Suffocating Suffolk. My hair falls over my shoulders, exposing my neck to the bristling night air. A new kind of fear reaches around me, its narrow fingers tinkling my scalp. Not the bitches in 11b whispering about me as I sit down at the front of the classroom, but a fear of what I might find if I lift my head. If I search too hard in the dark.

What if it's not Xanthe asleep in the cot, but some other kid? The one that was crying in my dream?

I know I have to investigate. I can't just sit here, crouched in the bed. I'll never get back to sleep like this. I slide out from the covers and tiptoe across the wheezing floorboards.

Xanthe is sleeping soundly. I know it's Xanthe by the sound

of her, by the way she breathes. How crazy is that? Knowing someone so completely you can recognise them just by their breath. As I lean over the cot, I can smell the Sudocrem Mum slapped on earlier when Xanthe had stupidly climbed into a scalding hot bath. 'No harm done,' Mum had said, looking shaken as she'd pasted the cream on for the thousandth time. The rest of the day had been subdued. We'd sat in the kitchen, eating soup, playing with the cats. The two cats. The white one and the tabby. But not the third. Not Alpen.

Guilt churns in my stomach, my gaze flitting to the closed bedroom door. The cat I'd let into the garden hasn't returned. What if he's scared? What if he hasn't found anything to eat? What if he's come back to the house and is sitting by the back door, waiting to be let in? I picture him in the dark, his straggly matted fur, his hungry meows. And I know what that feels like. I know what it's like to be alone, to go hungry, skipping dinner because I can't bear the eyes in the school canteen, to know that no one wants you.

I grab my phone and a jumper from the stack of clothes Mum organised earlier. *I'm coming to find you, Alpen.*

I tiptoe out of the bedroom and creep across the landing. The torchlight from my phone picks out the paintings on the wall, dark landscapes, misty faces, figures in dull red and green robes. Paintings that make the space even more spooky that it already is. If I owned a house like this, I'd fill it with sunflowers.

I reach the top stair, finding the edge of the runner with my feet, then hurry, not wanting to stay longer than I have to on the stairwell, half-falling down the final few steps. I press a hand to my chest, heart beating fast. Silence again. I'm aware of the doors on all four sides, all wedged open – Mum or Dad must have done that – and I don't know why, but it bothers me. Tiny shivers skip down my spine. I look up, drawn to the only source of natural light, the inky-greyness of the sky through the roof window. I imagine faces peering down through the panes, watching me, scrutinising me.

One thing's for sure, I can't stay here much longer. I run through the kitchen to the back door, draw back the heavy curtain, twist the key in the lock.

The night air sets me shivering again. There's a smell of cut grass and fresh dew. I can hear the rush of wind in the wood at the bottom of the garden and the hoot of an owl. I stare up at the moon, an almost but not quite perfect circle, at the canopy of stars. In any other circumstances – if we weren't staying in a creepy old house, if I'd not lost someone else's cat – this would be amazing.

'Alpen?' I call.

A gust of wind catches a plant pot on the patio, turning it over. A high-pitched rattle of plastic against stone. I take a step outside, wincing as my bare feet land on a scattering of pebbles. I wrap my arms around myself for warmth. It's so cold out here, so close to the sea.

'Alpen,' I call again. 'Alpen?'

I grab an uneaten bowl of kibble from inside, then stand on the threshold, shaking it gently.

The plant pot skitters towards me. I raise my phone, illuminating the area directly in front of the back door and to the sides, aware of space, openness, shadows darting away from the flashing light. No sign of a straggly black cat, just the old deckchairs Mum found earlier and erected on the terrace.

I give up, relocking the door, replacing the bowl of kibble on the floor. Switching off the kitchen light, I open the door to the hall, a door with two murky glass panels, and train my phone light on the bottom of the stairs, telling myself I can do this. It's no big deal, climbing the stairs.

I run, grabbing the banister, propelling myself upwards, but halfway up, I halt. Something's different. A shift in the air. I feel it on my arms, my cheeks, my forehead. An ice-sharp cold.

I swivel, catching hold of the banister on the opposite side, then move the phone light slowly around the ground floor. What I see doesn't make sense. *Can't* make sense. I shake my head, but it's still there, staring back at me like a sick joke.

Whereas before the doors had been wedged open, every single door leading off the hall is firmly closed.

8

Jess

It's morning and I'm watching Xanthe chase crunchy-nut cornflakes around a bowl of sugary milk. Round and round, round and round. The sound of the spoon scraping the bowl makes my head hurt. I think of yesterday, the bath, the scalding water, my hand scraping the ceramic as I'd fumbled to release the plug, the sense of something being deeply wrong. Scrape, scrape, scrape.

I force a smile. 'Did you sleep well?' I don't even know why I ask. Children always sleep well, don't they? It's one of the many things I envy about them. By contrast, I feel as if I barely slept at all, tossing and turning beneath the threadbare quilt, trying not to wake Liam. My head had been full of worries, although now I'm awake, I can't remember what the worries had been about. It wasn't the girls. It wasn't Liam. It was something else. Something on the periphery of my mind that I can't quite reach.

Xanthe doesn't answer, her mouth full of cornflakes, seemingly recovered from the bath incident yesterday. I busy myself with the junk on the table, reliving and then breathing through the panic I'd felt. Xanthe's skin had turned pink to the knees, but it had soon settled down when I'd run her legs under cold water. It's more what *might* have happened had Xanthe slipped. Had she panicked and not been able to pull herself out of the scalding hot bath. If I hadn't been there. If the bathroom door really had been locked. And then the baffling thought: the water had been tepid. I *know* it was tepid, I'd run the bath myself and tested the water with my own hand. Which meant the tap must have leaked, spilling sufficient hot water to make a sizeable difference. Because when I'd plunged my hand in and scrambled for the plug, my skin had been burning.

'I didn't dream,' says Xanthe.

'Everyone dreams,' I say. 'It's just you can't remember.'

She firmly pushes the bowl away.

The door swings open and Summer appears in hoodie and shorts, carrying the tabby cat. It leaps from her arms, leaving cat hairs on her jumper, and skitters towards the feeding bowls.

'Morning, love,' I say, trying not to mind the cat hairs still dusting the air.

'Hi.' Summer opens the jar of coffee, heaps two spoonfuls into a mug.

I switch on the kettle, then search for the saucepan I used yesterday to make porridge. Eventually, I find it, resting on a stack of pans towards the top of the cupboard where Liam must have put it. I take a chair from the table and position it against the cupboard, standing on tiptoes to reach it.

'Mum? Can I have a piece of toast?'

The sound of Xanthe's voice almost makes me topple. I grab on to the top of the chair. 'Yes, of course.' For some reason, I feel shaken; I could easily have fallen. 'With peanut butter? Actually, I think we've only jam. We can get some peanut butter, if you like? There must be a shop around here.'

I climb down and slice bread from the loaf I brought with us from home. I think about making a picnic lunch for later too. We could take it to the beach; there must be a way down from the coastal path and it will be fun exploring. I put the porridge on to boil, pleased with myself. The girls laugh at me for my lack of spontaneity. They see Liam as the laidback one, the one who takes them to McDonald's when I have a rare night out and he can't be bothered to cook, the one they turn to when they're bored, who buys them treats they can't really afford, who gets on the floor and plays ponies with Xanthe, who stays up late to watch films with Summer. The fact he always falls asleep on the sofa while Summer's still glued to the screen doesn't matter. It's not what you do, it's how you're perceived. But maybe this holiday, I can be the fun one too?

'Where's the other cat?' Xanthe says, bringing me back to the grubby kitchen. She's crouched on the floor, stroking the tabby. 'I've only seen Stripey and Snowy' – the names she invented yesterday – 'but there should be another one.'

'Maybe there are only two cats?' I say, nursing the niggle that, in an unusual move, it was Liam who booked the holiday. Liam who made all the arrangements. Maybe he was wrong about the number of cats?

'I think we should look for him.' Summer plonks her coffee on the table, letting it slop over the sides of the mug.

'Him?'

'The cat. He must be somewhere. Maybe he's in the garden. Maybe he got out somehow. Let's look for him after breakfast?'

'All right.' I reach for the St Anthony around my neck. The St Anthony I always wear. A gift from Mum for my confirmation. St Anthony, the patron saint of lost things. Only St Anthony's not there. The necklace has gone. I stem the rising panic. 'But this time, I don't want either of you running off, getting lost. I don't want a cat-hunt and a daughter-hunt on my hands at the same time.'

I reach for the necklace again, wondering whether it's somehow got twisted around my neck and is hanging backwards, or has unclasped itself and slipped down my clothing. But it's gone and I can't help thinking it's well and truly lost, like the cat.

We split up. Summer takes the garden, Xanthe takes the bedrooms, so I'm left with the ground floor. I'm already pretty sure from my earlier search that the cat's not here, so when I've exhausted all the nooks and crannies in the dining room and lounge, I poke my head into the study and find Liam staring at his laptop.

'How's it going?' I plant a kiss on the back of his head, on the place where the hair is starting to thin.

He sits back and stretches, catching my hands over his head, then pulls me around and settles me on his lap.

'I'm knackered,' he says.

'I'm not surprised.' I'd had a sense of him creeping out of bed in the early hours. When I'd rolled over and asked what he was doing, he'd whispered something about working, about getting on with the book. I glance at the stack of coffee cups next to his laptop. 'How far have you got?'

'Oh, you know, still editing.' He reaches around me and closes the Word document on his laptop. I sigh. He's so secretive about his work; he's only told me the bare bones of his plot. I know he's stressed, the pressure of writing a second book after a bestseller, and I try not to take it personally, but sometimes I can't help it. It feels as though there's a part of him I don't know any more. A part he's keeping secret.

'I wish you'd just talk to me,' I say, looking across at the books lining the shelves, the dark leather volumes printed with faded gold letters. Books that have probably never been opened, let alone read. 'I know I'm not a part of all this. But I can listen. I might even be able to help you with your ideas.'

'My ideas?'

'Your ideas for the book. You know. What happens next to Jake.' I think of the scene where the last book left off. The hero, Jake, scrambling about in a world full of monsters and untold terror.

'It's complicated. It's—' He frowns, for a moment looking truly lost. 'It's still a jumble up there.' He stabs his forehead with his finger. 'I need time to work it out. I need space.'

Space. I've given him plenty of space in the last six months. When we'd first met, he'd worked in the hotel industry, hating every minute of it, hating the management, hating every customer who was right regardless of how wrong they actually were. Then he'd taken a job in a bookshop and from then – or maybe it was deep inside him anyway – he'd caught the writing bug. Three years later, when his dad had died and left him enough money to take a few years out, I'd encouraged him to write full time. Now, he spends every spare minute in the boxroom at home.

'Okay.' I take a deep breath, trying to centre myself. 'I'm taking the girls out to the beach later on. Why don't you stay here and get on with things? A bit of peace and quiet?'

'Don't you want me around?' he teases me, planting light kisses on my neck.

I laugh. His moods are so unpredictable, like wind gusting in different directions. 'Of course I want you around. I just thought, a change of scenery, a new place to write.'

'If you really don't mind—'

'I *do* mind. But if it helps.'

'This helps.' He leans me backwards, trailing kisses down my throat and making me moan, then he reaches a hand up my T-shirt.

'Not now,' I say, thinking about the girls and the cat. But I barely protest. He's been so stressed recently, so distracted, it feels as though he hasn't had much time for me, and this feels good. Really good. I realise, I need to feel needed.

'This place is *huge*,' he says, reading my mind. 'The girls wouldn't hear a thing. We could lock the door.'

'I'm meant to be searching for the cat.'

'To hell with the cat.'

He lifts me on to the desk next to his laptop, pulls off his T-shirt, revealing the slight swell of his stomach, then walks across the room and locks the door. The sound of the key turning in the lock makes me tense. There's something about it I can't untangle. It's like a full stop after a very long sentence. It feels too final.

'What's wrong?' he says, reading my expression.

'I don't know. That sound. The sound of the key.'

He frowns. All the rooms are fitted with locks, which I suppose isn't unusual for a building of this age, for an old infirmary, but it feels like a shutting in rather than a keeping out.

'We can leave this until later,' Liam says, rubbing the back of his neck. 'I'm sorry. I shouldn't have insisted. I miss you. I miss the feel of you. We're always so busy with the girls and with work.'

'No.' I reach out and pull him towards me. 'Please,' I say, my voice a whisper. I glance upwards at the ceiling, at the shadows, the light shade rocking back and forth, caught in a draught. Not keeping my eyes off it, I run a hand over his chest, feeling him tighten his muscles and suck in his stomach. 'I need the distraction.'

NOTICE: ST CROSS INFIRMARY

The sickness afflicting your relative now
in the care of the nurses may still, in
some cases, be within your house or upon
your person. It is advisable, therefore,
that you open wide your windows and
doors for at least two hours, and wash
all clothes and bed linen that the sick
person may have touched. The washing
of such items in soap and hot water as
well as general cleanliness, including the
thorough washing of yourself and all other
members of your household, is imperative
for physical, mental and spiritual hygiene.
Further, it is advised that you do not visit
your sick relative without writing first to
the matron and seeking permission. Even
then, this visit may be denied due to his
condition and to prevent contagion.

9

SUMMER

———◦◦◦———

'Alpen? *Alpen?*' I push my way through the tangle of undergrowth in the wood. *Where the fuck is that fucking cat?* I run my hands through my hair, catching my fingers on a knot, yanking it out. My scalp stings as I shake off the twist of hair around my forefinger and watch it float to the ground. I need to calm down. No one knows it was me, do they? No one knows I let the cat out. I don't need to admit anything. I don't even need to mention I saw a black cat in the first place. Black cats are unlucky, right? Or maybe they're lucky? I can't remember which way round it is. Lucky for some, unlucky for others. '*Alpen?*'

'You lost?'

I swivel, heart pumping. There's a stranger standing between the trees. I feel an immediate swell of panic. *My classmates in the locker room where I thought I was safe.* 'No. I'm fine,' I snarl.

The stranger steps forwards. A boy a little older than myself with untidy brown hair and a sleeveless T-shirt. I relax. He doesn't strike me as a threat. The sort of boy I see strolling in and out of the sixth-form common room.

'You're the girl staying up at the house?'

'Yeah. With my family. We've lost one of the cats.'

'Shit.'

'I know, right?'

The boy takes an e-cigarette from his pocket, raises it to his lips, flexing his biceps. 'I'm Aaron,' he says through a plume of bubble-gum smoke. 'I'm staying with my nan and granddad in the cottage.' He nods towards the other side of the wood.

'Hi,' I say, suddenly self-conscious. 'I'm Summer.' I hesitate. 'Want to help me look for the cat?'

'Sure.'

He follows me through the brambles, deeper into the wood, the path I was following long since disappeared. I'm super aware of the boy behind me, the scent of his vape. How long since I was alone with a boy like this, just me and no one else in sight?

'So, you're just staying here,' I say, 'like, for the holidays?'

'U-huh.' He steps around me and pulls a bramble aside to let me pass. 'I got into trouble at school. My parents sent me here as a punishment. Not that Nan and Granddad are mean or anything. Just, there's nothing to do out here.'

My mind flits to France. 'What did you do that was so bad at school?'

'Oh, stuff.'

We reach the edge of a small lake. I've been so conscious of him behind me and then in front, the smell of him, the slight sweat of his skin, that I hadn't noticed the clearing until now.

'Oh,' I say, feeling stupid, 'a lake.'

'Fancy a dip?'

I giggle, unsure whether he's joking or not, but already he's stripping off his T-shirt. His skin is golden beneath, dappled where he's obviously half-heartedly rubbed in suncream. He looks like he spends every spare minute working out. I've a sudden impulse to run my hands over his chest, press my lips in the little dips between his ribs, reenact what I did in France with Harry. But instead, I just stare, wondering how old he is. Seventeen at a guess. He kicks off his trainers and pulls off his shorts revealing a tight pair of boxers, then he strides into the water, making ripples with his hands.

Without warning, he vanishes from sight, just a pool of inky water where his body should be. I hold my breath, waiting, watching, until he reappears, shaking the water from his hair. 'You coming in?' he calls.

I look around nervously, trying to think of an excuse not to.

'It's clean,' he reassures me. 'It's fed from the stream further up. Seriously, I wouldn't be swimming in it if it wasn't.'

I hesitate, for a mad moment wondering whether to strip to my underwear. Then, I throw off my hoodie and wade in in my shorts and T-shirt. I gasp at the cold, at the shooting pain in my ankles. 'It's freezing!'

'You just have to keep moving.' He dives under again.

I'm up to my thighs now, and everything beneath feels numb. Another step and I sink into the silty ground, the water rising up to my chest. I gasp again, fighting the urge to scramble out as fast as I can. A week ago, in the heatwave, this would have been welcome, but now it feels positively autumnal. The boy resurfaces, flashing a smile that lights up the parts of me that are still, incredulously, working.

'You see,' he says. 'It's not as bad as you think. You just have to move.'

I circle my arms through the water without lifting my feet from the ground. Thing is, I know I could easily outpace him; his stroke is all bravado rather than technique. He kicks his legs into a crawl, swims around me. My mind automatically flips to the night I went skinny dipping with Harry, the warm Mediterranean sea, the evening sun on our skin as we'd dried off afterwards. But I haven't had a single text from Harry for months, not since I'd told him we wouldn't be going back to the chalet after all.

'Swim,' the boy urges me. 'You'll freeze to death if you just stand there, waving your arms about. I don't want to have to lug a corpse back to the house. Hi, Mr and Mrs Kennedy. Nice to meet you. Here's your dead daughter.'

I move into a gentle breaststroke, brushing weeds and God knows what else with my feet. 'How do you know my surname?'

'Magic.' He dives under again then laps the pond.

I chase after him, hard and fast through the water, the effort taking away the edge of the cold.

'Seriously,' I say, through chattering teeth, catching him up. He looks around in surprise. 'How do you know who I am?'

He grins, treading water. 'My grandad gardens for the old lady, Mrs Clarence. She told him you were coming to St Cross.'

Mystery solved. I kick my legs. 'So, what did you do that was so terrible you got grounded for the entire summer holidays? Don't tell me it was just stuff. Stuff doesn't land you in that amount of trouble.'

He swims towards the bank, pulling his body from the lake, then he grabs his T-shirt and tugs it on. I gape at the way it clings to his abs, the water running off him, pooling around his feet. 'Do you really want to know?'

I follow, relieved he's given up on this ridiculous idea of swimming in the ice-cold lake. I grab my hoodie, struggle with it over my wet hair, conscious of the way it cleaves to my chest, the two sodden patches that appear almost immediately. 'Go on, shock me.'

He grins again. 'Have you ever looked in the mirror? I mean, *really* looked?'

I narrow my eyes, self-conscious. Is he taking the piss? 'What do you mean?'

'Come on, I'll show you.'

But I'm back on my guard. *The girls in 11b. The whispering. The mockery.* 'Show me what?'

He throws his hair back, sopping wet down his T-shirt, and cocks me a smile that makes me quiver inside. 'I can talk to the devil.'

The spare room in the red-bricked cottage – Aaron's bedroom – is small and cramped. From what I've seen of it, before Aaron drew down the blackout blind and closed the curtains, it's an almost empty space with not many clues as to the person he is, just a heap of clothes on a chair, a set of dumbbells, a couple of science-fiction books on the desk. In the darkness, with Aaron sitting beside me on the cushions on the floor, it also feels way too intimate.

'So,' I say, trying to disguise my nerves, 'what happens next? I bet you don't really speak to the devil.'

He leans forward so that I catch the scent of his skin beneath the cool earthy smell of the lake water. Then, he fumbles in his pocket and brings out a lighter, flicks it once, twice, three times, before coaxing the wick of a candle into life. He sets the candle in a little brass holder. 'Divination,' he says, moving his finger through the flickering flame.

'What?'

'Divination. Communicating with unseen forces.' He laughs darkly. 'Only the priest at school didn't see it that way. Devil worship sounds way more sinister. And it makes your parents freak.'

'The priest?' I slurp from the cup of tea he's given me, laced with whisky; according to Aaron, it's his granddad's recipe.

'It's a Catholic school.'

'And what do you mean by unseen forces?'

'The supernatural.' He runs his finger back through the flame. 'The spirit world. Me and some mates were bored one night in the dorm. My mate had been reading about it online and we thought we'd try it for a laugh. We made a Ouija board out of cardboard, and then we tried scrying.'

'You go to boarding school?' A gulf opens up between us, one I hastily try to ignore; from this short conversation I've gleaned Aaron's not only smarter than I am, but he's also rich.

He doesn't answer, just moves the candle in front of a small oval-framed mirror, set upright on a little box on the floor, tilted at an angle. Not the usual sort of mirror; the glass seems darker, almost black. The frame is elaborate and old-fashioned, painted gold.

'You have to stare at it,' he says. 'Stare at your reflection. Really concentrate. Then, ask it a question.'

'A question?'

'Anything you like, but in your head.'

'Okay. And then what?'

I sense him sitting back, giving me more space on the floor. 'Just wait and see.'

It feels awkward sitting there in the dark, looking at my ghost-like reflection in the mirror, trying to think of a question to ask it. *Mirror, mirror, on the wall, who's the fairest of them all?* But I'm being silly. I need to think of something else, something meaningful. I'm aware of Aaron behind me, the sound of his breathing, the smell of whisky on his breath above the waxy scent of the candle. It's impossible to concentrate. How long is this going to take? And what exactly am I waiting for?

Should I kiss him?

The question pops into my head and I'm immediately flooded with relief I didn't ask it out loud. Still, I'm too afraid to turn around, to search for Aaron in the darkness, in case it somehow transmitted from my mind to his. Instead, I focus on the mirror, focus on my flickering reflection, and despite everything, I start to relax, my weight sinking into the carpet, my backbone curving. I'm less aware of Aaron, less aware of the crack of light leaking beneath the bedroom door, less aware of the possibility of others in the house, the grandparents I haven't met.

Why won't you answer my question? I said, should I kiss him?

The reflection changes. Paler, greyer, a mist forming in the mirror. Is it meant to do this? I turn to Aaron, but I can barely see a thing courtesy of the blackout curtain.

'Carry on,' he says. I hear him settling back, relaxing on the cushions, stretching out his legs as if he's watching a show on TV. As if *I'm* the entertainment. The thought flits through my mind that he's laughing at me. I try blocking him out, blocking out the fear of being ridiculed. *Fuck him*, I think, staring at the mirror, deflated.

'It's not working,' I say, irritated. All I see is my own reflection and the black of the glass.

'Keep looking,' he urges, sounding serious, not laughing at all. 'It takes time.'

I concentrate again, focusing on my eyes in the mirror, my pupils wide. The glass changes again from black to light grey, my reflection misting over. I change the question, *Where is the black cat?*

Victus quoque rationem.

What the fuck? I spin towards Aaron. Had he spoken? But already I know the answer. The words were in my head, spoken in an unfamiliar voice, a deep voice, one that doesn't belong to me. One that belongs to the mirror. I turn back again, breathing audibly, focusing on the candle flame first before lifting my gaze to the glass. Behind me, I feel Aaron tense.

Neque vero cuiquam venenum mortiferum.

The words fill me with panic. I don't understand them. Don't understand where they're coming from, *how* they're appearing in my head. Surely it can't be the mirror? But they're spilling inside my brain now, a ramble of indecipherable sounds.

Verum caste, sancteque vitam meam.

I jump up, toppling the candle. My head pounds. My eyes sting. I stifle a scream.

'What is it? Shit.' Aaron's on all fours, scrambling to switch on the bedside light. I blink in its glare, making out the narrow single bed, the plain walls, the IKEA-style chair. 'Are you okay? Jesus, you almost burned the house down.' He picks up the fallen candle.

'I'm sorry. I thought I heard . . .' I swallow hard. What *did* I hear exactly? 'There was a voice in my head. I asked a question. I asked where the cat was, and it answered back in this other language. An old language. Latin, I think.'

'*Latin?*'

'I don't know.' I run my fingers through my hair, finding knots, tugging until my scalp twinges with pain. 'It was a man's voice.'

'Can you remember what it said?'

I shake my head.

'Try. Try to remember.'

But the words have gone, drifting from my mind as easily as the smoke from the extinguished flame.

'You said it was Latin.'

'Yes.'

'Have you studied Latin before?'

'No.' I swallow hard. My mouth has run dry. 'Maybe it wasn't Latin. I don't know. I don't go to public school like you. We study English and French and German. We don't study dead languages.'

He reaches over and lays a hand on my arm through my hoodie. 'Hey, calm down. Sounds like that was a bit full on. To be honest, I haven't known anyone to do that before, you know, hear voices. Normally, you just see stuff, like stuff in your mind. It was just meant to be a bit of fun.'

I need to get out of here. I need to get out of the bedroom. Go outside where I can breathe easily, where I can rationalise what just happened. Go to the seaside with Mum and Xanthe, pick sand out of cheese sandwiches and swim in the sea.

I stumble towards the door. 'I don't know what just went on. It's probably the whisky. I need some fresh air.'

He pulls up the blind, spilling sunlight into the bedroom. I blink, my eyes finding the little black mirror and the cheap red candle. The mirror's just a smeared bit of glass in a tatty old frame supported by its own stand, nothing special, and the candle is back in its holder. It's only the carpet that gives away what just happened. The carpet is splattered in bright red wax.

10

Liam

My head slides from my forearms and hits the desk. I jolt upright. The afternoon sunlight is heavy through the study window, making me feel sticky and unrefreshed. I must have fallen asleep, but I can't remember it, I can't even remember slipping into a daze. Whatever, I shouldn't have slept here. I should have gone upstairs and crawled into bed. Or maybe I should have gone to the beach with Jess and the girls after all. Better than just sitting here, doing absolutely fuck all. I haven't even opened my laptop since waving them off. I've only written a couple of paragraphs since I started work at 5 a.m. The thought pounds in my brain that I've lost the knack. Or maybe I never had the knack in the first place, just a stroke of good luck that's now over.

I tap my jeans pocket for my phone but it's not there, which sends me into a flurry of activity despite my banging headache: searching the desk, looking under the laptop, crawling on the floor, feeling the dark carpet for anything remotely phone-like. I just need a look. I just need to see my notifications.

Tap ... tap ... tap ...

I stop what I'm doing, hold my breath. Did I imagine it? A noise, right above my head. The same noise I dreamed the first night we were here. Yet, this time, I'm definitely awake. It must be something in the house. A pipe or a rattling window. There must be all sorts of hidden workings in a house this size.

Tap ... tap ... tap ...

I jump up, banging my head on the underside of the desk. Shit. I rub the back of my skull, sure I must have cracked something, but there's not even a lump. I stare at the ceiling, at the lightshade and the ceiling rose, as if they might signal what on earth is going on in the room above. *Our bedroom.*

The house is excruciatingly quiet again, like it's holding its breath, just as I'm holding *my* breath waiting for something to happen. I laugh to distil the tension. It's just a pipe, or one of the cats playing a game. I'll make myself a cup of tea, knock back some paracetamol, hunt for my phone again. There's no Wi-Fi in the house, so I can't use my laptop to search online. And I just need a quick look to check my notifications. Nothing more. I promise myself: absolutely nothing more than a brief glance.

The sound comes again, a distinctive tapping. I spin. What on earth? Not a pipe, I think, or a cat, but something banging on the floor above. I listen intently – quiet again – and steel myself. If I don't check it out, it will drive me mad.

I open the study door and listen. Complete silence. No meowing cats. No radio playing from the kitchen. Not even the quiet hum of electricity, the hum that is ever-present at home, in our tiny semidetached. I cross to the stairs and hesitate, trying to think of a good reason not to go up. But I know I won't be able to work until I've set my mind at rest.

I look around for something to use as a weapon and find a dusty broom handle wedged behind the hall table. I take it with me and return to the stairs. There might be an intruder. Someone might be rummaging through our things, rooting through Mrs Clarence's drawers for jewels I'm pretty sure from the state of the place don't exist.

I creep upwards, stopping now and again to listen. Still nothing. I wonder whether I imagined it, whether the stress of the last year has finally sent me crazy. But then it comes again, louder, rhymical, from right inside our bedroom door.

Tap ... tap ... tap ...

My heart thuds to the same rhythm. I reach the head of the stairs, my mouth run dry. Looking down at the entrance hall, I see how easy it would be to fall. How easy it would be to climb over the banister and go tumbling down *smack* to the tiles below. For a moment, the thought is exquisitely blissful. All my troubles over. Never the need to tell Jess the truth, to admit what a lousy human being I really am.

Then, I stop myself, repulsed by the image spinning through my mind: my dead body at the foot of the stairs, my blood splattered across the tiles. Even at my lowest point, I've never had such a desperate, dangerous thought.

I turn away, my gaze landing on the bedroom door, the white paint, the dark wooden doorknob. My chest squeezes, little spirals of pain that set me panicking all over again. Just a few more paces. I cross the landing, rest my free hand on the doorknob, the other still tightly gripped around the broom handle. The noise stops abruptly. A hollow gaping silence. Only the beating of my heart followed by a sighing creek as I throw wide the door.

Sunlight spills on the Turkish rug, on the chaise longue, on the bedsheets Jess has so carefully refolded and tucked beneath the mattress after our restless night. Nothing out of the ordinary. The room is deathly quiet. I take a tentative step forward. There's a slight, almost imperceptible rapping at the window, but it's just the ivy knocking against the pane.

I drop the broom handle, watch it roll to a standstill on the Turkish rug, then open the window as high as it will go, just a couple of inches. I look down at the drive, the turning circle with its stone fountain, the empty space where our car was parked before Jess drove the girls to the beach. I feel utterly stupid to have been scared witless by a plant, and yet at the same time, I feel relieved, because for a moment, I'd really thought—

Tap . . . tap . . . tap . . .

The sound comes from behind me, not from outside. I freeze where I am, hands gripping the window sash. Something's in the room making that noise. Something right behind my back. My scalp tingles. I feel the little hairs on my neck stand up on end.

Tap . . . tap . . . tap . . . And then, like a full stop, a single assertive: *TAP*

I whirl back towards the centre of the room.

Nothing.

Bloody hell. My hands feel clammy as I run my fingers through my hair. The air in the room seems suddenly too thin despite the open window. I gasp, gathering in as much breath as I can, my head filled with an unfathomable sense of dread as

I run across the Turkish rug, catching my feet on a book Jess must have dropped, sending it spinning. I yank open the door and sprint on to the landing, stopping dead in my tracks as I reach the banister. I look down at the hall, see the dust motes hovering in the afternoon sunlight. Everything is uncannily still. For a split second, I see something else: a ridge, a crop of sandy rocks, my father with his backpack. My heart beats wildly as I feel the fear. Cold, sharp, humiliating fear. Then, I jerk myself from the memory, back to the gallery landing, back to the tiles in the hall.

What if? What if I just jumped?

'No!' I shout the word out loud, pulling myself to my senses, taking the stairs two at a time until I reach the hall, then I make for the kitchen, wrench open cupboard doors, move contents aside, pile tins and bottles of sauce on the floor, not stopping until I find what I'm looking for. A single dusty bottle of sherry. I wipe the neck, crack open the top. Then, I find a small glass in the rack above the sink and fill it to the brim.

11

SUMMER

⸺⸺

I push my way through the sea, enjoying the stretch in my muscles and the tingle of salt on my lips. The muzzy feeling from the whisky-tea is gone, my tiredness forced to the back of my mind. I like the exercise, the ice-cold sea against my skin, the contrast of the lazy sun on my arms as I pull them from the water. Flipping on to my back, I stare at the cloud-streaked sky. It looks like it might rain and I like that too, the thought of water meeting water, the way everything connects.

I flip back again and kick my legs, thinking about Aaron, his taut skin, the ridge of muscle across his stomach. His boxers. God, I'd seen him in his boxers within five minutes of meeting him. I push myself into a vigorous front crawl, then wade towards the shore, towards Mum and Xanthe further down on the beach, building sandcastles. Shivering in my bikini, I splash through the smaller waves, kicking up drifts of watery sand.

'Hey.' I sink down into the sand beside them, wrapping myself in one of the threadbare towels Mum brought from the house.

Mum beams. 'Good swim?' She pushes a cheese sandwich into my hand.

'It was okay.' I take a bite. The cheese is hard and the margarine isn't the type I like.

'Only okay?'

'It was cold. And this sandwich is rank.' I dump the sandwich and stare out to sea, feeling Mum's disapproving gaze on my back.

'Want to help us build a sandcastle?' she says, wisely ignoring me.

I sigh and trickle my hand through the sand, my anger subsiding. 'All right.'

I force myself to get up, fill a bucket with wet sand, then help Xanthe build a gatehouse while Mum digs a moat.

The last time I was on a beach – literally the last time – I was in France, lying on the sun lounger next to Harry. There was no one else about. It was the last night of the holiday. Mum and Dad were in the bar with Harry's parents, and Xanthe was staying up late with them, taking advantage of the fact Mum was drinking. I lay next to Harry, drunk with sea air and his parents' wine, still kissed by the salt of the ocean where we'd just been swimming. Then he leaned over, unzipped my shorts and pushed his fingers right inside me. I was only fifteen at the time; I'd never let anyone do that to me before, only heard of it happening to other people.

'Summer, are you listening?' I become aware of Xanthe

staring expectantly at the bucket in my hand. 'I said, will you get me some more water?'

I throw off the towel and wade into the sea with the plastic bucket. Seaweed slaps against my thighs and brushes my feet. I step sideways, jamming the arch of my foot against something sharp.

Sancteque vitam meam.

I wince in pain as the strange words come back to me. For a split second, I've a weird feeling I'm still staring in that mirror, still hearing that voice. But I know it's just a memory; it's not for real. I stumble from the water, set the bucket down on the sand and inspect the underside of my foot. Blood springs across the skin from a fresh cut, but it's not as bad as it feels. Looking up again, my gaze lands on the chalets near the coastal path and the rocks further down. I press my hand against the cut, stemming the blood flow, then stand up, testing my foot on the sand. On the other side of the beach, Mum and Xanthe are still busy with the sandcastle, and there's only one other family, shivering inside a windbreaker.

I hobble towards the rocks and start to climb, the lower ones slick with the recent tide, the higher ones encrusted with seaweed. I've no idea why, but I've a feeling I need to reach the top, just below the level of the chalets; it's like there's something calling me up there. I glance back at the beach, at the abandoned plastic bucket in danger of being swamped by the surf, at Mum and Xanthe still building the sandcastle. I wave to them, and they wave back, puzzled.

I continue my climb. Almost there, just a couple more metres.

When I reach the top, I look down at the sea, breathless from climbing, taking a moment to enjoy the sense of success, the urgency gone. Then I sit down and lie back against the cool flat rocks.

I'm thinking about Harry again, how he'd messaged me, promising to keep in touch, promising to meet up again in France. Harry's parents always took the same villa, always stayed the same fortnight in August. But then Mum had landed the bombshell: we couldn't afford to go away this year, not to France, not to anywhere. Harry had stopped messaging after that, when I'd told him I wasn't going to France again after all. My WhatsApp messages to him had been read but he hadn't replied.

Tears slide down my face. I wipe them away, but the sand on my fingertips just makes it worse. I turn on my side, press my cheek to the rock. What the fuck is wrong with me? For what feels like hours I seem to lie there, unsure which are my tears and which are coming from the rock. *The rock is crying*, I say to myself, as I reach down and cradle the arch of my foot. And then I realise that doesn't make sense. I'm talking crap. Objects don't cry. I pull myself upright, wipe the tears from my face, smearing my cheeks with blood and dirt.

Back at home, I'm ravenous. While Mum's upstairs wrestling Xanthe from her swimsuit, I'm in the kitchen, raiding the bread bin. I slice a hunk of bread and spread it with real butter, then hunt in the cupboard until I find a jar of jam. Not the cheap jam from breakfast. This looks the real deal with a handwritten label: old-lady-handwriting spelling out 'strawberry'. But the lid won't budge. I try wrapping it in a tea towel, gritting my teeth as I turn, but nothing gives. Eventually, I hold the jar up high, staring at the angry red mark on my other hand where the lid dug in.

Then, I let the jar drop, hearing the satisfying crack and splinter of glass as it hits the tiles.

Extract from a letter written by Mr C. R. James, University College London, to The Times, *10 September 1847:*

I have been reading with interest the recent ruminations on the spiritual health of the diseased. The observations are, to an extent, correct – health is indeed both spiritual and physical in nature – but, to my mind, as a man of science, it is the advent of modern technology together with mass overcrowding that has brought a degree of suffering hitherto unknown. Loss of limbs sustained in mills and quarries, men crushed by falling scaffolds, the maimed and the blinded, and those unfortunates brought low by liquor and the ravaging deformities of syphilis are the tragedies of our industrial awakening. Whilst the theologians and, dare I say it, gentlemen of leisure, call for spiritual reform, it is the surgeons who patch up the broken bodies and who are the real heroes of our times.

12

⸺⊷⊶⸺

Liam

'Daddy. Daddy.'

It's nighttime and I'm lying awake, cocooned inside the bedsheets, hearing Xanthe calling for me from the room next door. But I'm too tired to move. I pray she'll fall asleep again, save me the bother of getting up and crossing the landing. It's not unusual for Xanthe to cry out in the night, but normally it's Jess who gets up, who makes a fuss, who doesn't complain when she's bleary eyed in the morning after a restless night. But tonight, Jess is sleeping deeply, and I'm wide awake despite my aching tiredness. I know I can't ignore Xanthe for much longer. That's not a sleeping cry. Xanthe's wide awake too.

'Daddy!'

'Okay,' I mumble, throwing off the covers. 'I'm coming.'

Jess shifts on her side of the bed. 'What is it?' she asks groggily.

'Xanthe,' I say. 'I think she's having a nightmare.'

'Do you want me to go?' She sounds exhausted.

'No.' I'm up now, grabbing my jumper from the chair. The nights are so cold in Suffolk, even in August. 'You go back to sleep.' I cast her a loving glance, then realise she can't see me, just as I can't see her. It's pitch black even with the curtains wide open. Instead, I hear her turning over, pulling the quilt to her side of the bed, muttering something I can't make out.

I search for my phone to use as a light, then remember it's missing. This afternoon, when Jess and the girls were back from the beach and I'd felt confident enough to traipse around the house, I'd looked everywhere for my phone. The kitchen, the study, the hall, the bathroom, the dining room. Even in rooms I'd only glanced in before. Rooms I *know* there's no chance of it being in. But it's vanished. I laugh inwardly at the phrase in my mind but that's exactly what it feels like: vanished into thin air.

Instead, I feel my way with my feet over the Turkish rug, and then the bare floorboards, stubbing my toe against the chaise longue and cursing.

'Daddy!'

'I'm coming, love.'

I stretch out my arms until I reach the door, twist the knob, step out on to the landing. The memory of looking over the banister to the hallway below, imagining my body splashed with blood, jolts through my mind. So I don't look, just keep my eyes pinned on the landing in front of me, the short walk between our room and the girls'.

I open the door.

'Daddy?'

'Hey.' I reach the side of the cot, touched that it was me Xanthe called out for and not Jess. 'What's up, Little Bear?'

'I had a nightmare.'

'It's all right. It's hot, that's all. The warm weather always gives you vivid dreams.' Except, it's not hot at all. It's even colder in the girls' room than in ours. If I didn't know better, I'd say it was the depths of winter.

'Do you want to sleep with me and Mum?'

'No.' Xanthe reaches up and grips me by my arms, so that I'm leaning right over the cot. My back protests, my muscles scream. Her breath is hot on my cheeks, and I wonder if she's coming down with something. 'I have to stay here with Summer. I can't leave her alone.'

'What were you dreaming about?'

'I was dreaming about you.'

'Me?' A chill runs up and down my pyjama top. 'What about me?'

'You were lying down.'

'Right.'

'And there was a man standing over you. He was going to hurt you. He was holding a knife.' She's crying, gripping me tightly, digging her nails into my skin. I imagine the marks I'll find there in the morning. 'I tried to stop him, but I couldn't move. I couldn't reach you.'

'Hey, hey. No one's trying to hurt me. It was just a dream.' But it stirs something deep inside me. A memory.

Space. Lights. A complex smell of skin and metal and blood.

Summer turns over in her sleep and I'm grateful for the distraction. It's too dark to see the room beyond the immediate space around me, but I'm aware of her, of the bed near the window, the wardrobe, the chairs. It strikes me this room was meant for children, it's not just the cot with its Mickey Mouse figure, it's the intimacy of the space, the wall-to-ceiling cupboards that suggest a never-ending cycle of laundry: clothes and bed linen and terry-towelling nappies. Perhaps the room has always been a nursery?

'He was holding a knife,' Xanthe says again between her tears. 'But it's okay, Daddy.' She reaches up to me. 'You're going to be okay. I'll look after you.'

'Oh, sweetheart.' I lean over even more, the side of the cot digging painfully into my ribs, and kiss her forehead. Then I stroke her hair over and over until she sighs and loosens her grip, allowing me to tuck her arms back beneath the quilt. I step backwards, landing on something. The sound of paper creasing. *Xanthe's diary.* 'No one's trying to attack me,' I reassure her. 'Go back to sleep, Little Bear, it was just a bad dream.'

13

Jess

It's early morning, and I'm in the kitchen, thinking about Summer yesterday, the argument we'd had after we'd got back to the house. It was a stupid thing. Summer had dropped a jar of strawberry jam on the floor and glass shards had flown everywhere, gloopy jam leaking out. I'd told her to take more care and she'd flown at me, called me an overreacting cow, said it wouldn't have happened if I'd made decent sandwiches in the first place. The argument had blown up after that. I'd sent Summer to her room and she'd stormed off, slamming the door. It had felt – I don't know – not quite like Summer. Like something was wrong. Something more fundamental than a smashed jar on the floor.

I circle my neck, relieving the tension. I know it's early days, but so far this holiday hasn't been exactly what I'd hoped it would be. I press my fingertips into the nape of my neck, finding the pressure points, and raise my chin. In doing so, I catch sight of the bell board near the ceiling. The labels seem brighter today, somehow more legible.

FRONT DOOR ‖ PARLOUR
DINING ROOM ‖ WOMEN'S WARD
MEN'S WARD ‖ ISOLATION WARD

It's like the ink is reinventing itself, layer over layer, but that's impossible. Involuntarily, I shudder. The bell board is a link to what this place used to be and I find myself wondering what sort of infirmary it was, and the exact point at which it stopped being an infirmary and became a normal house. There must be information about it somewhere, records in a museum, local memory. Not that there are many locals. The village of Blythe, from what I can work out, consists of St Cross, the church, the red-bricked cottage, the gatehouse, the handful of dirty-looking chalets near the beach. Looking at the bell board, I feel a connection to a past I know nothing about. I imagine the wires running through the walls, linking the bells in the kitchen to other parts of the house like a hidden map.

I turn away – the wiring is probably long gone, and I haven't seen any bell pulls, they're just a quaint reminder of the history of the place – and resume searching for the coffee. Liam's obviously been tidying up, which is unusual for him. I even look in the fridge. Then, in desperation, open the slim drawer beneath the workstation. It's stuffed to the brim with letters, envelopes, till receipts, a couple of ancient cheque books. At the top of the pile is a scrap of paper, penned with the handwriting I've seen in other places around the house: an old person's handwriting. It's an address in Edinburgh, prefaced with the name: 'Callum'.

Callum. I don't know why it bothers me, this tiny detail, only it nudges something in my brain, something I can't quite pinpoint. I've heard that name before, haven't I? Callum is probably Mrs Clarence's son. The son she's visiting in Scotland.

I shove the drawer closed again and immediately locate the coffee. It's exactly where I left it: on top of the microwave. I massage my temples. God, I must be going mad, or else I'm just tired. It's only 6.30 a.m. and I've a sense of the rest of the house sleeping deeply; even Liam had been snoring when I'd stolen across the bedroom in my socks. I should have allowed myself a lie in.

I make myself a drink and take it out on to the terrace along with the red-covered notebook, the one I found and brought down with me from upstairs – I want to take a closer look, make sense of the writing, get a feel for the mysterious Charles Keller, whoever he was. It's warmer out here than in the house and I settle myself in one of the deckchairs, trying to get comfortable. But the coffee burns the back of my throat, and the frame of the chair digs into my thighs. Although the writing is almost impossible to read, I soon realise what I'm looking at is some sort of diary. There are dates written throughout, from October 1847 through to August the following year. I struggle through the first entry; it seems Charles Keller had arrived in Suffolk from London. I flip a page. A dead daddy-longlegs falls out on to my lap, making me yelp. I dust down my dress and try reading again, but the writing makes my eyes dance, the strange looping 's's, the elaborate 'y's and 'g's.

I look up, and to my surprise find a woman is walking up the path from the wood, trailing a small white dog on a lead.

'Hello,' I call, closing the diary.

The dog stops to shit on the lawn, but it doesn't seem to

bother the woman. She pulls it onwards without picking up the mess, quickening her step.

'How can I help you?' I wonder if the garden lies on the route of a public footpath, though I haven't seen a sign.

The woman steps on to the terrace, her hair falling free from a ponytail. She's wearing an ankle-length dressing gown, hanging loose, revealing trousers and a blouse beneath. 'I met your daughter.'

'Oh?' My immediate thought is she's mistaken, but her expression tells me otherwise. 'I mean, which one? I have two daughters. Summer's the eldest. Xanthe's the youngest.'

The woman frowns, the little wrinkles on her brow knitting together. 'I think I frightened her,' she says, not answering my question. 'My dog . . .' She looks down at the Jack Russell straining on the lead, straining to get back to the wood. Is that the same dog I saw when I walked past the gatehouse? 'My dog can be a little nervous at times. But your daughter needn't be afraid. I came to see her. I came to tell her that.'

'They're both asleep. It's early. I'm sure—'

'Perhaps she'd like to visit me again?'

'Again?' I'm still confused. Neither Summer nor Xanthe have mentioned anything about meeting the locals.

'There are strawberries in the garden. Perhaps, she'd like to pick strawberries?'

'That's very kind.'

'Perhaps you'd all like to come? I'll keep Angel in the house.'

I eye the dog still pulling on the lead, quietly growling.

The lady taps it gently on the head with her walking stick. 'Be quiet you.' She smiles thinly. 'My house is on the other side of the wood, past the cottage, a little further down the lane. The old gatehouse. I think you've seen it.'

'Yes.'

'You were walking.'

It's an effort to return the smile; I hate the thought of someone watching me unobserved. 'I was trying to find the coastal path. My name's Jess, by the way. Pleased to meet you.'

'Roberta Silver. *Miss* Silver. But everyone calls me Robbie. How long are you staying in St Cross?'

'A fortnight. I believe the owner has gone to Scotland.'

There's an uncomfortable pause. Robbie stares at the deck-chair, and it takes me a moment to realise why.

'Is there something wrong?' I say, following her gaze to the notebook.

She shakes her head. 'Nothing wrong, but do say you'll come to the gatehouse? This afternoon? Angel won't bother you and your daughter can pick strawberries.'

'Okay.' I feel I haven't much choice.

'After lunch?'

I nod.

'We'll be waiting for you. Angel and I. We'll be waiting for you in the garden.' She turns around, pulled by the Jack Russell, walking fast across the lawn.

'She's weird.'

I look over my shoulder. Summer's standing at the back door, still in her pyjamas and hoodie, cradling a mug of coffee, her cheek creased from where she's lain on her pillow. I think about the argument yesterday, the fact Summer's yet to say sorry, and decide to let it pass.

'Ssh,' I say, 'she'll hear you.' But Summer just shrugs. 'She said she'd met you. But she didn't really explain. I think she's confused, poor love.'

Summer yawns. 'That first morning, she came to the back

door. She was just standing there, staring at the house, with that mangy old dog. Seriously, she freaked me out. She told me the doctor was here, or something like that. It didn't make any sense.'

'The doctor?' I laugh, but the words tumble about inside me. 'Well, I suppose this place used to be an infirmary.'

'Do you think she's properly crazy?'

I watch Robbie opening the gate to the wood, coaxing the dog. 'I think she's probably lonely. There's not much out here, is there? Not what you'd really call a community. Not much to do.'

A silence falls between us and I can't help thinking of the holiday we should have been having. The chalet by the sea, the beach, the bars, the buzz of a place alive with tourists. In hindsight, we shouldn't have promised the girls we'd go back. We should have been realistic. Success one year didn't mean success the next. Then there was the boy Summer had met. We'd got friendly with his parents, and I'd known immediately, they were people with money, people who holidayed on the French Riviera as a matter of course, as one of many holidays taken in a year. I'd only talked to Summer about Harry once. It was the last night in France, the evening air still warm, still tinged with expectation and the bristling hum of insects. I'd tried to give Summer the sex talk, realising she was growing up fast, but Summer had merely groaned, her face flushed with embarrassment, and said she already knew everything there was to know; they'd covered the topic extensively in school.

Looking down at the sloping lawn, I throw an arm around my daughter. 'Sorry, love. It's not exactly the holiday you were hoping for, is it?'

Summer swirls the coffee in her mug. 'It's cool. I like it here.'

'Really?' I try to meet her eye, but she looks away.

'I've already met someone my age. He lives in the cottage on the other side of the wood. He's called Aaron.'

'Oh?' I groan inwardly at the thought of the vaping teenager. Not Summer's age at all, I think warily, but a year or two older. But somehow I keep my views to myself.

'And no, before you ask, it's not like that. He's just a friend. I met him when I was out looking for the cat. He seems nice. We might hang out a bit.'

'Right.' What else am I supposed to say? I tighten my grip on my daughter, thinking again about the argument, the way Summer hadn't seemed herself. 'I love you, you know that don't you? And Dad loves you too. We might not always do the right thing, but we always try to do our best for you.'

Summer doesn't say anything, but I feel her relax and lean back against my shoulder.

Close up, the gatehouse is just as shabby as it had seemed from the road. The front windows are streaked with age-old dirt and hung with faded yellow curtains and white netting, which blocks the view into the house.

'We won't stay long,' I say, trying to sound enthusiastic as I push wide the gate into the narrow front garden. Xanthe hesitates, hanging back on the road. 'What is it, love?'

'It's nothing it's just . . .' she stares at her hands and I read the flush of guilt in her cheeks, 'I've been here before.'

'You've been here?'

'That time I got lost in the wood. I saw the old lady. She gave me tea. Weird tea. She made me stroke her dog.'

'You've been in the gatehouse?'

'I—'

'Hello!' Robbie Silver waves at us from the garden. 'Come round the back, I've got everything ready.'

I wave back feeling anything but cheerful. I glance at Xanthe. 'We'll talk about this later.'

The lawn is shin-high except for the little paths carved through the grass by the dog. There are a couple of untrained rose bushes by the wall and a stack of plastic plant pots lying on one side. Apart from that, there are no signs of any attempt to cultivate the garden. The place oozes sadness. A place that is lived in, but not loved, not cared for. As we pass the house, I see that the windowsill is a shrine to a macabre collection of tiny skeletons, the speckled blue and white of broken eggshells, the crisp yellowing skin of a snake.

We step around the side of the house to a small mown patch of lawn on which stands a table with four chairs. Robbie beams. 'Sit down. We'll take our tea out here. I've tea and biscuits and cooling lemonade for the little girl.' She fixes her gaze on Xanthe, and something about it makes me shudder.

'It looks lovely.' I try my best to be polite, wondering how long the tea and biscuits have stood here waiting for us. 'Where's the dog?'

'Angel's inside. He won't bother us. Sit down, make your-selves at home.' She fusses with the tea things, then smooths the cuffs of her dress. A pale blue dress with a narrow white belt and matching white shoes, cracked at the toes. Her cheeks glow with blusher and her lips are splashed bright pink. My heart sinks, guessing our visit won't be as swift as I'd hoped. Robbie has obviously been looking forward to this all day.

'Oh, look.' Xanthe runs towards a little rockery decorated with garden ornaments. A windchime tinkles softly overhead.

'There's a fairy!' She bends down and inspects the shimmering figurine planted between the rocks. 'She's so pretty. I wonder what she's called.'

'That one's Elvina,' Robbie says, pouring the tea. 'There's also Titania, Oberon, Pixie, Rosetta and Tinkerbell. But you will have to find them. Fairies are very shy creatures. They hide in the garden. Elvina's the only brave one. She's the only one who ever comes close enough to talk to.'

Xanthe squeals with delight and hurries off to explore and I swallow the urge to shout after her to watch out for dog poo. 'Have you lived here long?' I ask for something to say.

'All my life.' Robbie hands me a teacup. 'My grandparents worked in the manor. Then, when it was pulled down by the council, my parents kept the grounds.'

'Why was the manor pulled down?'

'The Massingham family lost their only son in the Great War. They had death duties to pay on top of mounting bills. It was the end of an era for a lot of the grand houses. The place was left to go to rack and ruin. Then in the sixties some youths got in and set fire to the place. After that, it was unsafe.'

'That's a shame.'

Robbie leans forward and fiddles with the tea cosy, stained black with old tea. 'It was the right thing to do, pull it down. There's only the foundations left now, in the field over there,' she nods towards the back of the garden, 'in what used to be the grounds.'

'And the infirmary,' I say, giving the house it's proper title. 'The infirmary's still there.'

'Yes.' Milk slops down the side of Robbie's cup as she fills it. She lifts the tea to her lips, dribbling milk on her dress. 'My parents didn't tend those grounds. That's always been the

Harrisons. Generation after generation. They used to garden for the manor house too. So, tell me,' she says, 'what brought you here for a holiday?'

'My husband found St Cross advertised on the internet.'

'You could have taken one of the static caravans further along the coast. They're very popular at this time of year. Good for families.'

'Maybe another time.' I don't want to admit we couldn't afford it. That this was the only chance of a holiday this year.

'Have you visited the church?'

'Not yet.'

'You should visit the church. It's always open. There are services once a month.'

We lapse into silence, watching Xanthe inspecting the hedgerow. I rack my brain for something to say. 'Tell me about St Cross. What do you know of it? Was it still an infirmary when you were a child?'

Robbie sets her cup down on the matching white saucer. 'The infirmary closed soon after I was born. After the Second World War, it was used for polio cases, and before that, it was a rehabilitation hospital for service men from the Great War.'

'And that's why it was built? Because of the war?'

Robbie shakes her head. 'It's much older than that. Built in the Victorian era. Originally, it was intended for poor people, and eventually it became a family home.' She pushes a plate of biscuits towards Summer. 'Help yourself, dear.'

Summer takes a pink wafer biscuit and nibbles the end.

'Do you know the family well?' I persist. 'The Clarence family?'

Robbie taps the side of her cup with her nails. Click, click, click. 'I knew Mrs Laurence.'

'Laurence?'

'Verity Laurence, the woman who lived there before Marianne Clarence. We were best friends.'

I sip my tea. It's boiling hot. Almost as if Robbie knew the exact moment we would arrive. I think about mentioning the diary, but then I remember the way Robbie had stared at it on the deckchair, the way she'd shaken her head.

'It was back in the seventies. I'd gone away for a couple of months to take a secretarial course in Bury St Edmunds and when I came back, I learned that the house had been bought by an American, Mr Laurence and his English bride, Verity, who was significantly younger than him. Caused quite a stir at the time. We met a couple of weeks later when Verity was walking the dog in the garden. I was in the wood and she called out to me.'

A breeze whispers through the garden, softly tinkling the windchime. For some reason, in my mind, I see the spidery old-fashioned writing in Charles Keller's diary.

'It was a hot day like today and Verity was wearing a sundress streaked with juice. I thought she was bleeding at first, but then I realised it was just tomatoes, she'd been picking them in the glasshouse. The dress was a gift from her husband, far fancier than anything I'd ever owned myself, and I helped her scrub it off in the big sink in the kitchen. She wasn't used to hard work. She was from a well-to-do family. Her father had recently died and the family had fallen on hard times. She never said anything, but I often wondered if that was the real reason she married Mr Laurence, to help her family out financially. But, bless her, she couldn't even work her way around a scrubbing board. Although we were from very different ways of life, we somehow hit it off.'

A wasp hovers over the covered jug of lemonade then makes its way to the plate of biscuits, buzzing loudly.

'Sadly, our friendship was short-lived. Mr Laurence didn't approve of me. He was a nasty piece of work. Controlling. Superior. The following summer, Verity had a baby. A healthy little thing, which grew up quickly. It didn't seem quite right when he died.'

'He died.' It comes out as an echo rather than a question.

'He was three years old, climbing a tree in the garden. He was a strong lad, physically advanced. He shouldn't have fallen, not from the low branches where he was standing. He hit his head on a stone and died a few days later. Verity had the tree cut down after that, she couldn't bear to be reminded about what had happened. Then three months after that, she died too.'

'I'm sorry. That's awful.'

Robbie nods sadly. 'So young. Verity was just a child herself, just turned twenty-two.'

'Why didn't Mr Laurence approve of you?'

'I wasn't the right sort. Mr Laurence was all airs and graces. A rich American playing lord of the manor, though the manor house was long gone by then. Verity just wanted to be young and have fun. I don't think she knew what she'd got herself into when she married him. He didn't think our friendship was appropriate. After she died, he married again, Marianne, the lady who eventually became the present Mrs Clarence – people said he couldn't stand being alone in the house – and this time, I kept away.'

'But you're friends with Mrs Clarence now?'

'We're neighbours.'

'How did Verity die?' I don't know why, but it seems important to know.

There's a screech from behind and I turn to see Xanthe running through the grass, cradling a painted metal fairy in her hand. 'I've found Titania!' she beams. 'This one *is* Titania, isn't it? *Isn't it?*'

Robbie slams her teacup down on the wasp. Biscuits crack. Milky tea slops on to the tray. She rises from her chair. 'You're to leave them where they are.'

'I'm sorry?' I jump to Xanthe's aid, seeing her crestfallen face.

'The fairies. You need to leave them where you find them. Naughty girl. Stupid girl. They're there for a reason.'

Notice, Lowestoft, 1847:

The governors of St Cross Infirmary, which lies on the site of the medieval hospital in Blythe and which serves the poor people of Suffolk including those from the workhouse at nearby St John's, are delighted to announce the employment of Mr Charles Keller, a surgeon from London, at the generous behest of Lord James Massingham of Blythe Manor.

14

Xanthe

Xanthe stares at the old lady, the words floating past her, not making any sense. The old lady's cheeks are the same bright pink as her lips. The same pink as the wings of the fairy in her hand. Xanthe makes a conscious effort to block it all out – the garden, the teacups, the biscuits, the pool of milk – as the tingling in her head rises and rises. A dam about to burst.

'She's an old witch,' she says when they're back in the big house. 'A stupid old witch.' She dumps a plastic carrier bag of strawberries on the kitchen table, and blinks back tears. Already the strawberries they were made to pick after Mummy had quietened the old lady down look like mush.

'She just doesn't like you moving her things, that's all.' Mummy throws an arm around Xanthe's shoulder. 'Some old people are like that. Stuck in their ways. You shouldn't let her bother you. She didn't mean to be unkind. I'm sure she didn't.'

'I hate her.'

Mummy lets go of her and grabs a knife for the strawberries. 'Want to help me with this? Take your mind off it?'

'No.' Xanthe turns and runs into the hallway and up the stairs, wiping away tears. She needs to be on her own. She needs to get away from Mummy and Summer. Just like when Grandma died and no one understood and everyone was pretending things were just the same. No one talked about the grave Grandma had gone to. The place where no one comes to find you. The coldness. The silence. It's only Xanthe who seems to even think about these things, to notice when things aren't right, when things need fixing.

'Hey, Little Bear. Daddy catches her on the stairs as he's coming down. 'Why the hurry?'

'I need the toilet,' she lies, and he lets her pass.

She closes the bedroom door and leans against it, breathing hard, thinking how much she hates that old lady and her horrible dog. She doesn't even like the garden with the fairies, or the strawberries they were made to pick in the rain. Most of all, she doesn't like the way the old lady looked at her, looked *through* her as if she knew what she was thinking. *No one knows what I'm thinking. No one has a right.* And she doesn't like the way the old lady shouted at her about the fairy, the anger behind her eyes.

It was the same the last time Xanthe had visited the gate-house. She feels bad about that, about not telling Mummy. She should have told Mummy before she got in the too-hot bath, only the words hadn't come, and she'd known deep down that her mother wouldn't understand.

She'd got lost and found herself wandering down the road, and the old lady had invited her in.

'My name's Robbie,' the old lady had said, holding out her freckled fingers. 'I want you to have tea with me and make friends with my dog.'

'You have a dog?'

'He's called Angel.'

Xanthe had seen movement behind the net curtains. A white-haired dog, pawing at the glass, scattering the assortment of shells and stones and what looked like bones. She didn't like the bones. She couldn't understand why they were there. Maybe the dog had found them and brought them inside? 'He doesn't look like an angel.'

'Come and see for yourself.'

She'd found herself inside the strange grey cottage, sitting on an upturned box, staring at the tea tray already set with two cups and a plate of pink wafer biscuits. It was like Robbie had known she was coming all along.

'It smells funny,' she'd said, forgetting her manners when Robbie had placed a steaming cup in her hands. The cottage was unlike anything she'd been in before with its cardboard furniture and haired-up cushions, which she knew Mummy wouldn't like, and the old lady had looked at her sternly, her pale green eyes narrowing into slits. Right then, she'd wished she hadn't gone exploring, hadn't gone wandering through the wood and found the rotten Wendy house and looked inside. She'd wished she hadn't fallen and snagged her T-shirt on the brambles as she'd run away again, out the other side, down the road, all the way to the gatehouse rather than back towards the holiday home.

'Sage tea,' Robbie had said. 'You can take it with lemon if you like.' She'd taken a pair of silver tongs, lifted a slice of lemon from a blue and white plate, dropped it in Xanthe's cup.

The cup was cracked around the edges, and the tea smelled exactly like the rest of the house, only stronger. A bit like stuffing inside the turkey at Christmas.

'I've never had sage tea before,' she'd admitted, taking a sip. 'Sometimes Mummy makes me strawberry.'

'And now I want you to make friends with my dog.' Robbie had leaned forward, the flaps of her dressing gown parting, revealing a chest as soft and rippled as a river. 'Don't be afraid.' Angel had growled up at Xanthe from the mat and she'd wondered, for the first time, if Robbie was mad. 'You need to learn. You need to learn to hold the fear inside you.'

But when she'd reached forward to stroke him, Angel had started to yap again.

Now, she leans against the bedroom door, trying to stop the yapping in her mind. She's staring at the cot, at the Mickey Mouse painting on the old white wood. Her mind begins to drift. She imagines the child who'd slept here last, not a baby but a child like herself in a stiff white nightie, with long slender fingers grasping the bars. And then an image swims in her mind. Mia Williams, the girl from her old school, the girl she always pictures in a bright blue sundress, jam sandwich in hand, jam smears on her sleeve. 'I can see you, Xanthe.' She shivers at the memory, remembering what she'd told her best friends Megan and Joe about Mia, and what Megan and Joe had told the teachers, and how everything after that had gone horribly, horribly wrong.

Footsteps up the stairs. Mummy coming to find her. Xanthe runs to the cot, pulls back the quilt, rummages beneath the pillow until she finds what she's looking for. The tiny pink bracelet with the silver snake charm – the bracelet Mia gave her. She holds the bracelet and rubs the tiny snake over and over.

15

Liam

I lock up for the night, taking care to check every room, every door, every window, ensuring that everything that can be is closed and latched. Not that anyone could get in, not with the windows only opening so far. But ever since I heard that tapping sound upstairs, I've been on edge. I can't shake the feeling we're under surveillance – someone or something is waiting to pounce. I examine the windows in the dining room, the study, the kitchen, the other junk rooms on the ground floor, scanning the space for my phone at the same time, just in case. It's driving me mad, not having my phone. I've asked Jess, I've asked the girls, but they've all denied sight of it.

I walk into the kitchen. The two cats, Snowy and Stripey, look up at me from the rocking chair by the window, but don't move. I check the back door, check the latch at the window.

You can never be too careful, I think, remembering the time the men had called at the house. It had been a Wednesday, a work day, Jess had been out and the kids had been at school. The doorbell had rung insistently. I'd presumed it was an Amazon delivery driver, or a neighbour wanting help. But when I'd opened the door, two men had thrown me backwards and pushed me up hard against the hallway wall.

'We're calling for a friend,' one of the men had said in answer to the question I hadn't had the chance to ask.

'A friend?' I'd somehow managed to gasp out the words.

'You owe him money. A lot of money. This is just a little,' the man had laughed and I'd smelled the stale nicotine on his breath, 'friendly reminder.'

An elbow had jammed against my windpipe, a knee had been shoved into my groin, and when I'd looked down through waves of nauseating agony, I'd seen the glint of a blade. Then, just as suddenly as it had started, the men had let me go again and walked casually away. I'd been too shocked to do anything but stand there, cradling my crotch, watching the fumes from their double exhaust misting the street.

Now, Snowy looks at me knowingly, extending and retracting her claws. I make a conscious effort to pull myself together. I'm meant to be the strong one, the man of the family. I need to keep my shit together in case we really are being watched. In case those men are back again. In case they've followed us here to St Cross. I glance at the bottle of sherry I secreted earlier behind a pile of Mrs Clarence's crap, so bloody tempted to have another drink. But I'm not about to go down that route again.

Instead, I step into the hall. The house is silent. Jess and the girls are in the lounge playing board games after giving up trying to get the old-fashioned TV to work. I glance at the roof window, the pale evening sky, the way the light illuminates the gallery landing and the door to the locked room. Mrs Clarence's bedroom. For some reason, the door holds me mesmerised — a sturdy wooden door like all the others in the house — but there's something about it. Something that gives me the weird impression of having stood here before, stood at the bottom of the stairs, looking up.

Mum, I don't feel very well.

Another memory flashes through my mind. I'm twelve years old again, just come in from playing rugby with my mates. My mum is wearing a bright pink tabard and doing the dusting. She looks down at me from the landing, feather duster in hand, worry furrowing her brow. *What is it, son?* My legs are shaking, covered with muck and grass from the pitch. I look up at my mum, pleading with my eyes. Then, slowly I sink to the floor, clutching my side.

I shake my head, dislodging the memory, dislodging the pain. That was then and this is now. St Cross is nothing like the council house I lived in growing up. Not remotely similar. I've no idea why my mind is travelling back to that time. Maybe it was Xanthe's dream last night and the drawing I'd glimpsed earlier in her diary: a man with a knife. 'What's that?' I'd said, but she'd seen me looking and closed the book.

I turn back to the kitchen. On reflection, maybe that glass of sherry isn't such a bad idea. Just a small glass to settle my nerves.

*Note penned by F. Fisher, governor, St Cross
Infirmary, 10 September 1847:*

*A suitable room has been identified for the accommodation of
the surgeon at St Cross – a light and airy room on the first floor
overlooking the entrance porch. It is the decision of the governors
that this room be fitted with furniture appropriate to the position
of surgeon: a bed and desk, a cabinet for storing medicine, a
wash stand and basin, a wardrobe for hanging such clothes and
garments deemed necessary for the undertaking of duties.*

16

Jess

I turn a page in my book, the words blurred, dancing. For some reason, I can't settle. I'm on edge, as if I know something is about to happen. I read a paragraph once, twice. I'm beyond tired and it's way past midnight – our fourth night in the house – but there's no point even trying to sleep, not yet, not like this. Liam had seemed on edge for most of the evening, worried about the book or so he'd said, and I'd been left to deal with the girls, finding an old Monopoly set in the cupboard, cajoling them into a game. It had ended in an argument: Summer accusing Xanthe of stealing money, swiping the counters off the board with her hand, then stomping off, leaving Xanthe in tears. At home, it wouldn't have bothered me so much – the girls often fight – but here in the house it had felt like our family was fragmenting, and I'd had to remind myself, despite Summer's overreaction, it was normal for siblings to bicker.

I yawn and turn another page. I need to relax before I even try to sleep, envying Liam who's deep asleep already. But, something whispers from the corner of the room. I drop the book in my lap, my eyes drawn to the wardrobe, to the door that's blocked by the chest of drawers. I shudder at the thought there could be mice in there or, worse still, rats. But it doesn't sound like rodents. It sounds like – I hold my breath and listen intently – material brushing against the back of the door, and a faint but distinctive tapping.

I peel back the quilt and slide out of bed, knowing I have to investigate or I'll never sleep at all. Icy air tingles against my skin as I tiptoe across the room, not wanting to wake Liam. I catch sight of myself in the freestanding mirror, catch sight of the bed and the half-lit painting of the Virgin Mary above it.

Tap ... tap ... tap ...

The sound is louder now. Louder and faster. I imagine a whole colony of rats leaping out at me when I open the door. But then I realise it's already open, the chest of drawers pulled away slightly from the wardrobe. Was it like that before? This morning, I was sure it had been flush. Liam must have edged it out for some reason and maybe one of the cats had got inside. The mysterious third cat who no one can find. That's it, I think. That must be it. Poor thing. It's probably starving.

Tap ... tap ... tap ...

My heart stammers. I consider waking Liam, but then I remember how tired he is, the weird mood that cloaked him all evening. Better to let him sleep and deal with this myself. I reach for the little brass handle, then crack open the door as far as it will go before hitting the chest of drawers.

Something falls from the peg on the inside door, landing at my feet. I stifle a scream. Staring up at me is a pair of tiny pin-prick eyes. For a moment, I think it's the cat, but then I realise it's a stole made out of fox fur, crowned by a real fox's head. I hold my breath again. The noise has stopped, just an eery stillness and the rippling memory of my own strangled scream.

The wardrobe is crammed with old-fashioned, fusty-smelling clothes. I pick up the stole and throw it back in with all the junk, but something else has fallen down with it, something still lying at my feet. I lift it up, immediately regretting it. The smell, oh God. It's repulsive, making me gag. A putrid smell of something rotten, like the smell elsewhere in the house, only far, far worse. But it's just another item of clothing: a jacket, light grey with a deep lapel, a jacket I'm sure I've seen some-where before. I fling it on to the chaise longue, then, tentatively, run a finger over the wool, turning it over one way then the other. It's pitted with moth holes and stained with age and dirt. The silk lining is ripped, the dull silver buttons on the cuffs dangling on their threads, the sleeves caked with whatever dirt is splattered all over the front panels. The smell is worse now, filling the room as if whatever evil is contained within the wool is seeping out.

I have to get rid of it.

I take my phone from the bedside table, switch it to torch mode, then drape the jacket over my arm. The deep chill fol-lows me from the bedroom, across the landing and down the stairs, the phone light picking out the stair runner, the stat-ues – saints, I think – on the newel posts, the terracotta floor tiles in the entrance hall. I hold the jacket far out in front of me, the light fragrance of the flowers I cut earlier and placed in a vase to brighten the place up unable to compete with the rancid stench of the old wool. Above me, I hear the sound of rain on the cupola and wonder whether it's been raining all along. Does that explain the noise in the bedroom? Water running into the house somehow, distorted through the walls? I move my phone so that the light picks out the glass panels of the kitchen door, and run towards them, desperate to get out, to reach the back door.

Outside, the rain is torrential. I throw the jacket on the path and allow the rain to soak me, feeling better just standing there, looking up at the starless sky as raindrops fall in my eyes, streak my cheeks, trickle beneath my pyjama top. A sudden stroke of lightning illuminates the wood and the garden and little stone wall. I breathe deeply, trying to capture the relief I felt just moments ago, feeling for the St Anthony around my neck before remembering I've lost it, the thing that calms me, that makes me feel in control. Instead, I count to three over and over, fingering my naked skin, the edge of my collarbone.

When I turn inside, the first thing I see is the diary – Charles Keller's diary – on the kitchen table. I stare at it, uncertain. It's like it's waiting for me, though I'm sure it wasn't there a moment ago. I would have noticed it, wouldn't I? Had I left it there without remembering? Or had Liam moved it there earlier? I reach out and open the front cover, seeing once more Charles Keller's handwriting on the thin yellowing paper.

Charles Keller's diary:

<u>4 October 1847</u>

Today, I journeyed from London to Suffolk, a miserable journey, the rain dashing the carriage windows and the horses churning muck. By the time we arrived it was evening and dark. The air was brittle with cold, but fresh – a stark contrast to the thick, wheezing air of London. I was shown into the manor at Blythe where I am to spend the night, and shook out my coat in a large entrance hall, lit by what seemed like a thousand candelabra. Lord Massingham greeted me heartily, apologising for the coachman with his rough ways, and asking me to dine with him despite the hour, a request to which I readily agreed, having eaten nothing since leaving Southwark. Over a hearty supper of roast meats and wine, Massingham talked incessantly and with great passion about his project, the infirmary at nearby St Cross where I am to be taken tomorrow. He has in mind an establishment to rival the most modern and illustrious of hospitals. It was past midnight when he bade me goodnight and I was shown to these comfortable quarters. Now I am weary, but not at all ready for sleep – I have drunk too much wine and am far too excited – and so, in a mood of anticipation, I am starting this diary.

5 October 1847

I awoke with the feeling of not having slept at all – parting aside the dark curtains of the bed and peering into the richly furnished room. I suppose I am still tired from the journey yesterday and our late night discussing Lord Massingham's plans. Still, I hastened to rise, not wanting to insult or in any way disappoint my host. I found him in the dining room with Lady Massingham who insisted I eat yet another big meal: curds, marmalades, kippers, ham. After breakfast, Lord Massingham requested I walk out with him, eager to show me his work at the infirmary. To my surprise, the storm yesterday had left little mark on the landscape, just a few stray twigs upon the lawn. The manor is in a most pleasant, rural spot, quite close to the sea. I fancy it is Jacobean with a number of later extensions. The garden is landscaped on two levels and there is a large kitchen garden to the rear.

The infirmary is a short walk from the manor, passing the head gardener's cottage, then taking a well-trodden path through a wood. It is an imposing building on the site of a former medieval hospital known as St Cross. The present building (which takes the same name) is not one I care for, but well suited to its purpose, being similar in design to a prison and thus affording the staff with a clear view of the wards. This, Lord Massingham was keen to press, was deliberate; the patients need to be watched at all times to ensure optimum recovery as well as the smooth running of the house. The contrast between St Cross and the manor is stark. The walls of the infirmary are painted in the muted tones of a servants' hall and the décor is plain.

Lord Massingham introduced me to the staff, who, I fear, are not of the quality I am used to in London, but poor, simple folk. The matron, Mrs Harker, is a tall woman with an irritating habit of jangling her châtelaine in response to any question asked. I was shown to the room that is to serve both as study and bedroom, a large room overlooking the porch. There is a bed and desk and a cupboard, more than large enough to accommodate my modest wardrobe, everything sturdy but simple (I had, it seemed, been spoilt last night at the manor and should have tempered my expectations). Soon after, I was introduced to my personal staff. I have at my disposal a young man who will act as dresser and another – a taller man with a gruff voice – who will act as ordinal, manservant and whatever else I wish. It seems I am to begin my work tomorrow, overseeing the arrival of new patients from the workhouse.

17

Liam

I creep downstairs, leaving Jess to sleep in. Today is a fresh start. I've woken up determined. No more procrastination. No more just sitting there, tapping my thumbs. Today I'm going to write the bloody thing.

I rub my hands together, blowing warmth into them, before pushing wide the study door. Sunlight streaks through the window, blinding me, reminding me, despite the chill, it's the middle of summer. August. *God.* The seasons are so messed up. The hall is like ice, and the study, despite the sun, isn't much better.

It takes me a moment to focus, taking in the mess of yesterday, my coffee cups, my doodles, my opened laptop, and then I remember I've lost my phone. Groaning, I do the usual patting down of my pockets, just in case. I feel naked without it, an itchy, creeping feeling. Jess has phoned my number several times, in different parts of the house, but I haven't heard my phone ringing. Knowing my luck, it's probably on silent.

I scratch the back of my hand, questions revolving in my mind. What if the stock market's turned? What if I've lost more money? What if I've been wiped out completely? What if I've *made* money?

Suddenly, I'm furious, flinging papers aside. Where the hell is the router? If I found the router and the Wi-Fi password, at least I'd be able to use my laptop to access my account. There's got to be a router somewhere. If I had my phone, at least I could ask Callum. I grab a pile of books from the desk, fling them to the floor, trample paper on the carpet.

My brain pounds as I stand back against the door, staring in horror at the mess. Still no router. I clutch my brow, telling myself it's all right. Everything's going to be all right. Later, I'll ask Jess if I can use her phone as a hotspot – I'll make an excuse about needing to check my emails or doing research for the book.

I open the door and march across the hall to the kitchen. Halfway across I stop dead in my tracks. There's a portrait on the wall, between the various religious scenes. A man in shadows I haven't noticed before, a man with pale almond eyes and a long moustache. I take a step forwards, read the label beneath it: Lord James Henry Massingham 1848.

I draw long scratches against the back of my hand, remembering the feeling I had yesterday, the vision – was that what it was? – of falling from the gallery landing, the sense of vulnerability, holding on to my willpower by a mere thread. It was here, I think; this was the place where my body would have fallen. I drag my gaze from the portrait and look up at the insipid light through the cupola, illuminating the wall above Mrs Clarence's bedroom. There's something there I haven't noticed before. A bricked-up window overlooking the landing. It must belong to an attic room. The urge to investigate tugs like a cord, but I've no idea how to get into the attic. There must be a staircase somewhere, probably servants' stairs, but wherever it is it's hidden from sight.

I resume my walk to the kitchen, less urgent now. I can't even remember why I was hurrying, why I was going there in the first place. It had seemed so important at the time. Evidently, Jess cleaned up after everyone went to bed. There are breakfast things laid out neatly on the sideboard, the cats' dishes are soaking in the sink, our coffee cups are ready for filling. Everything is perfectly ordered.

I retrieve the bottle of sherry I stored behind the row of Kilner jars. This time, I don't pause to think. I pour myself a glass and down it in one, feeling the sweet-bitter kick at the back of my throat. All these years I've been abstemious, convincing myself I can't trust myself to drink like a normal person. But is it really such a crime to have a small drink, just to get you going for the day, to dull a pounding headache?

I put the bottle back into the cupboard, and rub my hands together, jogging on the spot, not allowing space to doubt myself. 'Time to get going,' I say out loud, resisting the urge to pour myself another, larger glass. I make myself an instant coffee, take it across to the study, pausing once again in the hall. The outline of the window is clearer now, as if the sun is deliberately seeking it out. I've a strange sense of everything being connected, the sunlight, the house, the window. *Us.*

Abandoning my coffee on the table, I retrace my steps from earlier: up the stairs, along the landing, past the girls' bedroom, as silently as I can, taking care not to wake anyone. I just need to find that staircase, find out what lies behind the blocked-up window. I imagine an attic room stuffed with treasure, family heirlooms that have lain undisturbed for years – an attic room that has long been forgotten. What a thrill to discover it, to be the first person in a hundred years to open the door.

I turn the doorknob to Mrs Clarence's room. It's locked. I know it's locked. I've tried it before, the night we arrived, looking for the best places to sleep, but it's the most obvious way to the room above. I peer through the keyhole, not expecting to see anything, not in the milky morning light. But I'm surprised that I can: bare floorboards, a sash window arched at the top.

I feel itchy again, my skin crawling as if something's burrowing it's way inside. Callum told me his mother's bedroom was locked, that we are free to use any of the other rooms in the house except that one. But what I'm looking at isn't a bedroom. I remember the old-fashioned knickers in the room Jess and I have commandeered, the wardrobe stuffed with musty coats and hideous fur stoles. And then I get it. I fucking get it. The room I'm looking at right now through the keyhole isn't Mrs Clarence's room at all. It can't be, because we're sleeping in it. *We're sleeping in Mrs Clarence's bedroom.* It all makes sense: the little personal items, the hairbrushes, the handkerchiefs. Typical of an old person to forget to lock something, in this case a bedroom, when they said they would. And this other room is, well ...

I press my forehead hard against the door, move my gaze a little to the left until I find what I'm looking for: a short flight of steps leading to a closed door. A closed door that – I'm sure of it – leads into the attic stairwell. Leads directly into the room with the blocked-up window.

I rattle the doorknob, frustrated. I want to get in there. I *need* to get in there. I look around for clues as to the whereabouts of the key. There's a cabinet a little further along the landing, the obvious place. I wrench open doors, careless now of the noise. Another linen closet. God, how much linen does one old lady need? There's a deep musty smell as if this stuff hasn't been used in years. At the bottom of each drawer is a paper lining strewn with flowers that are so old they're almost disintegrated, just stalks and dust.

'Dad? What are you doing?'

'Oh, Jesus.' I jump.

Summer is standing in the doorway of the girls' room, looking at me with quizzical eyes. I hold my hands up defensively, as if I've been caught doing something I shouldn't.

'I was looking for a key,' I say, 'for the room next door.'

'It's five-thirty in the morning.'

'Sorry. Was I loud?'

'What do you think?'

She turns back into the bedroom and closes the door. The renewed silence is so penetrating, so almost-complete, I can hear the tread of her footsteps back to her bed. I turn to the cabinet, the doors pulled wide, the linen dumped on the floor, the smell of mothballs. The clear absence of a key. I taste sherry on my tongue and feel the dust of years on my fingertips. What the hell am I playing at?

18

SUMMER

I'm lying on the bed, quilt rolled to my feet, composing a WhatsApp message to Aaron.

Hi. It was nice to meet you the other day. Want to hang out?

I rub my eyes and re-read what I've written. Too formal. Too boring. I press delete and try again.

Remember me, the girl you tried to spook? Nice pants btw.

I laugh to myself, delete the message – obviously, I'm not going to send *that* – and replace it with a single 'Hi'. I press send and immediately regret it. 'Hi' could mean everything or nothing at all. I twirl a strand of hair around my finger and pull, feeling the quick nick of pain in my scalp, the blissful if short-lived aftermath. It doesn't matter, I tell myself. Aaron can either say 'Hi' back or choose to ignore me. And if he ignores me, fine. Although it would be nice to have someone to hang out with, someone my age – after all, it was him who suggested we swap numbers.

I roll on my side. I don't want to analyse my feelings about Aaron. I don't want to misread the signals or, worse still, end up getting hurt again. Being friends is cool. And if he doesn't want to be friends, I'll find something else to do for entertainment, work my way through the dusty books in the study, or find my way into the room with the blocked-up window. I grab another strand of hair and then another, twirling, pulling. Memories flicker mothlike through my mind: Harry; school; exams; the boy I kissed at the house party. Twirl, pull.

My phone vibrates.

Aaron: Do you always get up this early?

I smile and type back: Early bird catches the worm. It's one of Mum's favourite sayings and as soon as I press send, I cringe.

He responds immediately: Thought you were vegetarian?

Pescatarian actually

Fancy a walk? Or a swim?!!!

My gaze darts to my bikini, piled in a heap on the floor. Are you being serious?

Deadly. Meet you at the pond in fifteen minutes.

Fifteen minutes. Shit. I peel off my pyjamas, and fiddle with my bikini, still damp from the sea. The material clings to my skin and the clasp takes ages to do up at the back. I pull a hoodie and a pair of shorts over the top, push my feet into trainers. Now, I just need to get past Dad, avoid the inevitable questions about where I'm going and how long I'll be and who I'm going to be with.

I tiptoe downstairs. The house is silent, a muted silence as though someone's thrown a cloth over it. There's no sign of anyone about, only the white cat, Snowy, asleep in one of the chairs in the hall. Dad's probably in the study, working on his manuscript. I open the kitchen door and my heart sinks: Dad's standing at the workstation, pouring himself what looks like cordial.

'Hi, Dad,' I say, trying to sound casual. 'Couldn't get back to sleep. I'm going for a walk.'

He startles at the sight of me, downs his drink and wipes his mouth with the back of his hand. 'Sure,' he says, fishing a mug from the cupboard. He scoops out a teaspoon of instant coffee. 'Have fun.'

'You sure?' I can't believe my luck.

He cocks me a conspiratorial smile. 'Sure, why not?'

I make my escape before he changes his mind and starts asking questions, open the back door and step out on to the terrace. The sky is a dusty blue and the air feels fresh after the staleness of the house; there's a distinct feel of autumn, a coolness on my arms through my hoodie. I slow my step as I near the wood, pushing aside the thought of the encroaching school term and trying to remember my way to the pond. I take a track to the left, approaching what I think is the clearing, but it's not the space I'm looking for. It's a smaller opening between the trees, in the centre of which is what looks like a Wendy house.

It's *this* house, I think, recalling the building I've just left.

St Cross except in miniature. It's exquisitely constructed, the detail of the porch, the painted windows, the domed roof, but it's shabby with age. The paint is faded and peeling, and the wood looks rotten and riddled with insects. The impulse to open the door and investigate soon disappears.

I turn around and fight my way through the undergrowth, taking what I hope is a short cut, eventually meeting another track to the right. A minute later I'm standing at the pond, looking at my murky reflection in the water.

'Hey. You okay? You're shivering.' Aaron's gym-toned figure joins mine in the reflection.

I swivel. 'You shouldn't sneak up on people like that.'

'Sorry.' He takes a step backwards, then frowns. 'Didn't you bring a towel?'

'No.' I feel like such an idiot. 'I forgot.'

'Maybe we shouldn't go in,' he says, eyeing the water. 'It's colder today. I don't want to add enforced hypothermia to my list of crimes.'

'Try stopping me.' Without questioning myself, I tug off my hoodie, slide down my shorts, kick off my trainers. I want to prove myself. I want to prove I'm more than the girl I am in school. The girl who shies away from things, who tries to get through the day unnoticed. I'm aware of him staring at me, staring at my bikini top, and find I don't mind. 'Come on,' I say, 'if you're brave enough that is.'

I wade in, wincing at the cold, then throw myself under. What feels like a thousand icy knives slice my skin. I resurface, slopping my hair back from my forehead, my teeth chattering. I look around for Aaron, but he's not on the bank, not between the trees. For a moment, I think he's run off, but then I hear a splash from behind.

'Fair play,' he says, swimming lazily towards me, causing ripples. 'I don't know many girls who would get in just like that.'

I splash water in his eyes. 'It's the twenty-first century. Women have the vote. They become prime ministers and swim in the Arctic and do all sorts of stuff. Or maybe they don't teach you things like that in your posh school?'

He laughs, floating on his back. 'I was trying to give you a compliment.'

I move into a fast breaststroke. 'Actually, I'm in the swimming team at school.'

'Oh yes?'

'But usually we swim in a heated pool.' It's the one thing about school I actually enjoy. The only place it doesn't seem to matter I'm the new girl. The girls in the swimming team aren't exactly what I would call friends, but they're not my enemies either.

'Heated pools are overrated.' He flashes me a smile before ploughing into a front crawl. I follow, reaching him easily on the other side of the pond, then take a moment to look at him properly, his dark hair slicked back from his forehead, his eyes brown beneath long lashes. The sort of boy who, given the state of his clothes and the clear lack of a recent haircut, doesn't give a shit about fashion.

'So,' he says, 'have you given much thought to the mirror?'

'Not really.' I tread water to warm myself up. I'm lying, of course. I've thought a *lot* about the mirror. That weird fucking voice. I try to sound detached. 'The voice I heard, it definitely wasn't English. Only, how can I invent a language I haven't learned?'

'Did you see anything in the glass?'

'No, just a mist.'

'Did you feel anything? Anything touching you? Or moving around you?'

'No.' I bite my lip, because there was something, wasn't there? A feeling. A drawing in. Nothing I can explain. Nothing that won't stop me from sounding stupid.

'We should do it again.' He pulls himself out of the pond, on to the bank.

'I don't think so.' I follow him, sliding in the mud, smearing dirt along my thigh. I grab my hoodie, conscious of my nipples showing through my bikini top. 'It's not safe. Maybe the priest at your school was right. What if it was the devil speaking to me?'

He throws me a look that says, *Are you serious?*, then rubs his back with his towel. 'You know that's just bullshit, right?'

'Why?' I pull on the hoodie.

'Because for a start, the devil doesn't exist.'

'But you don't know that, do you?'

He stares at me hard, and despite the fact I'm still shivering, still thinking about the voice, I feel an energy travelling up and down my body. 'Trust me,' he says. 'The devil doesn't exist. It's just a story made up to frighten kids.'

'Then why did I hear a voice?'

'Maybe it was something you remembered from a movie. Or maybe it was a spirit.'

I laugh. 'You mean, like a ghost?'

'I mean, someone who died around here. We should do it again. You need to ask it who it is.'

I pull on my shorts, turn away to fix the zip, my fingers still clumsy with cold. The last thing I want to do is try the mirror again. The idea of a dead person hanging about, using me as a sort of radio, isn't much better than the devil.

I turn back again. 'If it was a ghost, what's it doing in your bedroom?'

He shrugs. 'The cottage is pretty old. There must have been births and deaths there. But maybe that's not where it came from. Maybe it's not the cottage. Maybe it's you.'

'*Me?*'

'Maybe the spirit is following you around.'

I laugh nervously. 'You're really into all this, aren't you?'

'Why? Aren't you?'

'Not really.' I remember other stuff beside the mirror: the feeling in the darkness when I'd gone in search of the cat; the unseen eyes watching me from the roof window. 'I've got enough going on without some spook following me around.'

'Like what?'

'Like stuff.'

There's an awkward pause. He slides on his flipflops and walks towards me. 'Hey, how about we get some breakfast? My nan makes these amazing cinnamon rolls.' He tightens the towel around his waist so that I'm drawn to the water gleaming on his chest.

I look back through the trees at St Cross and realise it's the last place I want to go. 'Your nan won't mind?'

'She likes visitors.'

'Isn't it a bit early?'

'You haven't met my nan. She's not like normal people.'

I frown. 'What do you mean?'

'I mean, I think you should talk to her. She's into all this too. Spirits and stuff. She might be able to help.'

I hesitate, hugging myself for warmth, making a conscious effort to still my chattering teeth.

'Come on,' he says, reaching his hand out to mine. Cold skin against cold skin. I feel a buzz deep down. 'I'm making the decision for you. You're bloody freezing.'

The rolls are good. Really good. I sit in the kitchen of the red-bricked cottage, huddled in one of Aaron's nan's towels, peeling off a strip of sugary cinnamon bread.

Aaron's nan, Mrs Harrison, smiles at me kindly. 'Spirits – the ones we *feel* – are just people like you or me who, for one reason or another, haven't passed over yet.' She leans over the kitchen table and pours tea from a proper teapot. 'Drink that. You look frozen to the bone, poor thing. Trust Aaron to make you go swimming.'

'I didn't make her.' Aaron helps himself to another roll. 'Summer's a feminist. She does what she likes.'

'Quite right too.' Mrs Harrison turns towards me. 'You mustn't listen to him. He's a troublemaker this one.'

Aaron pulls a face and I wonder how much Mrs Harrison knows about Aaron's school, about the Ouija board and the scrying. We haven't mentioned the mirror, and I've a feeling, despite Mrs Harrison's talk of spirits, Aaron hasn't told her either.

'Spirits are a fact of life,' Mrs Harrison says, 'just one they don't teach you about at school. It's easier, neater, for people to believe that when you die you're gone or you go to heaven. There's no in between.'

I sip my tea. It's sweet and milky and warms me up. 'How can you be sure about spirits?'

'Because if you look carefully, you can see them.'

'*See* them?'

'Usually they appear as little lights. There's one right now, sitting on your shoulder.'

I dart to my left, spilling tea all over my sleeve.

'Shit. Nan!' Aaron grabs a cloth and dabs at my hoodie, then he rests his hand on my arm. It feels like burning. 'Are you okay?'

'Yes.' I realise I'm shivering again despite the towel Mrs Harrison insisted I drape over my shoulders, despite Aaron's hand. I can't help thinking about the voice I heard when I looked in the mirror. 'I'm fine. It's just ... what do you mean?'

'There's no need to be afraid.' Mrs Harrison pushes the plate of cinnamon rolls towards me. 'Have another one.'

'No, thanks.' My default response when it comes to calorie-laden food.

Mrs Harrison takes a roll for herself, cuts it in two, and spreads butter on both halves. 'Peter doesn't like me talking like this. He thinks it's all nonsense.' She looks across at Aaron. 'And no doubt your mother wouldn't like me talking about this either.'

Aaron rolls his eyes. 'In case you hadn't noticed, Mum's not here.'

'Just don't tell your mother I told you all this.' She leans forward and fixes her gaze on me. 'People don't just die and disappear. They come back. Sometimes it's not even a question of coming back. They don't go in the first place.'

'Why did you say I've got a light on my shoulder?'

Mrs Harrison dunks her buttery roll in her tea and sucks off the sugar. 'Have you lost someone recently? Someone in your family?'

'There's my grandmother, but we weren't close. She lived abroad. Spain. In one of those retirement places. I'd only met her about five times.'

Mrs Harrison smiles and wipes the sugar from her finger.

'That's probably it. It's your gran on your shoulder. She wasn't close to you in life, so she's come to see you now. Maybe she feels guilty for living so far away? But, she's here now, looking after you. Maybe, she thinks there's some sort of trouble brewing and she's here to protect you.'

Aaron yawns dramatically. 'Don't tell me, you think that trouble is me.'

'No.' Mrs Harrison looks serious, her eyes still on mine, and I feel suddenly very cold. 'I don't think so. You need to take care. I haven't seen a light as bright as that for a long time.'

I hug the towel. 'But why can't I see it?'

'Most people close their minds to the spirits. As babies, we all see the lights. Have you ever seen a baby seemingly staring into space?'

I nod.

'Well, the most likely explanation is they're fascinated by a spirit bobbing about like a torchlight.' She bites into her roll, licks her lips. 'As we grow up we get brainwashed into thinking anything we can't explain scientifically isn't worth thinking about. We like things to be ordered. We see the world in terms of ideas that make sense to our pattern-seeking brains. Spirits darting about here, there and everywhere don't fit with what we're taught at school, so we close our minds to the possibility they even exist.'

'But you didn't.' I'm curious now. I find I want to believe. 'You didn't close your mind.'

'My mother died very suddenly when I was a little girl. The whole family was wrapped in grief. One day, when I was reading magazines in my bedroom, I smelled something. It took me a moment to place it. My mother's perfume. I looked up, and there she was: my mother standing at the foot of my bed.

Not a ghost, at least not the type you see in movies, but a real person like you or me. A second later she disappeared. It's the only time I've seen her since she passed to the spirit world, but I've *felt* her, just like a breath on my neck, and I've smelled her perfume at times when it's impossible.'

'But you said spirits were people who haven't passed over?'

'I said *some* spirits. The troubled ones. The ones with unfinished business to attend to. The others, like my mother, just pop back and forth.'

'You make it sound easy.'

'I suppose it is, for them. Like nipping to the shops. Talking of which,' Mrs Harrison stands up and pulls a shopping pad from the fridge door. The switch to normality throws me. 'I need to pop into Lowestoft later. We're almost out of tea. I don't suppose you kids want to join me?'

Aaron throws me a sideways glance. 'Have you got any plans?'

I shake my head. I'm about to say, it would be nice to get out, then realise we've only just arrived. Four days in St Cross and it feels like a lifetime. I pull my phone from my shorts pocket. 'I'd better tell Mum.'

Charles Keller's diary:

<u>7 October 1847</u>

I dreamed of Clara last night. It is the first time in many days that
I have done so. Clara sitting in the drawing room at home, with a book
in her lap. No other detail, just the movement of her fingers upon the
pages and the almost imperceptible rustle of her dress. On awakening,
I reached out to find that the bed was cold and, aside from myself,
empty. More than this, the room was not one I was familiar with. It
was only then that I remembered where I was: Suffolk not London.
How I missed my old routine and familiar room as I dressed and
brushed my hair and wondered when breakfast would arrive (at that
moment, a servant girl appeared with a tray of bread, porridge and eggs).
But there was little time to dwell on it. The day starts early at St Cross
and I was soon called upon to inspect the new arrivals and make
decisions as to who was worthy of medical attention and who was not.
Hard work and a change of air are exactly what I need. After all, is
this not the life I have chosen?

19

---∞∞∞---

Jess

I stare at the patch of lawn where the jacket should be, where I'm sure I dropped it last night. But there's nothing there, just grass still wet from the rain.

'It was here,' I say, knowing I sound crazy, knowing Liam's looking at me as if I've completely lost my mind. 'It fell out of the wardrobe and I took it outside. It was the middle of the night. It was raining. I left it right here.' We're standing on the terrace and everything feels out of kilter. 'You don't think this place, this house . . .' I feel it behind us, bearing down, ' . . . you don't think it's playing tricks on us, do you?'

'The house playing tricks?' Liam sounds remarkably together despite the fact I'm sure he's been drinking. Except Liam never drinks and we haven't even eaten breakfast. In the whole time I've known him, almost eighteen years, he's barely touched a drop. He's always maintained him and alcohol don't mix, but this morning, when he'd kissed me, I'd smelled alcohol on his breath. I'd almost asked him about it – it had been on the tip of my tongue – but whichever way I'd phrased it in my mind, it had sounded like an accusation.

'Don't you feel it?' I say. I glance behind him at the ivy creeping across the walls, fingering its way into the crevices. 'This house feels like it's watching us. I don't feel safe here. Maybe we should cut our holiday short?'

'What do you mean, we're being watched?' Liam looks suddenly tense.

'I mean,' I rub my forehead – what *do* I mean exactly? 'It feels like the windows and the paintings have eyes. Like the house is alive. I know that sounds stupid. But I guess there's just so much history here.'

'Right.' Liam laughs uneasily. 'History. Well, I'm afraid we can't just leave.'

'Why not?'

'The girls. They've been looking forward to all this. We can't cancel their holiday. And then, there's the cats.'

'The girls will cope. And you can just let the house-sitting company know we can't manage the rest of the fortnight.'

'No ... I ... I think we're being a bit rash.' He lifts his eyes to the house, and I see something written in the lines of his face, something I can't quite read. 'We should give it a few more days. The girls are loving it out here. The beach. The fresh air. Hey, what about I take the day off? We all go out? Do something together? Treat ourselves to a pub lunch?'

'We can't afford a pub lunch.'

'Yes, we can. We'll throw it on a credit card.'

I pull a face and immediately feel mean.

'Look, Jess.' He rests his hands on my shoulders, forcing them down. I hadn't realised how tense I'd become. 'We need to live a little. Let go. A pub lunch isn't exactly going to break the bank. The girls deserve it. We both know Summer's had a shit year even if she won't tell us about it, and after what happened with Mia, Xanthe's not exactly having the time of her life either.'

'I'm not sure ...' I think of Mia Williams, the kid in Xanthe's old school. I've tried so hard to push what happened to the back of my mind, to not mention Mia in front of the girls, but it's there. Mia's there. I can't pretend she isn't.

'Just one day, Jess. That's all I'm suggesting. One day when we let go a little, when we stop being so bloody controlled.'

The accusation stings. I breathe audibly and make a conscious effort to relax my shoulders. Why is it so easy for Liam? He can make a decision and stick to it, just like that, whereas I turn things over and over. But perhaps he's right. Perhaps, for once, I ought to stop worrying. 'All right,' I say, hating the reluctance in my voice. Even now, I can't let go. 'We'll drive into Lowestoft, find somewhere reasonable.'

He makes little circles on my neck with his fingers. 'There, you see? It's not such a hard decision, is it? And about the house, let's give it a little longer, okay? We're not used to old places. They're made differently to modern ones. There are more things to rattle and clang. I know what you mean, I've felt it myself. This place, it makes you *feel*. But it's not real. It's just our imaginations.'

I want to believe him. I want to think I've imagined all this. I want this to be the holiday we all desperately need. 'But what about the jacket? I know it sounds mad. Impossible. But I *heard* it. I heard something in the wardrobe, tapping to get out. And then the jacket, well, it just disappeared.'

'Someone must have taken it,' Liam says simply. 'Inanimate objects don't go walking by themselves. The gardener took it. Or Summer. She got up super early, said she was going for a walk.'

'A walk?'

He tilts his head and raises his eyebrows. 'I think she was going to meet that boyfriend of hers.'

'Right.' I remind myself Summer's old enough to take care of herself. 'Did she say when she was going to be back?'

'Nope. She just walked off.'

'And you didn't think to ask her?'

'No. I presumed—'

'God.' I pull my mobile from my pocket and dial Summer's number. No answer so I send a text: Where are you?

A message blinks back almost immediately: In the cottage. I'm fine.

Liam frowns. 'Everything all right?'

'Yes. Summer's fine. She's in the cottage, with Aaron, I presume. But he's not her boyfriend. Don't let her hear you say that. You know what she's like. One wrong word can spell a bad mood for a week.' I put my phone back in my pocket, resisting the urge to insist Summer returns immediately. 'We were talking about the house. The jacket.' I think about mentioning the diary too, Charles Keller's diary – the couple of entries I've been able to read – but for some reason I don't; it's far too medical. I need Liam to listen to me, not spiral into panic.

He steps away from me, bends down and pulls a weed from between the grouting on the terrace. It comes away easily, trailing its roots. 'Look at this place. It's totally unkempt. It needs a whole staff of gardeners, not just a man to cut the lawn.'

I stare at the swirl of his crown, his hair thinning, greying.

When he stands up again, he smells of earth and soap, not alcohol at all. 'All right,' I say, making an effort to sound calm. 'We'll stay a few more days and reassess after that. But if it's still not right, promise me you'll phone the house-sitting company?'

He wraps his arms around me, and breathes into my hair. 'You worry too much,' he says, kissing my forehead. 'But yes, I promise.'

20

Liam

After our conversation on the terrace, I'm on edge. Warily, I follow Jess upstairs to the girls' room. The eyes in the hall feel worse today, far worse since Jess said those things about the house, about the jacket. I think of earlier, staring up at the bricked-up window, seeing into the locked room with its bare floorboards and gaping nothingness. I should have jumped at Jess's suggestion of escaping St Cross. I should be packing our bags right now; better still, speeding away down the B-roads, my family safe. But I'm not. I can't. I made a promise and I'm too scared to break it.

'Hey, sleepy girl,' I say, leaning over Xanthe's cot.

Xanthe rolls over, her hair splayed across the pillow. 'Hello, Daddy. I was dreaming about mist.'

'Mist? That's a funny thing to dream about.'

Xanthe stretches and yawns, her fingers uncurling. She's holding something in her hand: a pink bracelet with a tiny silver snake charm. Have I seen it before? Probably. At home. Xanthe has so many toys and jewellery and bits and pieces for her hair it's hard to remember.

'I didn't like it.' Xanthe pushes herself upright, dropping the bracelet on the cot mattress. 'I didn't like the dream. It had a colour.'

'A colour?'

'A colour like this room.'

I glance at Jess who's busy picking Summer's pyjamas off the floor on the other side. She doesn't appear to be listening.

'But this room is just white.'

Xanthe looks at me puzzled.

I think of the steps next door leading to what must be the attic stairwell. I haven't told Jess I think we got it wrong about the bedrooms, that we're actually sleeping in Mrs Clarence's room. I realise I'm not going to tell her either. She'd only panic and insist we move, which, given the state of the rest of the house, would be more hassle than it's worth.

Xanthe climbs over the side of the cot, hopping down on to the wooden floor. She grabs her diary and pencils. 'I'm starving,' she says. 'I need breakfast.'

'I'm afraid it's cereal again,' Jess says, tucking the sheets beneath Summer's mattress. 'We're clean out of ingredients. We need to go shopping. Dad fancies a trip into Lowestoft for supplies and maybe, just maybe, a spot of lunch.'

Xanthe squeals, making me regret the fact that, due to my stupid financial decisions, a meal out is such a rare occasion. If only I could find my phone, at least then I'd know exactly how much money I have.

'Maybe we'll find a toy shop,' I say, feeling Jess glare at me as I grab Xanthe's hand. 'Come on, let's find you some breakfast.'

'I need a wee first.'

'Okay, Little Bear.'

I wait until she's left the room, her footsteps pattering down the landing, then turn to Jess. She looks tired, deep shadows beneath her eyes. 'I know what you're about to say, that we shouldn't promise her things we can't afford.' I reach for her hand, thread my fingers through hers. 'It's just I hate living the way we do, always counting our pennies, never really enjoying ourselves.'

Jess sighs. 'It's just life. Having kids. The school trips. The extracurricular activities. It all adds up.'

'It's not just life. It's me. I should have sold another book by now. I should have made more effort to finish this draft. I should have—'

'Ssh.' She releases my hand and presses a finger to my lips. 'It's not just your responsibility, you know. It's my responsibility too. Maybe I should look for a better job. It's all very well, working for a charity, but it doesn't exactly pay the bills.'

'It *is* my fault.' I want to tell her everything. I want to admit what I've done. But I can't. I can't find the words. I'm exhausted now the alcohol's worn off, and my head is thumping. The constant headache I feel in this house as if the very air we're breathing is bad.

I glance at the ceiling, at the spots of black mould. It's worse here than in other parts of the house. Should we move the girls elsewhere? I remember the junk in the other bedrooms. The other bedrooms which are so dusty, and so cluttered you can't even see the beds. Better here than in there. The girls will be okay for a fortnight.

Jess leans her head against my chest. 'You've got to stop

blaming yourself for everything,' she says. 'We've got each other, remember? That's worth more than money.'

Tap . . . tap . . . tap . . .

I spin away from her, causing her to stumble. 'Did you hear that?'

'What?'

I stride across the bedroom and open the door, listening hard, but all I can hear is the whirr of Xanthe's toothbrush. 'Nothing,' I say. 'I thought for a moment, but no, I'm wrong.'

'Thought what?'

'I said, it's nothing.' I can't let her know I'm freaked out too. 'I was mistaken, that's all.'

'Okay.' Her eyes narrow with suspicion.

She goes downstairs anyway to make breakfast, and I'm left alone on the landing. I see Xanthe in the bathroom at the far end, spitting toothpaste into the sink, then she closes the door, blocking me out.

Tap . . . tap . . . tap . . .

An image bolts into my mind. A cane striking the floor. A black cane with a brass tip.

I stagger backwards. How the hell did that image appear in my head like that? I try blocking it out, try thinking of France, the sun, the sea. I picture Jess in her swimming costume, the sway of her hips, sand in her hair, the white lines where her halter-neck vest-top has been.

Tap . . . tap . . . tap . . .

The sound is coming to my right, further along the landing, near the door to the locked room. But there's nothing there, nothing I can see, only sense. A figure. A presence. Someone who knows I'm there, who knows I'm listening. Who wants me to follow.

Tap ... tap ... tap ...

My mouth runs dry, my tongue feels like sandpaper. I can barely think beyond the racket of my own heartbeat.

Tap ... tap ... tap ...

The door to the locked room swings open. I *hear* it swing open. I hear the click of the latch and the creak of its hinges. I feel the air around me change as if there's a draught coming from the window opposite the door *inside* the room. But nothing actually moves. The door, as I see it, stays exactly where it is. Solid. Immovable.

It's all in my fucked-up mind.

I hear the door swing back again, clicking firmly into place. A final *tap ... tap ... tap ...* on the other side, fainter but just as sure.

I stare at the closed door, sweat slipping down my neck. What the actual hell? I run towards it, frustration overriding my fear, grasp the doorknob, twist it, yank it. When the door refuses to budge, I press my eye to the keyhole. The room is as I saw it earlier, the bare floorboards, the window, the stairs, the open space, the noticeable absence of clutter. *The window.* I move my gaze back to that central space. The window's open just a crack, just as far as all the other windows open in the house. Was it like that earlier? I can't remember, but it doesn't seem right. My mind is telling me something's happened. Someone has got inside the room and lifted the sash. Could that explain the noise? The sound of the wind distorting through the window and the cracks around the door? I know it's unlikely. I've known the wind to sound like a cat crying or a dog howling, but not something rhythmically striking the floor.

I move my gaze back to the stairs, the short flight of steps leading to the doorway that I'm sure conceals the longer stair-way to the attic. But the door isn't flush against the wall. It's open. I'd swear blind it wasn't like that before. I would have no-ticed, wouldn't I? I was so intrigued, I would have seen. Which means someone or something has been inside the room and opened it. Or – the thought pulses in my brain like a fever – someone has opened the door from the other side.

I stagger backwards, cradling my forehead, hitting the hard edge of the banister behind me. It *can't* be true. Because, unless Jess or one of the girls has found a key, or unless I'm mistaken about the window and the door, then – after what happened with the men back home, the explanation is almost too terri-fying to contemplate – someone else is in the house. Someone going back and forth between the room and the attic.

Extract from a letter written to Charles Keller from
Dr George Reynolds, London, November 1847:

My dear friend,

It is late but I must pen this letter. I have just returned
from Edinburgh, a long journey lasting several days. There,
not five days ago, I witnessed first-hand the administration
of chloroform. A young lady with a large facial abscess was
brought into the theatre and, with much ceremony, asked
to lie upon the operating table. A cloth was pressed to her
nose and mouth for inhalation. Several minutes passed before
the surgeon commenced the business of removing the abscess.
The patient awoke reporting no pain or consciousness from
the operation, only a small pain from the site of surgery
itself. Upon leaving the operating theatre, I was feverish with
excitement, eager to discuss the wonders of this drug with
any who would listen. Could this be the new age we have
been dreaming of?

21

SUMMER

'Here we are.' Mrs Harrison pulls up near Claremont pier. 'You kids hop out while I find somewhere to park. Go and enjoy yourselves. I'll meet you outside the bookshop in an hour. It's on the High Street.'

Aaron opens the passenger side door and steps on to the pavement. I jump out after him, grateful not to feel like the child in the backseat any more, ignoring my phone vibrating in my pocket, probably more messages from Mum.

'So,' Aaron strolls with his hands in his pockets as we follow the flow of pedestrians into town. 'What shall we do?'

I shrug, self-conscious and uncomfortable in my hoodie. It's a hot day but I've only my bikini beneath. I push my sleeves up as far as they will go and tug at the neckline. I would kill right now for a T-shirt. 'Coffee?' I say, then remember I haven't any cash. I should have gone back to the holiday house first, changed my clothes, put on make-up.

'Sounds like a plan.'

'One snag.'

'You don't have any money?' Aaron grins. 'It's fine. One of the few things my parents didn't do was to cut my allowance. I think they're waiting until I really mess up for that.' He laughs and throws me a smile. 'But, I'm behaving now, right?'

'Apart from the mirror. And the devil stuff. And the spirit talk.'

'Yeah. Apart from all that.'

I smile to myself, feeling my cheeks flush red, reminding myself this isn't a date, just two people with nothing better to do, hanging out.

We take seats upstairs in a café in a little side street, more intimate then I'd like. I'd rather a Costa or a Starbucks, somewhere familiar, somewhere where I could blend into the background, be one of many. Better still, somewhere with air conditioning.

'So,' Aaron says when we've both ordered iced coffees and I've filled him in on everything to do with St Cross. He drills his fingers on the table. The couple near the window – the only other people in the café – swap disapproving glances. 'So far, we've got the voice in your head and the foreign language. We think Latin. Then there's the feeling you've had of being watched in the house. And the house itself, an old infirmary, the history of which we know nothing about.'

I nod.

'Anything else?'

'I don't think so.' I take a spoon and play with the ice in my drink. 'Oh wait. The morning after we arrived, I met this old woman. She lives in the gatehouse, further down from your nan's. She said she'd seen the doctor in the house.'

'The doctor?'

'It was really weird. Ties in with the infirmary though, right?'

'Did she say anything else?'

'She just walked off. She seemed, I don't know, *scared*. Yesterday, she invited us round for tea. She completely freaked when Xanthe moved one of her garden ornaments. And she told Mum about this lady, Verity I think her name was, who used to live in St Cross.'

'Verity.' Aaron thumbs his chin. 'Rings a bell. I think Granddad's mentioned her before. Our family's lived in the village for centuries. Granddad's family used to work at the manor. Gardeners like Granddad is now. Could the voice have been hers? Verity's?'

I shake my head. 'No. Definitely not. It was a man's voice.'

'A man.' Aaron narrows his eyes. 'In the old days, a doctor would have been a man, wouldn't he? Maybe that's the link? There's bound to have been a doctor in the infirmary. Let's google it.' He pulls his phone from his pocket and taps the keypad. 'Here we are, St Cross Infirmary, Suffolk.' He scrolls through the entries. 'Built in the 1840s by the Massingham family to celebrate their son's twenty-first birthday. The Massinghams. I've heard that name before too. Granddad or Mum must have mentioned it. But kind of weird, right? Happy birthday, son, we built you a hospital.'

I giggle. 'Is there anything else?'

'Not much. A few old drawings by the look of things.' He turns his phone around and shows me the images. Black and white sketches of the front of the house – the stone fountain in the centre of the drive, the dark porch, the shadowed windows.

Ugly, I think. Even back then it was ugly. He puts his phone down and roots through the leaflet stand: the Maritime Museum, the Transport Museum, Snape Maltings, Aldeburgh. He fishes out a flyer from the back of the pile. 'Perhaps we should go here.' He hands it over: the Museum of Suffolk Life. 'It's just down the road. Maybe they can tell us something about the infirmary.'

'I suppose. The only problem is—'

'You haven't money for that either?' He splits open a sachet of sugar. 'It's fine. I think I can float a couple of museum tickets.'

'You sure?'

He nods and sprinkles the sugar into his drink. 'Believe me, this is the most fun I've had all summer. This time last year I was scuba diving in Borneo. What about you? Do you normally go house-sitting for your holidays?'

I spoon an ice cube into my mouth. Not this conversation. Not the bit where I'm supposed to explain we're meant to be in France. That, this year, we're poor. That Mum's new admin job and Dad's inability to sell, even write, a book means we have to live in a shithole, and I have to attend a shitty school. And then, everything that comes with that, the girls in 11b, the bitching behind my back. The boy. The other one, not Harry. The boy who really spelled the beginning of my troubles, who, as a result, made me fuck up my GCSEs. I suck the ice cube slowly, imagining telling Aaron everything: the boy who supplied me with drinks at a house party before leaning in to kiss me, whose girlfriend – the one I didn't know anything about – was watching from the balcony above.

'Not always,' I mumble. But Aaron looks at me as if he guesses there's more.

We finish our drinks and head to the museum, a narrow,

unassuming building further down the side street. Aaron takes charge, buying the tickets, asking for information about St Cross.

'St Cross?' The girl behind the desk looks up at us through heavily painted lashes. 'I'm not sure I know it.'

'The old infirmary?' I sense already this is going to lead nowhere. 'I'm staying there at the moment, and we thought it might be fun to find something out about the place.'

The girl shakes her head and pulls at the sleeves of her jumper. 'I don't know it, I'm afraid. Blythe is a bit far out for us. Why don't you take a look around and I'll see what I can find?' She looks pointedly at the empty entrance hall, then smiles at us as if we're the first customers she's seen all day. 'I'll have a root through our archives.'

'Thank you very much.' Aaron returns the smile, and I imagine him at boarding school, all charm and politeness. 'We'd be really grateful if you would.'

We traipse around the museum, peering half-heartedly at the displays of Roman and medieval artefacts. I try to focus, but I'm too aware of Aaron in front of me, the way the waistband of his shorts rides down at the back.

'Hey, look at this,' he says, bending over a small display cabinet. The band of bronzed skin above his waistband widens. 'Old medical instruments.'

I lean next to him, my arm brushing his. 'Oh my God. Forceps.' I laugh nervously, my skin prickling where we're touching, I turn my attention to something less obviously anatomical: a long rod with a wide metal head. 'I wonder what that was for?'

Aaron reads the label out loud, his voice cool and unflustered: 'Cauterising iron. For sealing wounds. The larger end was heated until red hot, then pressed against the wound for sealing.'

I grimace and point at a black case lined with purple velvet. The label reads: 'A surgeon's instrument case'. Inside is an array of knives and tiny silver saws. 'Those were for amputation.'

We spin around at the voice, knocking against each other. The girl from the desk is standing behind us, jumper discarded, displaying a sleeve of tattoos. 'Sorry.' She sweeps her fringe from her eyes. 'Didn't mean to startle you. I see you've found our medical section. There's not much I'm afraid, but those little saws were for amputating limbs. Pretty gruesome before the advent of anaesthesia. See that cane at the back?' She points to the top end of the display case: a black walking cane with a little brass tip. 'It's a surgeon's stick. Before general anaesthesia, ether and then chloroform in the late 1840s, the best a patient could hope for was a leather stick to bite into while the surgery was performed.'

I shudder, observing the marks still visible on the stick.

'Hospitals were houses of death back then. Lister didn't discover antiseptic until 1867. Most people who ended up on the operating table died there, or soon after. Surgeons didn't wash their instruments between each patient, they'd only wash their hands if you were lucky. If you didn't die from the shock of the surgery itself, you'd most likely die from infection afterwards. Which brings me to St Cross.'

'You found something?'

'Not much. We've barely any records from that area in the museum. But I did find out that St Cross was an infirmary for poor people, mostly inmates from the nearby workhouse. In the late 1840s, a time when medicine was moving forwards, and more was known about disease and infection and how it was spread, it was extended to include an operating theatre. It would have been pretty unusual at the time. Operating theatres were generally the reserve of the big hospitals. It was announced in the local newspaper – I found a clipping in our file of the area – and even attracted a surgeon from London.'

'Wow.' I feel a beat of something I already know, but then it's gone, and all I'm left with are tendrils.

'As I said, it would have been pretty unusual. But that's the only thing I've discovered so far. If you want me to take a phone number, I could give you a call if I find anything else?'

'You don't mind?'

'Not at all. Gives me something to do.' The girl laughs. 'To be honest, I'm bored out of my mind here. I'm studying history at uni. I'm only here for the holidays. I'm Lucie, by the way.'

'Summer,' I say. 'And this is Aaron. Nice to meet you.' I jot down my number in Lucie's notepad and hand it back to her. 'Thank you very much. We really appreciate it.'

Lucie shrugs and blows her fringe from her forehead. 'No worries at all. As I said, it's a bit quiet here for my liking. Fingers crossed I find something for you. Anything particular you want to know?'

I shake my head. 'Just anything. Anything at all.'

We step out on to the street, hit by a blast of hot air. I tug at my neckline, push my sleeves further up. Aaron flashes me a grin then pulls out his vape. 'An operating theatre. How cool is that?'

I look away from him, back towards the museum. I'm not sure I like the thought of all that blood in the house, but at the same time those old instruments are fascinating. I've always seen myself as a creative type – I'm planning to study art, drama and English A levels – but this has given me another idea.

Verum caste.

I shudder at the Latin words that float through my mind. At the same time, it feels right us being here and finding the display, like it was meant to happen. I'm about to say something about it to Aaron when he lets out a low whistle. I follow his gaze up the street. My good mood plummets. Mum, Dad and Xanthe are strolling in the opposite direction, Xanthe clutching an ice cream. As soon as she sees me, she lets out a small yelp of surprise and starts running.

'What are you doing here?' She dances excitedly on my arm, ice cream flecking the ground. 'We've been looking for you *everywhere*. Mum even called at the cottage but there was no one in. Mum and Dad are taking us out for lunch. Don't you check your phone?'

I think of the vibrating messages in my pocket. 'I was busy.'

'Mum's angry.'

I look over Xanthe's shoulder and there's Mum fiddling with the strap of her bag.

Sancteque vitam meam.

'Fancy meeting you two here,' she says curtly.

'Hi, Mum.' I can't help wondering if she's here on purpose, whether she's keeping tabs on me in more ways than I realise. 'This is Aaron.'

'We met before. At the cottage, I believe?'

Aaron threads his thumbs through his belt loops. 'Yeah. We did.'

Mum flashes an unconvincing smile. 'Didn't you get my messages?'

I shrug. 'I was busy. I *am* busy.'

'I was worried.'

I groan. 'I'm not a child any more.'

'Strictly speaking, you are.'

I grit my teeth, my world turning red. For a split second, I'm back in the museum, staring at the surgeon's stick. *Verum caste, sancteque vitam meam.*

'I don't mind what you do.' Mum's voice is a taut as a knot. 'Within reason, that is. All I ask is for you to tell me where you're going.'

'Fuck's sake,' I growl. 'I'm sixteen. Isn't it about time you trusted me?'

Dad scowls and I've a feeling if it wasn't for Aaron, he'd be livid right now. He probably *is* livid, just trying not to show it.

'That's not the point,' Mum says, 'and you know it.'

'Hey, hey.' Dad steps between us, laying a hand on my shoulder and one on Mum's arm. I hadn't realised I was shaking. 'Calm down. No one's died.'

Mum and I simmer at each other.

Aaron's laughter cuts through the silence. 'Well, it's nice to meet you again, Mrs Kennedy.' He leans over and gives me a quick hug that feels way too intimate in front of my parents. 'You'll have to excuse me.' He puts on the same voice he used with Lucie. 'I've got to meet my nan. I'll see you around.' He throws me a wink before walking off, and I'm left staring at Mum through the blaze of red.

Charles Keller's diary:

<u>26 November 1847</u>

I have been busy, far too busy to write this diary. Although there is a physician, Dr Marne, who visits weekly, I am, for most days, surgeon, physician and apothecary! The needs of the poor in this part of the country are many. Today, I have pulled teeth from five different mouths, cauterised and bandaged wounds, bled two women with leeches, and delivered one child. Tomorrow I will ride out on one of Massingham's fine horses and visit the clients who have requested my private assistance. I am tired but, I dare say, content. Is this not what I desired? The reason I am here? No time to dwell on my own misfortune but to minister with a true and industrious heart to the far greater misfortune of others.

<u>1 December 1847</u>

I am to have my own operating theatre! Not a table in the dining room as I have been using until now, but a whole room dedicated to the purpose. I have spent the afternoon ordering furniture – a table for operating upon, medicine cabinets, a desk, a wash bowl, hooks for hanging coats – and medical supplies. Massingham visited me after supper, eager to acquaint himself with my plans. It seems the operating theatre was his suggestion. I thought of the theatres in London with their spectator stands and room for several students, dressers and assistants, and the theatre I have recently visited in Edinburgh, and wondered to what degree I could imitate that. Of course, there is no such demand for observation of surgery in the countryside, the populace being, in the main, entirely unscientific, but Massingham is ambitious and encourages me in all that I desire.

22

Liam

The tapping in my dreams is incessant. *Tap ... tap ... tap ...*

Tap ... tap ... tap ...

Tap ... tap ... tap ...

I'm acutely aware of everything: the rope around my wrists, the stinging sensation as it cuts into my skin, the way my body rebels, every bone, muscle, sinew straining to get away. I'm in the room with the bare floorboards – the locked room – and two men with gruff voices are manoeuvring me towards the stairwell. I tug away from them, hoping to throw them off with my jerky movements, but they hold on fast, digging their fingers into my biceps, leaving marks through the sleeves of my shirt.

'It's for your own good,' says the man to my left, the smaller of the two.

The man's holding a candle, its flame flickering in the draught from the window, spilling splodges of white wax on the floor. In front of us, beneath the splodges, is a trail of dirty footmarks. Footmarks from the others who are waiting for me upstairs. One of them must have trodden in dog shit and the smell makes me gag.

'You're making things worse for yourself,' says the man to his right, the man in the cloth cap who yanks me upright whenever I stoop. The man coughs and spits on to the floorboards.

I half walk, half allow myself to be carried to the steps at the far end of the room. The steps leading to the door.

'Now, are you going to behave?' says the cloth-cap man. 'Or are we going to have to drag you all the way up?'

I pull at the restraint around my wrists, twisting my hands one way and then the other, trying to wriggle out. But the pain of the rope makes me cry out. *'Please.'*

A chorus of throaty laughter. The two men hoist me on to the first step, then the second, then the third, all the way to the open door. I peer around the corner into the stairwell beyond. It's lit by a single oil lantern that casts a shadowy glow along the bare wooden steps. The wallpaper is peeling and the stair-case is speckled with damp, black permeating the green. The first man blows out his candle and leaves it on the lower step. 'Right, then,' his tongue jabs. 'Up the stairs.'

I hear the congregation of men before I see them, hear their excited whispers from the attic room. They crowd their faces towards me when I emerge, still guarded, into the brighter space. To my surprise, the window in the room isn't bricked up after all, and light spills from both sides into the centre.

'Ah, Mr Kennedy.' A man steps forward from the depths of the room. A middle-aged man with a long pale face. He's wearing a light-grey jacket with dull silver buttons, a jacket I've seen somewhere before. 'We're so glad you could join us this evening.' He signals for the two men to release me, to untie the rope.

I shake out my wrists, relief flooding my arms. I think about running, legging it down those stairs, but I'm bound by the man's magic. Apart from my shaking hands, I'm rooted to the spot. The man's hair is slick with pomade, his moustache gleams with grease. I smell the oil in the lamp above his head, the sweat of the other men in the room, the faint odour of flowers.

'Tonight,' the man in the light-grey jacket turns to his audience, 'we have no need of this.' He lifts the cane in his hand – a black cane with a brass tip, embossed with the impression of a snake – then lands it on the floor with a final *TAP*. He lets it fall. The cane rolls away from him and stops at my feet. The men hold their breath. 'For tonight, gentlemen, you will observe the miracle of chloroform.'

The grey-jacketed man steps aside, revealing a table in the centre of the room. A table set with glinting knives and a little green bottle.

The company of men lean forwards, faces twitchy with anticipation.

The lantern sways. The room blurs.

I scream myself awake into the midnight dark.

23

⬦

Xanthe

Xanthe hears the scream in her sleep, a piercing scream followed by silence. Daddy, she thinks. She *knows*. She opens her eyes and listens hard, but there's nothing more, just the wheezy old mattress beneath her when she moves. It sounds like lungs, like someone struggling to breathe. She hunts around for the snake bracelet, pushing her hands beneath the pillow and quilt, but she can't find it anywhere. She's sure she put it beneath her pillow before she went to sleep. Maybe it fell between the bars of the cot? She tries sliding her hands through the bars, but they don't quite fit. In the end, she stands up and climbs out.

'Summer,' she whispers. 'Summer, wake up.'

But her sister doesn't stir. She gropes in the dark for the bracelet, her fingers stumbling through the dust beneath the cot, making her sneeze. The bracelet isn't there. Her mind whirls with worry. She'd promised Mia she'd keep the bracelet safe. What if Mia finds out she's lost it?

She runs across the room, climbs into bed beside Summer, slips beneath the thin sheets, and pulls the quilt higher. Summer throws an arm around her, but doesn't say anything, doesn't wake, but she feels safer here, the two of them together.

24

Jess

It's early morning and day five in the house. I'm staring at the wood at the bottom of the garden, the wood with the hidden lake, which Xanthe refuses to walk through. I feel cold run right through me. 'There's something wrong with the wood, Mummy.' Xanthe had said that yesterday, and I'd frowned at her, not understanding. The trees aren't managed, but they're harmless enough – harmless beech trees – and the wood is too small to get really lost in. But as I'm staring at them, I start to wonder if Xanthe has a point. The wood doesn't seem quite right, it seems . . . I wipe my eyes . . . it seems to be shimmering.

I walk towards it, slowly, fearfully. When I reach the gate, I look back at the house. It's a beautiful day. The brief spell of bad weather has come and gone. The garden is serene. There's a blackbird hopping along the low stone wall, stopping now and again to peck at the moss, and, although I can't see the sea from here, I can smell it. The freshness in the air. The slight but perceptible tinge of salt.

So why am I so afraid?

I rub my eyes again. I barely slept last night, not after Liam shouted out, waking us both.

'What is it?' I'd said, disorientated, not sure where I was, catapulted into wakefulness from some deep-deep place.

'I'm sorry, love. I was just dreaming,' Liam had mumbled into his pillow.

But it hadn't sounded like a dream. It had sounded like a nightmare. 'Are you okay?'

'I'm fine.' His voice was muffled. 'Go back to sleep.'

I'd sensed him rolling away from me, checking his pulse, silently counting. I hadn't even needed to watch him do it, I'd known by the movement, by the sound of his lips. His fear of hospitals runs deeper than a fear of blood, the superficial phobia he jokes about whenever a hospital scene comes on the TV. Although he's never mentioned it, I know he's scared of falling seriously ill or, worse still, dying. More than most people are scared of these things. I don't even know *how* I know all this. I've never asked him about it. He's never told me.

I open the gate, drawn by a movement: a black cat slinking along the path, disappearing as it bends out of sight. The cat we've all been looking for.

I run, my flipflops sliding along the path, catching stray stones and clumps of dirt. The cat is nowhere to be seen, and I'm starting to doubt myself. Did I imagine it? Could it have been some other small animal? I look left to right, peering into the undergrowth. There's a narrower track branching off to the left. Is that the way to the pond? I risk it – if the cat's not on the main path, then it makes sense it's gone this way. A couple of minutes later, the track begins to thin, difficult to pass in places, overgrown with brambles that scratch my legs. I'm about to turn back when I spy a clearing ahead of me.

'No!'

Someone steps into my path. I scream.

Robbie Silver looks wild. Her hair is loose. Her dressing gown hangs open revealing a ghost-white nightdress and olive-green wellies.

'God.' I press a hand to my chest. 'You gave me quite a fright.'

'Go back.'

'I'm sorry?' The Jack Russell pushes its way between Robbie's legs and bears its teeth. Instinctively, I step backwards. 'I thought I saw a cat.'

Robbie narrows her eyes. 'There is no cat. You should keep away from here. Your daughters will be waking up. They'll need you.'

'Robbie, are you okay? Is there something wrong?' I look beyond the old lady to the clearing. Not the pond I was expecting, but a smaller space with what seems like a garden shed.

'They don't want to be disturbed.'

'*They?*'

I realise the shed isn't a shed at all. It's a Wendy house designed to look exactly the same as St Cross. It has the same windows, the same grand porch, the same glass roof, except it's entirely made out of wood, and the windows and the glass roof are painted on.

Robbie reaches out, grabs my arm, pinching me through the sleeve of my cardigan. The Jack Russell circles my feet, yapping. 'Go back to your family. Look after them. Look after your daughters.'

I shiver beneath the thin cotton of my cardigan. Those words. The same words Peter Harrison used when I'd met him in the garden, fiddling with the mower. *Look after your daughters.* I think of Summer, her mood swings. The way she's seemed even worse out here, like all the rot in this place has got inside her.

'Are you sure you're all right?' I say, wondering if the old lady has some sort of dementia. 'I could walk with you back to the gatehouse? Or you could come to the house? I could make you a cup of tea. There's the cats, of course, but we could shut them in the dining room.'

The Jack Russell yaps furiously, pawing my bare legs as if it understands the word 'cat'. I take another step back.

'Angel, be quiet.' Robbie bends down and lifts the dog into her arms, smearing dirt on her nightdress. The Jack Russell growls its discontent.

I try to regain my composure. 'So, how about that cup of tea?'

Robbie shakes her head, then straightens up, stiff with hostility. 'We're leaving now, aren't we, Angel? I just need to see you on your way.'

I turn, brimming with exasperation, but also wanting to get back, needing to get back, to see Summer and Xanthe, to know they're okay. I hurry down the track, then up the main path into the garden, breaking into a run. It's only when I open the back door that I relax. I'm hit by the smell – the mustiness, the mould, the bitterness of coffee cutting through it all – but the place is silent. The danger I'd imagined dissipates in the gloom. No one else is awake – Liam seems to have given up on his early-morning writing. I reach my hands to my neck, massage down to my shoulders. Everything so taut, so painful. I try to smooth away the stress of the last few days, the argument yesterday with Summer about not telling us where she was going, the awkward meal out where I'd argued with Liam over what we could and couldn't afford on the menu, Liam's refusal to speak to me when I'd quizzed him about his book, the second book in the duology – the part where Jake wins the girl and slays all the villains and, against all the odds, stumbles out into the light. And now that I'm thinking about it again, I can't push it from my mind, though I've tried. I've desperately tried to tell myself that Liam's silence on the matter is just a need for artistic privacy, but I can't any longer. Not in this house.

I open the kitchen door and cross the hallway, not pausing to lift my eyes to the roof window. I can't articulate why, but the space frightens me – it's frightened me ever since we first stepped inside St Cross. That first night, my compulsion to get the children to bed, and sort our things, and stack our tooth-brushes in the glass in the bathroom, it was all because of this. This fear. This thing that sits in the house like a monster.

I enter the study and close the door, waiting for the soft click behind me. Liam's laptop sits open invitingly on the desk, dispelling any doubts I might have. I power it up, then stare at the blank screen, stumped momentarily by the password bar. Will Liam know if I type in the wrong password? Will it be flagged the next time he powers it up? I push my worries aside and type in the word 'Summer', then 'Xanthe', then finally, when neither of those work, 'Jess'.

The screen immediately flashes to his home screen: a photo of the four of us in France last year. We look so relaxed out-side the chalet. I'm holding an almost full glass of red wine, Liam is sipping an orange juice, the girls are clutching cans of Coke Light. I open My Documents and find the folder 'Book

2'. Inside are three blank documents as yet unnamed, and one fourth document entitled 'Ideas'. I click on the latter and find a single page of broken sentences. Nothing else. The realisation punches me full throttle: *There is no second book.*

I close the files, close the folder, open Internet Explorer, my fingers trembling lightly on the keyboard, my breathing shallow. I think about all the hours Liam's spent cooped up in the box-room at home, all the times he's made excuses not to help out with the girls because he's writing. The search engine opens on Google, but there's one other window labelled IG, a name that means absolutely nothing to me. I click to open it, then groan.

'You are not connected.'

Of course, no Wi-Fi – but at the same time, I'm relieved: I don't want to look any further. I don't want to search his browsing history. I don't want to be the sort of wife who doesn't trust her husband. And maybe I've got it wrong about the book? Maybe there's another folder, buried deep in all the other folders in My Documents? Maybe he keeps his book stuff entirely online? I power off the laptop and open the study door just as Liam walks across the landing above.

I run towards the stairs, away from the study, about to call out, to offer a cheerful good morning. But something stops me. A noise from behind. I turn, expecting to see one of the cats. But it's not, it's Xanthe. I blink in confusion. Xanthe is standing on the hall table amidst the magazines and piles of old post, still in her pyjamas with messed-up hair. She's reaching up to the painting on the wall, one of the dark religious paintings, fingers fumbling above the gold frame. But then – it makes no sense to me now, it makes no sense later when I replay the scene in my mind – Xanthe falls, catapults from the table as if lifted up by invisible hands and lands with a thud upon the terracotta tiles.

25

Liam

There's a rush of movement. My brain can't work fast enough. The hallway. The eerie white light from the cupola. The painting of the man with the pale grey eyes. Xanthe. Jess. The table. The tiles.

My mouth sours with bile as I run down the stairs two at a time, my hand gliding over the banister, bouncing off the newel post, the saint who looks like a shrouded nun. 'What the fuck?'

Jess is beside Xanthe, smoothing hair from her eyes. I know she's counting up to three in her head. I can almost hear her ticking brain.

'Don't move her,' I shout. All the information I've picked up over the years, googling symptoms on health information websites, spins through my mind.

'What?' Jess's eyes glisten with concern as she turns towards me.

'Don't move her, whatever you do. She might have broken her neck.'

'Mummy.' Xanthe opens her eyes and searches for Jess.

'I'm here, love. It's okay. You had a fall. Can you wriggle your toes?'

Xanthe pulls herself up to sitting and I feel a wash of relief. 'My head hurts.'

'It would after a tumble like that.' Jess sounds so in control. She touches Xanthe's head, moving her hand gently from her forehead to the crown to the nape of her neck. 'You've got a lump, right here.' She indicates the bit just below the crown. 'What on earth were you doing, standing on the table?'

'I can't remember.' Xanthe shakes her head. 'I feel sick.'

'Lie down again.' Jess gently guides her head back on to her lap. 'That's right. Lie still.' She looks at me and mouths the word 'hospital'.

I'm shaken out of myself. I've just been standing there, staring at the two of them, frozen in my anxiety. Now the word 'hospital' shocks me like a jolt of electricity. 'Right. Yeah.'

'Concussion.' Jess makes the word sound almost gentle. 'Ought to get it checked, just in case.'

'Right,' I say again, feeling utterly helpless. This is Jess's domain, not mine. I bend down, take Xanthe's hand. Her fingers are freezing. 'Are you okay to walk to the car, Little Bear? Mummy's going to take you to hospital. Just to get you checked over.'

Xanthe nods slowly.

'I'll stay here,' I say, trying to unravel the knot of panic in my brain. 'Look after Summer. I'll carry you to the car.'

'No.' Xanthe's eyes are shining. 'I want Mummy to carry me. I want Mummy to sit in the back with me. You drive.'

Fear slides all over my body, a slick film of sweat. 'I have to stay with Summer.'

'*Please.*'

'No. I—'

'What's going on?' Summer appears at the top of the stairs, wiping sleep from her eyes. 'What's wrong with Xanthe?'

'Your sister had a fall.' Jess sounds so matter-of-fact. I envy her control, her ability to keep everything together. 'She was standing on the table. We're taking her to the hospital. Just in case. Will you be okay on your own?'

Summer heads downstairs in her fluffy slippers. She smooths the bed-hair from her eyes. 'Sure. But what was she doing on the table?'

I follow the instructions on Google Maps, switching my gaze between Jess's phone and the road ahead. I tell myself that's all I need to do, drive them there safely, let Jess do the rest. But even as we leave the B-roads and head towards Lowestoft, I feel my chest tightening, my hands slipping on the steering wheel. I glance in the rearview mirror. Jess has taken the seat in the middle and Xanthe is next to her, head on her shoulder.

'Is she okay?' I ask anxiously.

I see Jess smile down at Xanthe. 'I think so. How are you feeling, love?'

'A bit sick. Can I go to sleep now?'

'Not yet. Stay awake a little longer, if you can, just until we've seen the doctor. Can you remember yet, what you were doing on the table?'

'I was looking at the painting.'

Jess frowns and I try to picture the painting above the table, but I can't.

'And then I slipped,' Xanthe says, her face contorting in confusion. I feel the confusion too. I can't explain what I saw, Xanthe at the back of the table, not slipping, but *flipping*. I'd been half-awake at the time. Still drowning in the weight of my dreams. Those horrible dreams. I still have a sense of them hanging over me. I can still picture the room with the pale green wallpaper in my mind, and those men, the oil lamp, the table. The man in the light-grey jacket.

Tap ... tap ... tap ...

I swerve. A horn blares from the other side of the road. Jess cries out from the back.

'Hey,' I say. 'Sorry.' I bring the car back between the lines, lift a hand in apology to the other driver. 'Nearly there,' I say, risking a glance at Jess's phone. Four miles according to Google Maps. I just need to keep my shit together for another four miles. 'Nearly at the hospital.'

It's the smell more than anything. The wipe-clean smell of disinfectant and the undertone of overcooked hot dinners. It makes my head hurt. The lights are too bright. The colours are too stark. My brain keeps fizzing with what feels like tiny electric shocks. I sit in a hard plastic chair in the waiting room with Jess and Xanthe, while Jess asks me for the hundredth time whether or not I'm all right.

'I'm fine.' I dig my hands beneath my buttocks, press them into the seat.

I think of the school counsellor, clipping and unclipping

her pen on the desk. 'I hope you don't mind me saying, but I don't think you're fine at all. Can you explain why you ran out of class today?'

Class. Anatomy. The workings of the heart.

'I didn't feel very well.'

The counsellor leans in and lowers her voice. 'Describe it. How did you feel?'

Sweaty hands. Itchy palms. Heart pounding.

'Sick.'

'I see. Anything else? Any other sensation? Would you say you felt panicky?'

Shaking my head. 'Just sick. But I'm better now. Can I go?'

I shift in the plastic chair, feeling the pressure on my fingers, breathing through the memory. I can do this. It's just a question of facing my fear, like people with proper phobias. Phobias of rats or spiders or heights. Only those fears seem legitimate, whereas this – this random sequence of memories and feelings – is utterly, *utterly*, ridiculous.

'You sure you're okay? You can wait in the car, you know?' Jess holds me with her eyes and sees me. She really sees me.

Right then, I think about telling her everything. Here in the hospital. In the place of all places I hate the most. The book. The day trading. The thousands of pounds she still thinks are squirrelled away for a rainy day, but which no longer exist. I feel the familiar twisting of guilt in my gut as I practise what I want to tell her in my head, about all the money I've lost on the stock exchange and the gambling that has become my full-time occupation. All this time, she thinks – it's almost laughable – I've been writing my book. But the book doesn't even exist beyond a few rough notes. Instead, I've been sitting at my laptop placing bets on the stock market in the hope of a massive win, then nail-bitingly watching the stock market index go up and down.

I close my eyes, feeling my weight sink into my fingers, pushing harder against them until it's almost painful.

For a while I'd done okay. More than okay, I'd done bloody brilliantly, but it had made me reckless. I'd started taking risks, placing massive bets while waiting for the perfect time to tell Jess the truth. I'd imagined spinning her around in some expensive hotel room, plush sofas, carpets so thick you could sink your feet into them, imparting the fact we weren't just wealthy, but millionaires. But the perfect time had never come, and now . . .

Suddenly, I feel sick. I know I can't do it. I'm kidding myself. I can't tell Jess what I've done and I can't just sit here either, pretending I'm normal, patiently waiting for the triage nurse. Even when Jess was pregnant, I'd not been able to accompany her to scans and prenatal visits. I must have come across as a right bastard. The only father in the whole town who hadn't heard his children's heartbeats before they were born. Even during the homebirths I'd felt traumatised, seeing the midwives invade our space with their gadgets and cylinders of gas and air, listening to Jess scream in the next room as I'd silently prayed the midwives wouldn't call me in.

'You're right,' I say, standing up, giving Xanthe's hand a squeeze. 'I'd better get back to the car. I might have to move it. I'm not sure where we're parked is legit. We don't want a ticket on top of everything else.'

She smiles thinly, playing the game, then looks up at me pleadingly. 'You understand now why we have to leave?'

It takes me a moment to realise what she means. She doesn't mean leave the hospital, she means leave St Cross. I battle the doubts in my mind. This was just an accident. No one's fault. Although I still can't explain what I saw in the hallway, I can't risk doing anything rash.

'Let's just see what the consultant says, okay?' I squeeze Jess's hand, then lean over and kiss Xanthe's forehead. 'Take care, Little Bear,' I say, hoping I sound braver than I feel. 'Be a good girl for the doctor.'

Extract from a letter written to the British Medical Journal *by Dr G. Reynolds, physician, February 1848:*

The trouble with chloroform is its unpredictability. Administration needs to be precise so as to induce the desired heavy sleep. The problem is in the administration. The typical method is to soak a cloth and hold it over the patient's nose for inhalation. Too small a dose and the patient will awake too early. Too great a dose and the lungs and heart cannot cope and the result is almost certain death. There needs to be some sort of machine or pump that can regulate the dose and thus avoid unnecessary distress or, in worse cases, fatality.

26

SUMMER

—⊗⊗⊗—

I brush my lashes with mascara, push the wand back in its tube and inspect my reflection in the bathroom mirror. Turning my head one way and then the other, I smile at the way the light catches my cheekbones – I've lost weight since the start of the holidays, which can't be a bad thing. I think of Aaron yesterday in the museum, the museum guide who'd obviously fancied him, who'd gone out of her way to search the archives. I imagine kissing him, the way he'd taste of coffee and toothpaste and cinnamon rolls. I imagine pulling him on to his bed in the cottage, giggling at the sound of the mattress rocking against the frame.

My phone buzzes. I pull it out, still smiling. But it's not Aaron, it's Harry. How are you? I stare at the screen in shock, transported to a different world, a different time. It's been weeks since Harry texted. My last four messages to him have gone unanswered.

I reply: Fine.

The minutes tick by. I stare and stare and stare at the screen, willing it to ping into life. Have I lost him already? I send another message: How about you?

His reply is immediate: Are you alone?

I hesitate: Yes.

Can we videocall?

I frown at the screen. What the fuck? In the whole time I've known Harry, we've never videoed, just messaged on WhatsApp. And now, after weeks of silence, he wants to speak to me. More than that, he wants to *see* me.

I don't know. There's no Wi-Fi where we're staying. The signal's crap.

A long pause. I wonder whether I've lost him completely. I tuck my hair behind my ears, arrange my fringe in the mirror, telling myself I'm fine.

My phone buzzes: Let's try. I'll call you, okay?

Okay.

I'm flustered now, unsure what to do, checking my reflection again in the mirror, wetting my lips, rubbing life into my cheeks. A moment later, my WhatsApp rings with Harry's face. My skin prickles with heat as I press the accept call button.

'Hi.'

'Hi.' His voice is deeper to how I remember, but it's been a whole year. He's grown up. *I've* grown up. He looks different too, angular and slightly gaunt.

'Where are you calling from?' I try to sound casual.

'France. My parents are out. I'm bored.'

I picture the chalets, the sun loungers, his parents' minibar. 'I'm in Suffolk,' I say, wishing it didn't sound quite so dull. 'We're staying in this weird house.'

He tilts his head at the screen. 'It looks odd. Where are you? It looks kind of white.'

'I'm in the bathroom.' I move the screen around, showing him the sink, the old-fashioned toilet with its dangling chain, the huge iron bath.

'Get in,' he says.

'What?'

'Get into the bath.'

I giggle nervously. He's joking, right? 'I'm not getting into the bath. Don't be ridiculous.'

'Please.' He sounds needy. 'I want to see you in the bath.'

I giggle again, wondering what he's playing at, whether this is some sort of game. He *must* be bored. 'All right,' I say, though I don't really want to. I clamber into the huge iron tub, still grasping my phone, then lean my head back beneath the taps. The enamel is uncomfortable and damp from the bath I took earlier. I try to imagine bubbles and tealights.

'Not like that,' Harry says. He runs his tongue over his upper lip. 'Take your top off.'

'What?'

'Take off your T-shirt. I want to see all of you.'

'Are you serious?'

'I told you, I'm bored.' He takes a swig of beer from a bottle.

I want to resist. I want to tell him to go fuck himself. But, at the same time, I don't want to lose him, and maybe this is normal? Maybe this is what everyone is doing? I pull my T-shirt over my head and fling it on to the floor. The cold of the bath shocks my back. I try not to flinch, moving my phone to my eye gaze, then lowering it slightly, glad I'm wearing a decent bra.

'You look good,' he says, slurring his words. It's only 11 a.m., although it's an hour later in France. I wonder if he's been out all night and is just carrying on. 'Really good. Mmm.'

An even longer pause. I don't know what to do. Don't know what to say. I suck in my stomach, though he can't see it anyway, grateful for all those hours I've spent swimming and starving myself.

'But that's in the way.'

'What?'

'Your bra. Take it off.' He sounds impatient.

'*What?*' A million warnings about internet safety fly through my mind. But this is Harry. Not exactly the perverts we've been warned about at school.

'Go on,' he moans.

I unhitch my bra from my shoulders, feeling behind for the clasp, awkwardly arching my back. My mind races. The bathroom light dazzles my eyes. I wonder what my parents would say if they came home right now. I imagine the shock, the embarrassment, the inevitable lectures. And then that feeling again – although I know it's impossible because the door is closed and there's no one else in the house – that feeling of being watched. But the only things watching me are things without eyes: the bath tub, the toilet, the mirror above the sink. *The mirror.*

Suddenly, Harry yelps.

I scramble upright, knocking my head against the taps. Instinctively, I draw one arm across my chest. 'Harry? What's wrong?'

'Your screen.'

'*What?*'

'Look at your screen.'

I study my phone, but all I see is Harry's shocked face, and next to it, the small window with my own reflection.

'I saw ... I ...' He rubs his eyes. The longing in them is gone. He looks knackered. Sunburned. There are two white circles where his sunglasses have been. Suddenly, he seems incredibly young – younger even than me – a kid playing games. 'I saw ... just now.' He stands up from wherever he's been sitting and paces. I see flashes of the summer I should have been having: the stylish décor, the sunlight pouring in through the wide windows of the chalet. 'You must have done something,' I say. 'You must have pressed something.'

'No. I swear ... He was looking at me. Staring at me. He had these horrible, evil eyes.'

'Who?' I say, desperate, panicky. For some reason, I'm thinking about the mirror. 'Harry, please, you're frightening me. Who was staring at you?'

He runs a hand down his face. 'Did you do something?'

'What?'

'Did you do something to the screen? You must have messed with the screen.'

'No. I swear—'

'Look. This isn't a good idea. I've got to meet my parents. I'll call you, okay?' He hangs up.

I dress as fast as I can, grabbing my bra from the bath,

pulling on my T-shirt. I need to get out of the bathroom. I need to get away from the mirror. I run across the tiles, unlock the door and pull it wide.

Sunlight pours through the roof window, a shaft of silvery light pooling in the hallway. I stop in my tracks, looking down at the tiles from the gallery landing, then drawing my gaze upwards, resting it on the blocked-up window near the roof. I've an impulse to run, to escape the house, but I'm pinned to the spot. *Openings, openings, openings.* Except there are no openings. No places to hide. No places to run to. Because everywhere leads to the landing or the hall, just like the pictures of Victorian prisons I've studied in history class: the surveillance platforms, the cells leading off from each floor, everything clearly visible. Cells, I think, not rooms. And the light from the roof window is deceptive, because more than anything, it intensifies the feeling, like a torch thrust into the dark. I've a feeling that wherever I go, I'll be followed, I'll be *seen*.

The sound of my ringtone startles me. I pull my phone from my pocket, expecting to see Harry's number, expecting to hear Harry's voice on the other end, apologising or explaining or both. But the number isn't one I recognise, and the voice is a woman's.

'Hello. Is that Summer Kennedy?'

'Yes.'

'It's Lucie from the museum.'

A pause while I try desperately to pull myself together. 'Oh, hi.'

Lucie clears her throat. 'Is this a good time? I can always call back.'

'Yes ...' I shift my gaze down to the tiles. 'Yes ... It's fine.'

'It's just, I did some research for you, after you came in

yesterday. I found something in the archives about the house you're staying in. The old infirmary.'

I don't say anything. Right now, I don't want to know. I'm not sure I want to learn anything else about this strange old house.

Lucie fills in the silence. 'I told you there was an operating theatre, right? Well, the surgeon's name was Charles Keller. His family were German, but he made a name for himself as a surgeon in London, was well respected in the profession which was emerging at the time, the foundations of the practice we know today. He came up here, I suppose, to make a difference. There used to be a large workhouse nearby, and I guess there would have been a lot of illnesses and injuries. Anyway, Charles Keller died in Suffolk.'

'Keller. Dr Keller.' The name comes alive on my lips. What did the old lady say? *The doctor's here.*

'Strictly, he would have been known as Mr Keller. Surgeons were, and still are, known as mister rather than doctor. It's a small technicality.'

'Where did he die?' But even as I ask the question, I know the answer. I stare at the terracotta tiles in the hallway, the way the light warms them, making them look more red than brown.

'He died in St Cross. According to the newspaper clipping, he died from falling from an internal window.'

Charles Keller's diary:

An unclaimed cadaver arrived from the workhouse this afternoon – in life, a waif of a man who had suffered from convulsions. No one knows who he is, having knocked upon the workhouse door for admittance only days ago, and then promptly collapsed. He has not been sensible since and eventually succumbed during one of his spasms. I have spent the hours since dissecting first the heart and then the lungs, trying to find a cause for the death. Despite everything I have seen – despite all that Clara endured – my fascination with the human body never tires, indeed it grows with each dissection, with each incision, with each organ removed. I called Thomas Percy, the dresser, to my side, and showed him the arteries and ventricles, the bronchi and lobes, watching with amusement as he paled and found an excuse to stand back. Massingham arrived soon after, dismissing Percy, and taking great interest in the cadaver himself, showing no such weakness, even cutting into the heart muscle under my instruction. By the time we had finished, our hands and clothes were caked in blood.

20 December 1847

A child died upon the operating table today. Whilst not an infrequent occurrence, the case was a straightforward one – amputation of two fingers crushed in the mechanisms of a cider mill. I am yet to discern a cause, but the question plagues me: did the child succumb to too great a dose of chloroform? Thomas Percy is somewhat unsettled – he is fond of the children, having lost three himself, and is often found on the wards attending to their needs or, more often, providing some kind of frivolous entertainment.

23 December 1847

Late afternoon, I was called to the home of John Harrison, the head gardener, a red-bricked cottage beyond the wood. He had got in the way of a wayward horse and fractured his arm. With little fuss from the patient, I set the arm straight, then took tea with Harrison and his wife in the parlour. All manner of things were discussed, the Harrisons being agreeable if uneducated people. We got on to the matter of my work and my frustrations with anaesthetising my patients, the right dose of chloroform being somewhat evasive. Harrison suggested a machine could be used to administer the drug – would I care for his assistance in the matter?

On returning to my room, still mulling over Harrison's suggestion, I withdrew the cork from a vial of chloroform and, out of curiosity, inhaled. It is a pleasant smell – a scent of flowers that reminds me of the garden in London. I soon fell into a vivid sleep. Bright colours, crisp outlines, an unadulterated feeling of elation. I awoke just before midnight without headache or any other malaise, only a sense of calmness I cannot recall feeling for a very long time. Perhaps, there is more to this drug than mere sedation?

27

Xanthe

X anthe doesn't remember where she is at first. The room feels different, smells different. A smell like vinegar. The quilt feels thinner and reminds her of old people; reminds her of the few times she stayed over at Grandma's house. And then she remembers: she's in the room over the porch, sandwiched between Mummy and Daddy. Mummy had insisted she spend the night here because she hurt her head, but it all feels wrong, the three of them together, and Summer on her own in the room next door.

She thinks about the doctor's words, the doctor in the hospital with the kind smile and big teeth, who gave her a unicorn sticker, *You need to rest*, and she feels the heat of Daddy lying next to her. 'Daddy,' she whispers, but he doesn't move, doesn't wake. She turns the other way. Mummy's breathing is slow and raspy, and a sheet is pulled over her eyes. In the moonlight, she looks like one of those dead people in the movies Summer likes to watch.

'Daddy,' she says more urgently. She tugs on his arm but he bats her away. 'Please, Daddy. I'm scared.'

'Get off me,' he growls, tossing beneath the quilt, rolling away from her. 'Leave me alone.'

Something strikes the floor outside on the landing. *Tap . . . tap . . . tap . . .* She buries her head beneath the quilt. That tingly feeling in her brain again, like a fuzz of electricity, the feeling Mummy took her to the doctor's about before. Another doctor who talked about things she didn't understand.

Tap . . . tap . . . tap . . .

She thinks about the house and the garden and the wood, the way the wood calls to her, the way it makes the tingling worse. And she thinks about what the old lady told her: *You need to learn to hold the fear inside you.*

But she's not brave enough to do that yet. She edges closer to Daddy, feeling the sadness oozing from him like blood from a cut. If only she still had Mia's bracelet . . . if only she hadn't been so careless . . .

She pictures Mia in the garden, twirling the bracelet round and round her wrist, the snake charm tinkling against the plate when she reaches for another jam sandwich. She remembers the heat, the flying ants, the sound of the radio playing through the kitchen window. When Mia had given her the bracelet, she'd felt a warmth in her tummy like she'd been given something special despite the bad things that had happened. Those bad things she doesn't like people talking about, but which find her anyway, at the end of the school day, or alone in the garden, or in her room in the dead of night.

The bracelet. The one thing that might have helped, and she's lost it, and now there's no knowing what might happen. She screws her eyes closed, blocks out the room, blocks out the tapping sound, and tucks her head in the dip next to Daddy.

28

⟐

Liam

A sharp clutch of pain makes me scream inwardly. I throw back the quilt, grab my lower calf, rub it furiously until the cramp subsides. God, that bloody hurt. I fling myself back against the pillow and groan. Daylight stings my eyes, my mouth tastes sour. What day is it? Wednesday. Day six in this house. I run a tongue over my teeth and wonder briefly whether I remembered to brush last night. *Last night.* It comes back to me in nauseating waves: finishing the bottle of sherry after everyone else was in bed, searching through the cupboards, first in the kitchen, then in the study, until finally I'd found a bottle of whisky.

I remember pouring myself a large glass, before switching on my laptop and staring at one of the blank documents in my book file. I'd poured myself another, and then another, until half the bottle of whisky was gone. After a while, I'd given up pretending to write, and crept upstairs, tiptoeing across the bedroom, knocking into the chaise longue. I'd held my breath, waiting anxiously for either Jess or Xanthe to awake. When they hadn't, I'd renewed my mission, finding Jess's phone on the floor next to her side of the bed, and then stupidly checking my IG trading account. Only, I hadn't been able to remember my password. The password stored automatically on my phone and my laptop. My stupid, clumsy fingers had stumbled over the tiny keyboard.

I roll over, reaching past my sleeping daughter, past the empty space where Jess should be, fingers groping in the dust beneath the bed. Eventually I find Jess's phone, pushed far under. I sit upright and stab in her password, then check the browsing history. My emails. God, I remember now: logging into my account, deleting my junk mail, then, finding nothing else of interest, writing an email to Callum. I open my sent box and read the words I'd written.

Callum, you're a bloody liar. I'm not afraid of you any more.

I feel pinpricks of anxiety. How can I have been so reckless? I delete the email from my sent box – not that it will do any good – delete my emails and IG Trading homepage from Jess's browsing history. Then I fall back against the pillow next to Xanthe and gently stroke her hair. I think about this time last year, the last night of our holiday in the bar in France. I'd felt good about myself, basking in the triumph of my first book, buoyed by the success of my day trading, drunk on my achievements rather than the shots everyone else was downing. I'd got talking to Giles, the father of that gawky teenager Summer had seemed taken with, stayed up long after Jess had gone to bed, drinking tonic water while Giles ordered champagne. Giles had introduced me to a friend of his, an old friend he'd bumped into in Cannes: Callum. A chance meeting that had changed everything.

A good twenty years older than me, Callum and I had struck up a friendship based on the same interest in stocks and shares. I admit, I was flattered. Callum seemed exactly the sort of person I should be hanging out with, with his expensive clothes and expensive choice of drinks. We'd kept in touch after the holiday, swapping texts, then emails, then videocalls. Only, whereas Callum had been doing well in the day trading – more than well – I'd started to flounder. I'd even talked about jacking it all in. Except, of course, I couldn't because Jess thought I'd invested my book money and her inheritance in blue-chip stocks, only slightly more risky than premium bonds. I didn't have the heart or the guts to tell her the truth.

So, when Callum offered me twenty thousand pounds just to keep me afloat, I'd leaped at the chance, promised to pay him back double. I was so bloody sure I could make it. But three weeks later, I'd lost the entire amount. All that money disappeared into thin air. A month after that, the men had turned up, knocking on my door when Jess was out, threatening me with their fists and the glint of a blade. It was a mistake, Callum had said when I rang him panicked later that night, my throat still hurting from when they'd rammed my windpipe. The men weren't meant to hurt me, just shake me up a little. And then, as if to prove the point, he'd offered me a house for the summer holidays. His mother's house in Suffolk. A couple of weeks in the countryside, time with the family – didn't that sound grand? Besides, it would be doing his stepmum a favour; she was coming to visit and needed someone to look after the cats. I'd agreed because I'd had no option, because the threat was still there even though he said it wasn't. Because it had seemed like an olive branch, Callum's way of an apology for the men turning up like that. And of course I'd not told Jess, just fudged some story about a house-sitting company.

The house is amazing. Callum had said. *Huge. A place to get lost in. You won't be disappointed.*

I close my eyes and swallow back bile, wondering if I'm still drunk. I picture going downstairs and finding Jess, telling her everything, admitting I've lost her inheritance and more, that I owe a man I hardly know twenty thousand pounds. That, despite her objections, we've no choice but to stay in this shithole of crumbling brick and stone, because if we just up and leave there's no telling what those men might do.

Except I just can't. I don't have the nerve.

I lift the quilt carefully so as not to wake Xanthe and stand upright, hit by a wave of dizziness. For a moment, I'm back in my twenties: the alcohol sweats, the nausea, the pounding headache. The first time I'd met Jess had been in a bar on my way home after a big night out. It was lunchtime and the city was alive with an energy that made my headache worse. I'd intended to buy myself a beer, a hair of the dog, but then I'd seen Jess at the bar with a tray of drinks, and there was something about her – her confidence, her clothes, her hair and barely-there makeup – that had made me stop and stare. Maybe it had been the fact I was still drunk, but I'd struck up a conversation, then purposely knocked over her glass of wine.

'I'm sorry,' I'd said, resisting the urge to mop up the splash on her shirt. 'Can I buy you another?'

She'd flicked her fringe from her eyes, and I could tell she was amused, that she knew I'd done the drink spilling on purpose. When I'd ordered her a drink, I'd ordered one for myself as well, a tonic water with lime. Despite the alcohol still coursing through my system, despite my desperate need for a hair of the dog, it had seemed like the right thing to do. A fresh start. I'd been meaning to give up drinking for months. Years in fact. I'd reached a low point, and hated myself for it. And Jess seemed like the perfect excuse.

Now, I stare at the floorboards in St Cross, my stomach flipping, sweat rolling down my face. My stomach muscles squeeze. I run to the bathroom, groaning at the ache in my belly, squatting over the toilet just in time. Then I flush, scrub my hands, splash water on my face, feeling a million times better. A headache, but I can deal with that. I'll swallow a couple of paracetamol, alternate pints of water with coffee. Jess need never know. I grab my toothbrush and stare at my grey, washed-out skin in the mirror. I pull down my lower eyelids, checking for signs of jaundice. But my eyes, though vaguely bloodshot, are predominantly white. I check my pulse.

'Mr Kennedy, I'm so glad you could join us this morning.'

Jesus Christ.

I swivel to face the empty bathroom. That voice. The same voice I heard before in my dream. Only I'm not bloody dreaming. I'm wide awake. I press a hand to my head, my temples pulsing. My eyes dart to the bath, the toilet, the mirror, the little shaving cabinet above the sink. The shaving cabinet – the only space that's concealed. I open the door, tip bottles of lotion and shampoo, dental floss and cotton wool buds into the basin, desperately searching for something, *anything*, to explain the voice. Maybe there's a radio that's been left switched on. A faulty miniature radio. Because if it's not something external, it's me. *Me.* Which is even more terrifying.

A bottle of perfume smashes against the taps, the contents dribbling out. The smell makes me retch. Harsh. Acrid.

I run to the toilet and dry heave, my stomach knotting in pain.

'Such a pleasant aroma, don't you think?'

Bloody hell. I dart upright, scanning the room. But everything is as it was. I touch my forehead, damp with sweat. I'm running a fever. Maybe it's not just the whisky, maybe I'm coming down with something too? I stagger backwards until I meet the wall, taking large deliberate breaths.

The room swims pale green, the silence muted like I'm swimming under water. In its place, I hear the high-pitched whine of the tinnitus I haven't suffered from for years. Not since before I met Jess. I think of the landing, the banister rail, the tiles below, the solace they offer. All this could be over. All this could disappear, replaced by a soothing nothingness.

I run to the bathroom door, slide back the lock, step on to the landing. The memory rolls inside me as I look down at the hall. *The ridge, the rocks, the sunshine, Dad with his backpack egging me on.*

My stomach churns, but this time I'm not fast enough. Vomit splashes down my chest and on to the carpet, the landing swaying in the same pale green light. I bend over, unable to think of anything else, ignoring the way the house watches and judges, just fighting the urge to vomit again.

Charles Keller's diary:

<u>2 January 1848</u>

It is a year to this day that Clara died. A year I have cursed myself for not saving her, for not seeing the cancer before it was too late. The memory of Clara is forever shadowed by her final breaths, the pain in her eyes as she begged me over and over to end her misery.

I have spent the day in a malaise, performing my duties without care or attention. Exasperated, Mrs Harker ordered me to my room, but I cannot rest. From here I can hear everything: doors slamming, women wailing, children crying for their mothers. It is as if the whole place is intent on feeding my misery.

<u>5 January 1848</u>

I am persuaded by my new friend, Dr Marne, the physician who visits the infirmary frequently, that the malady from which I currently suffer is one of the mind. The cure is simple: fresh air, exercise, and a break, however small, from my labours. Thus today, despite the cold weather, we walked for miles along the coastal path, stopping only for refreshments at a seaside tavern. It is indeed a pleasant country – undulating arable fields, dormant in the winter sun, and clear skies above blue water (*I must take greater pains to acquaint myself with Suffolk!*). We talked about many things, the recent advances in our respective professions, the rise in typhus, the latest news from parliament. By the time we returned to St Cross it was four o'clock in the afternoon (we had been walking all day) and dark. I fell upon my bed and slept, rising only a little before six. I feel restored if aching from the exercise. Perhaps Dr Marne is right?

6 January 1848

This morning, Massingham came to see me in my room. He has been somewhat unwell and asked for my assessment. I am well aware of his condition, having treated him also in London, and yet I was shocked when he stripped his clothes. The signs of syphilis are now many, the bodily sores that mark his chest and legs and even his hands. He complains of fever and fatigue and yet he has no trust in Dr Marne who prescribes him only mercury. Rest was all I could suggest, to which he shook his head. Not rest, he said, but hard work is needed.

7 January 1848

Massingham assisted me in the operating theatre today, a complicated procedure removing a patient's breast and occasioning much blood loss. Thomas Percy stood nearby with bandages wearing what can only be described as a ghostly pallor – and he has seen many things! By contrast, Massingham was steady throughout, unaffected by his own illness, handing me knives when I requested them and relieving Percy of his duties. The patient is now recovering in the ward, but I fear the blood loss is too great and, whilst I have applied bandages, infection may soon set in.

<u>10 January 1848</u>

Our patient on the women's ward died today. I thought of Clara, the tinge of suffering upon her lips, how they had moved without speaking as she took her final, shallow breaths. Clara, dear Clara, how I failed you!

<u>11 January 1848</u>

I awoke to bright sunlight. I had slept in and my breakfast tray was already upon my desk. Next to it was a vial of chloroform. I had forgotten to stopper the bottle after inhaling and the vial was empty. I must have inhaled the substance all night, which explains the dreams – vivid, wonderful dreams – and the headache I am now troubled with. What happened last night? I am trying to piece it together, but there is little to go upon. Only the opened bottle, the memory of the patient dying, and Clara. I had been thinking of Clara, hadn't I?

29

⚬⚬⚬

Jess

FRONT DOOR ‖ PARLOUR
DINING ROOM ‖ WOMEN'S WARD
MEN'S WARD ‖ ISOLATION WARD
CHILDREN'S WARD ‖ OPERATING THEATRE

I stare at the servant bells in the kitchen, the words on the bell board running through my mind. The labels are bright today, clearer to read. I wonder if it's something to do with the light, the way it spills at an angle through the window, pooling on the wall to the right of the door. But it's only six-thirty. Not full sunlight yet, not for a number of hours. Unsettled, I fill the kettle with water. The air feels charged with an energy I can't see, a pulse like the house is beating with its own heart. The water splutters into the sink and splashes my dressing gown. I screw off the taps and listen to the pipes groaning in the walls.

I reach out, press one hand against the paintwork above the sink, feeling the coolness of the plaster beneath.

'Hi, Mum.' I jump, spilling water from the kettle. Summer's behind me, rubbing sleep from her eyes. She heads straight for the coffee. 'How's Xanthe?'

'She's fine. Sleeping in. How are you?'

'Good.' Summer flicks on the kettle. 'Thought I'd hang out at the cottage today.'

'Okay.' I look away, hiding my dislike of the boy Summer seems intent on spending the holiday with. Hating the way he seems to have infected her mood. 'Why don't you invite Aaron around here? He could join us for lunch?'

Summer takes her time selecting a mug from the assortment of stained, chipped ones in the cupboard. No doubt my offer must sound ridiculous to a teenage girl, but if she's going to hang out with him, I'd rather it was here where I can keep an eye. I brace myself for yet another argument or snide comment but, instead, Summer turns around and smiles. 'Thanks, Mum. Yeah. I think I will.'

I hide my surprise, thinking about the conversation I should be having with my almost seventeen-year-old daughter. The conversation about safe sex and only saying yes when she really means it; the one she assures me has already been covered extensively in sex education at school. But right now isn't the time. 'I'll fix us lunch on the terrace,' I say instead. 'About one-ish?'

'Sure.'

The light changes, a cloud passing the sun. I grab a pile of dirty cutlery and throw it in the sink, washing it in threes – three spoons, three forks, three knives – knowing that whatever doesn't fit into my rhythm will remain there until later. I pick up the glass I retrieved from the study, stare at the neat ring of liquid at the bottom of it. Whisky. I'm sure of it. I think of Liam presumably still asleep upstairs, the distinct boozy smell in the bedroom. I can't understand it. Liam's practically tee-total, always has been. I plunge the glass into the sink, scrub around the rim, take it out again and hold it up to the light.

Something catches my eye near the ceiling through the glass.

The bell at the far end, the bell above the words 'Operating theatre'. The clapper is swaying gently, the coil of metal above pulsating. I take a step backwards, lowering the glass. The servant bells don't work – I've even tried tugging the bell pull I found behind the dining-room door – and when I look again, it's still. I glance at Summer, stroking the white cat, completely oblivious, and draw my hands down my face, leaving soapsuds on my cheeks. It's me. I'm driving myself crazy.

30

SUMMER

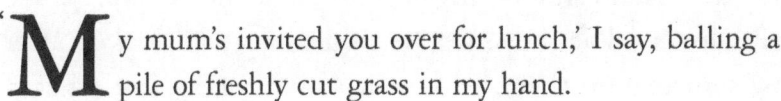

'My mum's invited you over for lunch,' I say, balling a pile of freshly cut grass in my hand.

Aaron grimaces.

'I thought it would be a good excuse for you to have a look around the house?'

His frown turns into a grin. 'We should take the mirror.'

'I'm not sure my mum would agree to that—'

'Well, we're not exactly going to tell her, are we?'

I shake my head. Mum would freak.

'We'll sneak it into the house and try it again after lunch. Remember the words you heard? The Latin? They're bound to be connected to the infirmary in some way. This time, you need to write them down.'

I pick at a flake of wood from the bench, feeling a splinter dig beneath my nail.

He nudges me with his elbow. 'Hey. What's up?'

I force a smile, focusing on the pain. 'Nothing.'

'You're not still worried about scrying, are you? It's completely safe.'

'You don't know that, do you?' I peel a long strip of wood from the bench.

'According to my nan, it is.' He directs his gaze to the far side of the cottage garden, to the washing line where Mrs Harrison is pegging out sheets.

'You told her you've been scrying again?'

'Not exactly.' He chews the end of his thumb. 'Anyway, strictly speaking, it wasn't me who was scrying, it was you.' He grins and picks at the dried skin on his thumb. 'When the school flipped out about the Ouija board and the mirror, and my parents grounded me for the entire summer holiday, Nan came on my side. Told me not to worry.' He tilts his head at the sky. 'She thinks we're all looked after by someone up there. I know it sounds crazy, but what if she's right?'

'And what if she's wrong and there's nothing out there at all?' I think about the hypothetical light on my shoulder, the gran I hardly knew following me around like a surveillance camera.

'Then there's nothing to worry about, is there? You can't have evil without good. Everything has to balance.' He stands up, dusts the cut grass from his shorts. 'So, what shall we do now? Lunch is hours away.' He stares into space, then looks down at me and smiles. 'I know, I can show you the grounds of the old manor. You can still see the foundations.'

I shrug and suck my finger where the splinter's dug in. I suppose it beats sitting here, talking about ghosts.

The heat wraps around us as we walk, a dizzying breathless heat. I taste sunscreen on my lips and my T-shirt feels damp. We pass the gatehouse and take a small path between the fields on the right. Insects swarm between the hedgerows, and more than once, I feel the sharp bite of something attacking my legs. The path is overgrown with brambles and grass, and runs only a short way before it ends at a fence.

'You okay?' Aaron looks behind him as he straddles the stile into the neighbouring field.

I slap my right thigh. 'Fine. Except for the flies.'

'You need to eat Marmite. That's what my nan says.' He grins. 'But then, we've already established my nan's bat-shit crazy.' He jumps down on to the other side.

I lean over the fence. No public footpath sign. 'Are we allowed here?'

Aaron sighs. 'You coming or not?'

'I'm coming.' I straddle the stile. The field beyond is covered in stubby stalks of wheat and there's a clear lack of a walkable path.

'We need to cross over there.' Aaron points at the far corner of the field. 'According to Grandad, the driveway used to run from the gatehouse through that field on the right. I guess the house would have been huge.'

We make our way to the other side of the field, climbing over a gate, landing in a narrow boggy section.

'The stream,' Aaron says. 'It runs from the lake at St Cross. There are stepping stones over there.'

He leads me a little further up, where the stream is deeper, then balances on a series of well-positioned rocks. Halfway across, I lose my footing, one trainer slipping into the water below. Aaron reaches out and grabs hold of my hand. 'Are you all right?'

Heat rushes through my body. 'Fine.' I pull away in embarrassment.

He jumps the final rock to the other side, and I follow, still feeling the flush in my cheeks.

'So, here we are.' He gestures at the field ahead, beyond another gate, open this time. The field is a tangle of tall grass and weeds, completely uncultivated. The grass pricks my legs as we walk, and more than once I stumble down an unseen dip. Aaron strides ahead as if he's been here many times before. Halfway through the field, he jumps up on to a platform, half-hidden by grass. 'The foundations of the old manor,' he says, tapping his foot against stone. 'Nan said it burned down when she was a teenager. Then they pulled down what was left for safety reasons.'

I join him on the platform. 'That's what Robbie Silver said too. You know, the old lady who lives in the gatehouse?' I inspect the remaining stones, the outline of what was obviously once an imposing building. But there are no walls, no floors except for what we're standing on now. I feel a wave of disappointment; I'd expected more. 'It feels sad, don't you think?'

Aaron sits down and pulls a bag of weed from his pocket — obviously, he didn't bring me out here for a history lesson. I watch him roll a joint before lighting up.

'Depends what you call sad,' he says. 'I mean, it would have been great to own a place like this. But, I guess most people who lived here would have been servants. Poor people working long hours for almost nothing. So, yeah, I guess it is kind of sad.'

'But what about you?'

'What do you mean?'

I sit down next to him. 'Well, you're not exactly poor, you go to boarding school. You learn Latin.'

'That's my parents, not me. I never wanted to go away to school.' He hands me the joint. I put it to my lips and try not to cough – it's a long time since I did this, not since my old school. After a couple of drags I hand the joint back to him and stretch my legs, feeling the intense heat of the sun. Aaron strips off his T-shirt and lays it beneath him on the stone. Then he leans backwards, blowing smoke circles into the stagnant air. I lie down next to him, my body heavy and sleepy, feeling the burn of the stone against my lower back.

'I could get used to this,' Aaron says when we've finished smoking. He leans over and kisses me.

For a fraction of a second, I tense, thinking about Harry, then I allow myself to respond, tugging his lower lip, tasting his tongue. Energy charges through my body, intensified with each kiss.

'Hey,' he pulls backwards abruptly, the movement making me panic. Am I doing something wrong? I push myself up to sitting.

'I guess we better get going,' he says, grabbing his T-shirt, pulling it over his head. 'We don't want to miss lunch.'

'It's hours until lunch.'

He rubs the back of his neck, then busies himself with tidying his weed and tobacco. 'I'm sorry. I shouldn't have done that.'

'Why?' Panic grips my chest.

'It's just,' he pulls at his fringe, 'you're going home soon. And I'll be stuck here for another month. And we'll never see each other again. I don't want to mess you around, that's all.'

I almost laugh. He's trying to do the honourable thing; unlike Harry, he's trying to be a decent person. 'But what if this *is* what I want?' I say, emboldened by the weed.

He looks me straight in the eye. 'And is it?'

I think of the girls in school, the boy I kissed because I was drunk, the shit year I've had as a result. I reach over and pull him towards me. 'Yes. I think it is.' I kiss him again. He responds, fumbling with the hem of my T-shirt, his hands gliding over the dip of my stomach, moving upwards, cupping my breasts. Suddenly, I let out a small yelp of surprise.

'What is it?' He jerks away, following my gaze over his shoulder. A dog is running towards us, leaping through the grass. Aaron grabs the bag of weed, stuffs it in his pocket.

'It's Robbie Silver's dog from the gatehouse,' I say, pulling down my T-shirt. The Jack Russell scrambles on to the platform and crouches a metre or so away, growling. 'It must have escaped.' I scan the field to the left and the right, then down towards the stream. It's then that I see her: Robbie Silver, watching us from the gate.

'Call him back, will you?' Aaron shouts, anger ringing in his voice.

Robbie Silver doesn't move. She's enjoying all this, I think. She's enjoying the fact we're too scared to move for fear of having a leg or an arm ripped off. Aaron jumps to his feet. The dog snarls. 'Get away,' he shouts, lobbing an imaginary stone. 'Go on. Get away from us.'

The dog starts yapping and wagging his tail as though he thinks it's all a game.

'Come on,' Aaron reaches for my hand. 'Walk slowly. No sudden movements. It shouldn't be let off its leash.'

But the dog settles on the stone, suddenly disinterested,

making no attempts to follow us as we walk. The thought flickers through my mind that he's achieved exactly what he intended to achieve. We cross the field to the gate, Aaron tightening his grip on me as the old lady takes us in.

'Where is she?' Robbie hisses. Despite the heat, she's wearing the dressing gown with the faded blue flowers. 'Where's the little girl?'

'What little girl?' Aaron snaps.

But Robbie's eyes are on me. 'The one who stole my fairy.'

I bristle. 'Xanthe's in the house. And she didn't steal your fairy. That's a lie. She was just looking at it.'

'She shouldn't come here. *You* shouldn't come here. This place is a dead place.'

I glance at Aaron, the muscles tense in his neck, his veins bulging. 'You shouldn't let your dog off the lead,' he growls. 'It's dangerous.'

'And, young man, you shouldn't be in this field. Don't you know you're trespassing?'

'Well, if we're trespassing, then so are you.'

Robbie straightens her spine. 'My dog ran off. He must have sensed you were here. I had no choice but to follow him.' As if on cue, the Jack Russell runs up behind us, obediently settling at his owner's feet.

I take a step closer to Aaron, my shoulder brushing his arm. 'What did you mean by this place being a dead place?'

A breeze ripples through the hedgerow, lifting brambles. Despite the saturating heat, I shudder with cold. Robbie bends down and fastens a lead to the dog's harness. 'You should come with me,' she says. 'You should take tea with me in my garden.'

*

The tea is disgusting. Herbal tea but not the nice minty variety I sometimes like. It's savoury and strong with a bitter aftertaste, and the addition of honey makes it only slightly more palatable.

'The manor house burned down in 1965.' Robbie Silver sits stiffly, saucer in one hand, teacup in the other. I sit opposite her next to Aaron, feeling vaguely sick from the tea or the weed or both. 'It was a hot day like today. The heat was unbearable. There were hippies in the ruins, setting up camp, dragging huge speakers into the space of the old ballroom. I watched them from the stream.'

'You were there?' It's hard to imagine Robbie Silver as a young woman in the sixties. Mini-skirts, platforms boots and flower-power headdresses seem a world away from the woman in the threadbare dressing gown.

'It wasn't just me. Susan was there too.'

'Susan?'

'Mrs Harrison. Only she wasn't Mrs Harrison back then. She lived in one of the new houses by the sea. Her family had recently moved into the area.'

Aaron frowns. 'Nan saw the manor house burn?'

'Back then, we were friends. Not friends like me and Verity, the girl who married Mr Laurence, the girl from St Cross – that came later. We were friends who went to dances together, who sat next to each other on the bus. We had the same interests – the church, the spirit life; we were both curious about what comes after – so it was natural we became friends.' She taps her cup, her fingernails yellow and brittle. 'It was our sixteenth year and we'd just finished school and the hippies turning up was the most excitement we'd had in weeks. Susan wanted to join them in the manor. She wanted to dance and maybe find love. But I was happy just to watch. Then, the hippies built a fire, and it caught one of the old timbers, and the place went up, whoosh.'

I swallow some of the awful tea. 'Was anyone hurt?'

'No one was hurt.'

'Then why did you say the field is a dead place?'

'Couldn't you feel it?' Robbie closes her eyes and lays a hand on her chest, and maybe it's the after-effects of the weed, or maybe it's just the bizarreness of the situation, but I fight the urge to laugh. 'Couldn't you feel the silence? You should have seen it when the place went up in flames. Sparks like a firework show. You wouldn't have thought there was that much to burn with all the furniture moved out and half the roof missing. But you could feel the heat of it for days afterwards. The timbers still smouldering despite the efforts of the fire brigade. Months after it happened, when we went there to see what was left, there was nothing.'

'It was reduced to ruins?'

'I mean the soul of the place had died along with the fire. Its heart had been smothered in the flames. Now, nothing grows over the foundations. The weeds only come up so far. They don't sprout between the old paving stones. The only things you'll ever find there are dead things. Skeletons. A mouse or a bird dragged on to the platform by some creature or other and mauled to death.'

I glance at the gatehouse, but I can't see the front window from here. I can't see the collection of animal bones. I've visions of the old lady taking them from the manor house, tucking them in the pockets of her dressing gown, then cleaning them up and displaying them on the windowsill like seaside ornaments.

'You children shouldn't go there,' Robbie says. 'It's not a place for young people. You could easily awaken it. It's a place for the dead.'

I smother a smile, thinking of Aaron's fingers brushing my belly, the hardness of his muscles as I'd run my hands over his biceps, the taste of him as I lay back, heady with heat and dope, the way his pelvis had grinded against mine. Nothing dead about that.

'Can you tell us about Verity?' I say, changing the subject. 'You said you were friends.'

Robbie's face closes up. 'Verity died. Sepsis they said it was. She cut herself badly in the kitchen at St Cross and the wound wouldn't heal. She was afraid. Very afraid. Her child died in a freak accident and she thought there was something wrong with the house. She found a diary—'

'A diary?'

'Written by someone from the old days. She never told me what was in it, only that it was bad. That something terrible had happened there. After she died, I tried to find it. I let myself into the house when Mr Laurence was working and had a rummage around. But it was impossible. There was so much clutter. Mr Laurence obviously couldn't look after himself without a woman.'

'Why did you fall out with Nan?' Aaron cuts in and I look at him in surprise. I didn't know there'd been a falling out.

'You should ask Susan that.' Robbie's eyes flicker with anger. 'Verity was nothing like Susan. Verity was kind and sweet. I thought I could trust your grandmother. I thought Susan was like me, but she wasn't. She ran off and told everyone my secrets.'

'What do you mean?' Aaron stands up, knocking the tray.

I reach for his hand but he shrugs me off. 'It's okay,' I say.

'It's not okay. Didn't you hear her? She practically called my nan a bitch.'

'I'm sure she didn't mean—'

'I mean everything I say about Susan Harrison.' Robbie glares at Aaron. 'Susan turned everyone against me. Poisoned them with her lies. She's a bad woman. A bad, bad woman.'

Aaron laughs and runs his hands through his hair. 'Oh my God. Whatever my nan's said about you, she's obviously right. You're a freak.'

He stalks away, striding through the garden. I stumble after him, ignoring the old woman, mumbling behind me. For some reason, I'm thinking about the cauterising iron in the museum, the rounded end of it glowing red hot. *Venenum mortiferum.* The Latin words dance through my memory, as I trample through the rockery, kicking over the tiny fairy – Titania – in my haste.

'Aaron,' I call after him, the sound of my own voice a welcome distraction from the terrifying ramble of Latin in my mind. But, by the time I reach the road, Aaron's already halfway to the cottage.

Charles Keller's diary:

<u>15 February 1848</u>

It is only through my dreams that I can escape. In my dreams, I see Clara again, more real than in life. I see her clearly: the sheen of her skin, the red of her cheeks, the blue of her eyes, the brilliant white flowers in her hair, the way her dress narrows to an impossible hand-width at her waist. I see that she forgives me for not seeing the cancer sooner, for not daring to end her suffering swiftly, only dosing her with enough laudanum to silence her cries.

I am using two drachms of chloroform daily, my tolerance having increased, but I am perfectly able to perform my duties, and the headache upon awakening is merely trifling. Indeed, I do not think I could sleep without it. I came to Suffolk to escape my memories but find they have only followed me here.

It is bitterly cold weather still. The patients huddle together in their beds although such fraternising is strictly prohibited, but who has the heart to chastise them?

17 March 1848

Once again, I have been too busy to write this diary. My days are filled from dawn until dusk with the needs of my patients, those at the infirmary and those further afield. Deaths are many. The operating theatre has become one of the busiest rooms in the house. We are all worn out and Thomas Percy is sick, a fever that troubles me greatly and which resists my efforts to treat it.

20 March 1848

Massingham visited me today and saw, upon my desk, my design for a machine to administer chloroform. He was greatly impressed with the idea and insisted I show it to John Harrison at once. Thus, I returned once more to the red-bricked cottage and sat with the gardener and his wife and explained my plan. It is simple in its construction: bellows attached to a rubber hose, the air flow divided in two, one part directed to a sealed container of chloroform, the other directed to a cloth mask and connected to the rest by means of a glass tube. The whole lot, I explained to Harrison, would be contained within a wooden box. Harrison listened diligently, suggesting various improvements. With Massingham's blessing, he will commence work on the project at once.

31

Jess

They're late, of course. I should have known it. I shouldn't have been so prompt with lunch. I watch Summer and the boy sauntering up the lawn from the wood, taking their time as if the omelette I've made with the last of the eggs will keep for ever, and the broccoli I've steamed will stay perfectly hot. Everything's ready. I've wheeled a little fold-up Formica table from the kitchen on to the terrace, dusted down glasses, found matching cutlery.

'Hi.' I raise a hand, trying to act causal. I should be grateful they remembered at all. 'We're having lunch out here. Aaron, isn't it?'

'Correct.' The boy smiles politely. 'Mrs Kennedy, right?'

'You can call me Jess.' At least he seems to be remembering his manners today. 'I'm afraid Summer's dad won't be joining us. He's gone to bed. Not feeling too well. I think it's the heat.' I turn my face to the sky as if I can convince myself as well as the others of the lie. 'I'm sure he'll be fine later.' *When his hangover's gone.*

There's a squeak of excitement from behind. Everyone turns. Xanthe's running towards us across the lawn, clutching her diary. The prospect of having someone join us for lunch, even if it's just a friend of Summer's, is clearly enthralling. She obviously recovered from her fall, and, I remind myself, as soon as Liam surfaces, I need to speak to him again about leaving.

I grin. 'Aaron meet Xanthe. Xanthe meet Aaron.'

'We met before, Mummy. Remember? In Lowestoft?'

'Of course. Silly me.' The narrow street in front of the museum, the argument with Summer, the amusement on Aaron's face. I fuss with the cutlery on the Formica table, feeling unduly nervous. I can't remember ever bringing a boy home as a teenager, only hanging out with boys in the woods, staying out far too late after school. And then, the inevitable kissing, the awkward fumbling, the whispered promises that made me both embarrassed and hungry for more.

'What's for lunch?' Summer leans over the dishes on the table, and lifts a lid, revealing the rapidly cooling omelette.

'Bits and bobs. Sit down. I hope you're hungry.' I try to sound upbeat, turning to Aaron. 'We don't seem to have settled into a routine here. There's broccoli and new potatoes and cheese and ham and chutneys. Can I pour you a drink?' I indicate the decanter I found in the dining room and spent half an hour soaking in soapy water before washing and polishing. 'Lemonade?'

He licks his lips. 'Lemonade. My favourite.'

I can't miss the obvious note of sarcasm. I lose some of my

composure, sloshing lemonade into glasses, spilling some on the table. Should I be serving something else? Should I be offering the boy beer? 'So, Aaron, you live in the cottage?'

'No.'

'Okay.' So, we're back to the monosyllabic answers. I try a different tack. 'Where are you from?'

'Bristol.'

'And you're in Suffolk because ... ?'

'My parents wanted to get rid of me.'

I laugh. 'I'm sure they didn't.'

He smiles and lifts his lemonade. The bubbles fizz and spit against the glass. 'Only joking. I'm visiting my grandparents.'

'Aha.' Finally, I'm on familiar ground. 'The Harrisons? In the cottage? How long are you staying?'

'Mum!' Summer groans. 'Stop the Spanish Inquisition.'

'I was only asking—'

'It's fine.' Aaron places the glass down, leans over and helps himself to broccoli. He stabs a floret and watches with obvious delight as it slides down the fork and disintegrates into overcooked sludge. 'I'm here for the entire summer holidays. I live on the outskirts of Bristol with my sister and two younger brothers. My parents have a dog called Bruce. My mother's a barrister and my father's an architect. I'm studying Spanish, French and Latin A level. My favourite food is chilli con carne.' He spears another floret, this one slightly more successful. 'Have I missed anything?'

I raise my eyebrows, unsure whether I'm meant to be amused or offended. Summer drags a fork across her empty plate, a noise that grates. 'Well, that's quite a list,' I say, attempting a smile.

The meal is awkward, the conversation stilted. Thank God

for Xanthe, chattering away, asking Aaron questions about Bruce. To my relief, he responds, doing doggy impressions to demonstrate how Bruce begs for scraps.

'I'm going to draw Bruce,' Xanthe announces at the end of the meal, grabbing her diary from the table, then running off to find a shady spot on the lawn.

Summer pushes her plate aside. She's barely eaten a thing, just shuffled her food around with her fork. Her lack of eating is a constant source of anxiety, but out here it's worse. A statement of independence, like she's trying to tell us she can do whatever she likes. I feel her pulling away from me just a little bit more. 'I'm going to give Aaron a tour of the house,' she says.

'Okay.' *Just remember, it's not ours*, I want to add, *and don't take him into your bedroom.* But instead I bite my tongue, and pray for the best.

Aaron picks up his shoulder bag and traipses after Summer. I watch them go with an ache in my heart. Will it always be like this? Watching our girls grow up? Gradually allowing them liberties? Will it always be so hard? Would it help if I *liked* Aaron? I watch them disappear into the house, Aaron's hands thrust in his pockets, the shoulder bag bouncing against his back. Summer looks over her shoulder and throws me a look of pure triumph. It's as if she knows what I'm thinking, but I don't react. I don't have the heart for yet another argument.

I pick up the dishes and carry them inside – already, no sign of Summer and Aaron – scraping chutney off plates, throwing leftover broccoli into the bin. I fill the sink with water, pile cutlery and pans into the sink. More than once, I stop and listen, trying to locate Summer and Aaron in the house. But the house is quiet. A heavy, oppressive silence. I wipe soapsuds off my hands and open the kitchen door.

The stillness makes my skin tingle. I can feel the house. I can feel it breathing. I listen hard – still no sound. I almost call out, *Summer, Aaron*, except I realise I want to surprise them. I want to catch them at it, whatever *it* is. I slide off my sandals, then creep up the stairs, listening, waiting. Where are they? Where are they hiding? I lift my gaze to the landing. I can see everywhere from here, all those closed doors on the ground and first floor. The doors I'd purposely wedged open to get the air moving. All closed. I climb another couple of steps, then stop and listen, aware only of my own heartbeat, the sun dizzying through the cupola, the thick asthmatic breath of the house.

Something hits the roof, a bird landing full pelt on the glass. A solid thud. I look up, expecting to see the bird crack through the glass, come plummeting into the hallway through the shaft of light. But there's nothing, just a shadowy patch on the roof that could be the bird, that could be anything.

I place a hand on my chest, and let out a long uneven breath, counting in my head, counting up to three.

What am I doing? Why am I on the stairs?

And then I remember: Summer and the boy. I was going to spy on them. It suddenly seems an incredibly untrusting thing to do. I take a step backwards, back towards the hall, shaking and disturbed. It wasn't me, I think. This need to see, to catch Summer doing something she shouldn't.

It wasn't me. It was the house. It was the watching eyes in the hallway.

Extract from an unpublished letter written to the British Medical Journal *by Dr F. J. Hunter, July 1848:*

Those who have studied the recent advances in surgery, will be aware of the transformation currently taking place. Hitherto unimagined procedures such as abdominal surgeries are being performed under the anaesthetising effects of chloroform and ether. As a physician, attending to the needs of patients post-surgery, I can but offer a cautionary tale. Whilst the surgeons seem delighted to operate at increasing speeds and levels of complexity, the outcomes are nothing short of horrific. The stench and filth of the operating theatre permeate the air even from a distance. The surgeons strut about in their blood-soaked jackets, their arrogance clouding their commonsense. Men, women and children are dying unnecessarily. Only yesterday, I attended the death of a child brought in for the simple removal of a tooth. How many more unnecessary deaths must occur before this folly disguised as scientific advancement is made to cease?

32

SUMMER

⸻ ∞ ⸻

'You ready?' Aaron sits next to me in the bedroom and my whole body tenses. I glance around, trying to find an excuse to delay what we're about to do, but all I see are the piles of clothes, hairbrushes and books, my make-up bag, Xanthe's pencil case. After a week of sleeping here, this space feels too personal, too almost-ours. *Kind of creepy*, Aaron had said when he'd seen the old cot with the Mickey Mouse figure. The room still has that sickly-sweet scent like the smell in the bathroom when Dad broke the perfume bottle, except different, lighter and somehow more permanent like it's buried in the very fabric of the place. And yes, it is kind of creepy, but I've got used to it now and I certainly don't want to make things worse. But it's hard to resist, when Aaron's right beside me, his knee brushing mine, the smell of his skin seeping into my space.

'I'm not sure,' I say.

'It's fine. Relax. It's just a bit of fun.'

A bit of fun. That's not the impression he gave me before.

'You do it,' I say. 'Go on. You don't have to sleep here, it doesn't matter to you.'

He sighs and takes the little mirror from his shoulder bag and places it on the floor. Then he fishes out the candle, and the lighter from his pocket. 'All right,' he says. 'Close the curtains.'

I do what he says, casting the room into semi-darkness. 'Just don't burn the house down.' I sit back down, crossing my legs, mimicking him.

'This might take some time,' he says. 'You'll need to be quiet. I need to concentrate.'

He leans forward, lights the candle and stares at the mirror. The minutes stretch by as my eyes adjust to the altered light. But it's impossible to concentrate on anything other than him, the sound of his breathing, the smell of sweat and deodorant and sunscreen.

'Don't,' he says.

'What?'

'Don't look at me like that. You're putting me off.'

I feel my face redden in the dark, wishing I *could* put him off. There are so many better things I could be doing alone with Aaron in my bedroom. Besides, I don't want to find out anything else about this weird house. We've still another week here and I need to survive it.

'It's not working,' Aaron says, sounding pissed off. 'You'll have to try. It was you who heard the voice before. If there's anything here, it will be you it wants to connect with.'

'I dunno.' I search desperately for an excuse. 'Maybe we shouldn't be doing this at all?'

'I thought this was the reason I'm here? The reason I endured that awful lunch?'

I swallow hard. The lunch wasn't great, but I know the effort Mum went to. 'All right,' I relent. 'I'll give it a go.'

We shift positions. I stare into the mirror beyond the candle-light, trying to keep my thoughts at bay, blocking out Aaron and the possibility of someone coming into the room and finding us like this. Just the mirror, I think. Only the mirror. The glass greys over as it had before, a mist forming in the shadowy reflection, but it's barely been a minute.

'Ask it a question,' Aaron whispers hotly.

Et cultus.

'Shit,' I say. 'It's happening.'

'What?'

'The voice. The man's voice. I didn't even ask it a question.'

Aaron scrambles across the room, but I don't take my eyes off the mirror. I can't drag my gaze away. Aaron thrusts a scrap of paper and one of Xanthe's pencils into my hand. 'Write it down.'

'*What?*'

'Whatever it's saying, write it down.'

Quae vitae integritas.

'I can't.' I hear my voice tremble. 'It's Latin or something. This is too weird. Too fucking weird.'

'TRY.'

Juro Apollinem Medicum,

I grab the pencil and start to write, trying to make sense of the words, trying to keep my eyes on the mirror at the same time. But the words are coming too fast.

et Deos omnes,

itemque Deas testes adhibens,

me ratum pro viribus,

judicioque meo jusjurandum hoc,

hancque contestationem effecturum.

I throw the pencil down, cover my eyes with my hands, breathe into my palms. 'I can't do it. I can't do it any more. It makes no sense. I can't write fast enough. I don't understand the words.'

'You're doing fine. You're doing great. Don't break the connection.'

I go back to staring, feeling the stinging heat of the candle flame.

Primum non nocere.

I fumble for the pencil, waiting for the next words or phrase, regardless of the fact it sounds like nonsense.

Primum non nocere. Primum non nocere. Primum non nocere. Primum non nocere. Primum non nocere.

I drop the pencil, and press my hands to my ears, but this time it doesn't stop the words because they're inside my head. Not coming from the mirror. Coming from *me*.

Gravibus somnum.

Gravibus somnum.

Gravibus somnum.

'Stop it,' I shout. 'Stop it, stop it. I can't look any more.' Then the voice comes again, but this time in English.

THEY NEED TO DIE.

Charles Keller's diary:

<u>20 April 1848</u>

The machine failed! The patient – a boy of seven – awoke just as a I cut into his abdomen. Thomas Percy was quick to sedate the patient once again whilst the gruff porter held him down, but the child died upon the operating table. No doubt, the shock and the blood loss were too great.

<u>21 April 1848</u>

Despite the trouble yesterday, Massingham is eager to see revisions to the machine, and thus I have written to my old friend Dr George Reynolds at University College London for his advice on the matter. Meanwhile, Massingham assists me daily in my duties, pushing aside his own ill health. Thomas Percy is sick again, a return of the dreaded fever, which is a great inconvenience. Not only am I anxious for his wellbeing, but Massingham, acting in his stead, requires constant instruction, which demands more of my time.

<u>30 April 1848</u>

Tonight I dined at the manor, a lavish meal consisting of mock turtle, pigeon's compote, veal, jellies and burnt cream, one which I fear will upset my constitution greatly. Afterwards Lady Massingham retired to her room, and Lord Massingham and I stayed up late, smoking. I showed him my new design for the machine. A pin will control the flow of chloroform and a nozzle will restrict and then expand the airflow, resulting in a suction mechanism. Massingham insists that I must begin the revisions at once - he will see to it that Harrison diverts all his attention to the business until it is complete.

On another matter, the air in the infirmary is bad and I have ordered all rooms to be ventilated for the purposes of ridding miasma.

<u>8 May 1848</u>

Thomas Percy died today. The infection, no doubt acquired from one of our patients, was rife throughout his body. It is a hazard of this occupation, but I cannot help but feel his death deeply, it has weighed upon me all afternoon. And yet, when I saw him, laid out in the morgue, his expression was peaceful. He was simply asleep.

33

SUMMER

—⚬⚬⚬—

*G**ravibus somnum.*

The words stir me from my dream, but I can't place them immediately. I'm confused, still drugged with sleep, from the feeling of something – cloth, I think – being pressed over my face. It feels early. Far too early to be awake. The dead of night. I look around the almost-dark room, using the greyer light from the window to orientate myself: the cot containing my sleeping sister, the wall-height cupboards, the space on the floor where I'd sat with Aaron. Sat with the mirror and the little candle.

Gravibus somnum – the words I'd heard when I'd looked at my dark reflection in the mirror and seen the swirling grey mist. That voice. It had felt exactly as if someone had been standing next to me. No, worse than that. As if someone had squeezed themselves into my head. Afterwards, after I'd screamed at Aaron to open the curtains, he'd picked up the sheet of paper with my scribbled attempts to record what I'd heard, and taken it back with him to the cottage to decipher. But not those words – *gravibus somnum*. Those words, I hadn't written down.

'It's definitely Latin,' he'd said before he left, studying my almost illegible scrawl. 'But what it means, I'm not quite sure. I don't think you've quite mastered the spelling.' He'd laughed, but it hadn't felt funny. I'd thought of the other words I'd heard spoken in English, but I couldn't bring myself to say them out loud. Instead, for a long time, I'd sat hugging myself on the floor. When Aaron had joked about doing a Ouija board, I'd wanted to grab the mirror and bring it crashing down on his head.

I fish for my phone beneath my pillow, type the words into Google Translate. A couple of tries while I play with the spelling and I have a translation:

Gravibus somnum: Heavy sleep.

Heavy sleep? What the hell does that mean? My skin tingles all over when I remember those other words, the words spoken clearly in English: *They need to die.*

I shift my gaze to Xanthe in the cot, then throw back the bedsheet. Fear courses through my veins as the night air tingles against my skin. I run, feeling for the side of the cot with my hands, then reach over and touch Xanthe's forehead. It's cold to the touch. I reach further, pulling back the quilt.

'Go away,' Xanthe shrieks at the touch of me.

'Xanthe?' Relief washes through me. 'It's me.'

'Summer?' Xanthe's voice is thick with sleep.

'Yes, you know? Your sister.'

Xanthe tosses her head vigorously on the pillow. 'Sister. No. No. Not my sister. The other children.'

'Wake up.' I shake Xanthe by the shoulders. There's something not right. She's still asleep. 'You're dreaming.'

She grabs on to my arms. Her breath smells stale; not sweet like a child's but old and sick. I remember the feeling in my dream, the feeling of cloth on my face. *Heavy sleep.* 'Please help them. Please. I need you to help them. They need to hide.'

'Who needs to hide?'

'The children. Please. The little children. They all need to hide. He's going to kill them. He's going to kill them all.'

The words chill me. I take a step backwards, shaking Xanthe from my arms. The action seems to undo whatever spell she's fallen under.

'Summer?' Xanthe suddenly sounds small and frightened, but awake. This time, properly awake.

I move back to the cot. 'Hey, sis. I think you had a nightmare.' It's an effort to keep my voice steady. 'You were talking in your sleep.'

'Was I?'

'What were you dreaming about?'

'I can't remember.'

'You were talking about the little children. Tell me about the children.'

'I don't know.' Xanthe stands up, dragging the quilt with her. 'I'm cold,' she says. 'Can I sleep with you?'

'Sure.' I don't mind. I'd rather feel the warmth of Xanthe sleeping next to me, hear the steady in—out of her breath, than spend the rest of the night worrying.

She reaches out and grasps my hand. Her fingers are icy. 'We'll never leave this house, will we?'

'Of course, we will. We're just here on holiday, remember?'

Xanthe doesn't reply but climbs out of the cot and into the bed. I follow, wrapping an arm around her. I want to ask her what she was thinking, why she thought we'd never leave. But I don't.

34

Liam

*T*ap . . . tap . . . tap . . .
     Tap . . . tap . . . tap . . .

I've been listening to the sound for hours, wide awake in bed, thinking about the drink I denied myself earlier. I've easily slipped back into my old ways. In the old days, there'd always been an excuse. Just a tipple to get me to sleep. Just a couple of drinks to commiserate a hard day, or to celebrate a good one. Never a true estimation of the amount I'd actually go on to drink. Deep down, the need to numb has always been there, sometimes strong, sometimes a mere whisper, but never ever going away. When I'd given up the drink, I'd found other ways to cope. The symptom checking. The half-hearted attempts at hypnotherapy and reflexology and all other manner of crap. But none of it had worked. It was all still there, the memory, the pain. No magic method could obliterate it. Not even Jess. Not even our daughters.

My mind turns to my father, a big man who liked a drink himself. I've an image of him standing on the side of the rugby pitch. 'Go get 'em, son.' And just like that, I'm running for the ball, my legs working hard, completely focused, no other thoughts than to win the game, to make my dad proud, to make up for all the times I know I've disappointed him. But then someone smacks into me from the side. I fall, jarring my shoulder, banging my head, grazing my knees. Someone helps me up and I hobble off the pitch. 'You all right, son?' Dad pats me on the injured shoulder. I feel sick, my vision swimming, threatening a surge of familiar panic. Automatically I reach for my appendix scar. 'I don't feel very well.'

'Course you do.' Dad ruffles my hair.

'I don't want to go back on.'

'Nonsense.' He gives me a shove, back to the pitch. 'On you go. That's my boy.'

Tap . . . tap . . . tap . . .

Tap . . . tap . . . tap . . .

I'm in another place, this time on holiday in Devon, staring at the rock face. My father's behind me, egging me on. But I can't do it. It was easy climbing up the other side of the ridge, but this seems too hard, too tricky. I'm not even sure where I'd place my first step. 'You can do it, son. Don't let me down.' My gaze flits to the ground below me, the craggy outline of rocks. I think of Mum and my aunty taking the obvious route down on the other side, the easy route, the sensible route. The route we should all be taking. 'Come on, son.' Dad prods me in the back. 'We're not going to let the girls beat us to the car.'

Tap . . . tap . . . tap . . .

I fold the pillow around my head, hands clasped on either side, muffling but not completely eliminating the sound. I want it to go away. I need it to go away. Because it's nearer tonight, just like the memories. Nearer, and louder than it's ever been.

Extract from a lecture given to students at University College London by Mr Stewart Harding, surgeon, 3 July 1848:

The surgeon's jacket is a thing of pride. This simple woollen frockcoat is worn to perform all surgical procedures, thus protecting the surgeon's clothes beneath, and bears the marks of his labour. Whilst some may regard this jacket as a sordid item, caked as it is in blood and other undesirable human fluids, it is, to the surgeon, his badge of honour.

35

⸺ ∞ ⸺

Jess

The jacket is waiting for me on the terrace. The light grey jacket with the ripped silk lining. I walk towards it fearfully. As usual – now that Liam's given up his pretence of writing – I'm the first one awake, the first one to tiptoe downstairs, to venture into the garden. Even the cats, Snowy and Stripey, are asleep, curled up together in a chair in the hall. But the jacket is there, sprawled on the Formica table, waiting for me like a living thing. Even from a distance I can smell the rancid stench of the wool. I can feel the evil.

I scan the lawn and the garden shed, hoping to catch sight of the gardener. It's the only explanation I can think of: Peter Harrison must have taken the jacket, then brought it back again. But there's no sign of anyone about. I run my gaze along the fence. Something moves: a black cat disappearing into the field beyond, the black cat I'm sure I saw before.

I dart forward, stepping on something small and hard: a silver button trailing a short line of grey thread. A button that's come loose from the jacket, that feels somehow familiar. I pick it up and roll it round and round in my hand. It feels like a message, only one I can't read. One I'm not sure I *want* to read. I look up again, scanning the field, hoping to catch a glimpse of the cat, but it's disappeared from sight and all I can feel is the house behind me, the windows at my back, the unrelenting unease.

I put the button in the pocket of my shorts and walk.

It feels good to stretch my legs despite my tiredness. I take the route through the field on the left, keeping my eyes peeled for any sign of movement, then powerwalking along the wood at the bottom of the garden, eventually meeting the road. It's the first time I've exercised since the morning after we arrived. That day, I'd walked all the way to the sea, but today I turn in the opposite direction, back along the winding road towards Lowestoft, pausing at the gates to St Cross. I stare at the snakes on the pickets, their twisting sinister form, before directing my gaze along the overgrown path, seeing the house in my mind's eye at the end of the driveway. I remember the first night I'd seen it, how strange I'd felt when I'd awoken and stretched my legs in the passenger-side seat, and Liam had said we were here. I'd been full of anticipation and nerves. Nerves because I'd wanted this to be a good holiday. A holiday to make up for the shamble of a year we've had, to make things right with Liam.

Because this year, we've drifted – it feels so good to finally admit it – and I miss him. I miss the closeness of him, the nights we'd stay up late talking over cups of tea, discussing his writing, discussing my day at work, discussing the children, trying to navigate the tricky world of parenthood between us. Now, it seems, he does his thing and I do mine, and we hardly ever really connect.

I think of the book that isn't actually a book at all, the secret drinking, the shadows beneath his eyes. I know I need to talk to him. I just need to tread carefully, choose the right moment.

I leave the gate and climb the steep bend to the church, a white stone building with rounded Norman arches, remembering Robbie Silver telling me to check the place out. And I think, why not? There's no hurry to be back. I open the gate to the churchyard, take the footpath to the door at the side. To my surprise, the church is open. I step inside and find the building empty, my footsteps echoing on the uneven stone floor. The place is obviously well cared for. There are flowers on the altar, and it smells of fresh polish. I step up to the chancel, drawn by the large monuments on either side behind the choir stalls, beside the old-fashioned pump organ. When I investigate, running my hands over the smooth marble and reading the carved letters on the sides of the tombs, I find they're memorials to the Massingham family.

The Massinghams of Blythe Manor.

Massingham – the name in Charles Keller's diary, the diary I have put to one side because the pages are too damaged, the writing too hard to decipher. But here, the engraving is clear. I close my eyes, welcoming the cool of the stone, imagining the threads of time, linking the church to the manor, the manor to the infirmary. When I open them again, my eyes rest on a name on the memorial: Lord James Alexander Massingham, died 1849 at the age of fifty-five. The same Lord Massingham as in Charles Keller's notebook?

I retrace my steps to the churchyard and take a moment to study the graves near the path. I note they're all old graves, nothing more recent than 1900. I wander to the back of the churchyard where the grass isn't mowed and the graves are closer together, surprised by the size of the space and the sheer number of graves. Presumably this was where those who died in the infirmary were laid to rest. I take my time, reading the inscriptions, wondering at the lives of those who lie buried beneath. Most of the dates are mid-nineteenth century, and so many had died young.

I reach the end of one row and begin another, reading the names, the ages, the dates of death. There's a large collection of graves from July and August 1848, mostly children. I go back to the first row and re-read the names and dates again: at least half of those buried here had died in the summer of 1848. What had happened to cause so many deaths close together? An outbreak of disease? Cholera? Typhoid? I move to the next row and find the deaths spaced further apart, but all young children, leading right up to twenty years ago. *Emily, George, Anne, Elijah, Sophie . . .*

I feel a sweeping sadness, as I turn and turn the thing in my hand, rolling it between my palms. It takes me a moment to realise what I'm doing. When I look down, I see it's the little silver button with the length of grey thread. The button I'd put in the pocket of my shorts. Impulsively I drop it, not wanting to feel it any more, rubbing furiously at the place where it's dented my palm. I must have taken the button from my pocket without realising it. I must have clenched it as I walked. I must be even more tired than I thought.

*

When I get back to the house, Summer ploughs into me. She's going out and I'm coming in and our shoulders jar in the open back doorway. I turn around to apologise, though I'm pretty sure it wasn't my fault, but already she's heading off into the garden. 'Good morning,' I call after her but she doesn't respond, and I can't help feeling hurt. Is a bit of respect too much to ask?

In the kitchen, the sight of Xanthe eating her cereal lifts my spirits.

'I made you a smoothie,' she says proudly, pointing at the bowl in the centre of the table, one of the dusty bowls from the dresser. I peer at the slop of banana, spinach and milk. 'Only I didn't have anything to whizz it up with. Not properly. So, I used a fork.'

I give her a squeeze. 'Oh, Xanthe. Thank you. I'll go hunting for a blender.' I'm touched by her gesture, despite the unappetising contents of the bowl; for some reason – maybe the contrast between Xanthe and her sister – it almost brings me to tears.

'Is Daddy better today?' Xanthe sounds genuinely concerned as I search through Mrs Clarence's jumbled cupboards.

I feel a flush of anxiety as I pull out an assortment of plastic kitchenware, cracked and dirty. 'I'm sure he's going to be just fine. He had a bug or something yesterday.'

'So, he's not sick any more? Everything's going to be okay?'

'He wasn't really sick. Just feeling a bit off.'

Xanthe wrinkles her nose, and I can tell she's not convinced, then she lifts the cereal bowl to her mouth and drinks the sugary milk. I shake my head disapprovingly, but I don't have the energy to tell her off.

Xanthe slides off her chair. 'I'm going to wake Daddy up now. I'm going to check he's okay. I'm going to pretend I'm the doctor.'

'Well, do it gently, won't you?'

'I'll try my best.'

As soon as she's gone, I give up looking for the blender, pouring away the milk, then carefully scraping the unappetising mush of banana and spinach into the bin. Turning back to the table, I spy Xanthe's diary open beside her cereal bowl. Xanthe's been drawing the garden from the terrace: the lawn, the stone wall, the flowers.

I find myself turning the pages, although I know I shouldn't, know I'm breaking an unspoken rule. There's a drawing of Liam in a meadow, smiling but looking slightly startled at a horse behind him; a drawing of the beach, Summer splashing through the waves; a drawing of Mia Williams eating sandwiches that has me quickly turning the page; a drawing of a black cat scribbled through with pen. I flick to the first day of the holiday, a double page covered in a black and white drawing.

A room, a table, a lamp, Liam.

I trace the outline of the drawing with my finger. It's wrong. All wrong. Liam is lying on the table, his head resting on a plinth, straps binding his arms to his sides. But what makes my finger tremble on the page, what makes even less sense, is the man Xanthe's drawn standing behind him, looking down at Liam with a knife in his hand. I've seen his face before although I can't think where. Those eyes. Those dark unsettling eyes.

I step backwards, stumbling over one of the cats' bowls, dropping the diary. The pages stare back at me as I take a deep breath, feeling the thud-thud-thud of my heart. What on earth has Xanthe drawn?

Charles Keller's diary:

2 June 1848

To my great surprise, George Reynolds arrived at the infirmary sometime after luncheon. He is travelling in this part of the country, having an ailing uncle living this way, and appeared without announcement, giving me quite the surprise. How good it was to see my old friend again! He was, however, much alarmed by my appearance and insisted on examining me at once. The country air is not doing me any good, he concluded on completing his assessment, before urging me to return with him to London.

London! The very thought made me quiver, for is not London a memory both bitter and sweet? And yet, I admit my health has suffered grievously in the country, my skin is sallow and I am troubled daily by headaches and loose bowels. But I cannot leave so readily, so flippantly! I promised Reynolds I would give the matter thought and write to him soon.

5 June 1848

A complicated surgery today, involving the removal of an eye. The patient – a simpleton from the workhouse – was already blind in both, but one was riddled with infection, weeping and causing the patient great distress. 'Take it out, take it out,' he implored me, grasping my shirt with his filthy hands. The surgery was protracted, occasioning much blood loss, but necessary, the eye being cancerous. The patient was hard to rouse following sedation, and on awakening was delirious, screaming wildly and uttering all manner of profanity.

7 June 1848

Our eye patient has died and the wards are quiet once again to the unveiled delight of Mrs Harker. Today is glorious. Patients are sitting in the grounds, enjoying the sunshine and the restorative effects of nature. There is a deep calm that, I confess, I find unsettling. It is the calm that precedes death. The calm before Clara took her final breath. The calm that befell the delirious eye patient before he fell forever into sleep.

36

Liam

I'm sitting on the terrace, stirring my coffee, eyes averted from the jacket on the Formica table. Jess swears it's nothing to do with her, that it just appeared there, fell out of the sky. But, seriously, how can an object appear by itself, just like that? If it's nothing to do with Jess, it's to do with the girls, or that boy from the cottage, or – the most likely explanation – that mad old woman I've seen more than once, sneaking around the garden with her crazy dog as if they own the place.

But though I know it's just a dirty old rag, I can't bring myself to touch it, to carry it to the bins at the side of the house. There's something about it that makes my skin crawl. It's eerily familiar, like something I've known for a very long time – and that makes no sense. I'll ask the gardener to take it away when I see him. I'll tell him to burn the bloody thing.

I sigh heavily. I should feel better today now my hangover's gone – I even resisted a drink last night – but I don't. I feel worse. My mind is clanging like one of the knackered servant bells in the kitchen. I clutch my coffee like my life depends on it, trying to breathe through the pain in my head, trying to think clearly.

'Hey.' Jess comes up behind me and I jump, spilling hot coffee down my T-shirt, splashing my hand, scalding my chest.

'Fuck.'

'Sorry.'

'Don't creep up on me like that,' I say, not meaning to snap.

'I didn't creep up on you.'

I shake the rapidly cooling coffee from my hand, then dab my wet T-shirt, making it worse. What the fuck is wrong with me? Wrong with this house? It makes us all jumpy. For a moment, I forget why we're here. Forget why we don't just pack our bags up and run. And I'm about to suggest we do just that, pack our stuff and get the hell out of here, make Jess's day. To hell with Callum and his mother and her mangy cats. But I know I can't.

Tap . . . tap . . . tap . . .

I spin around, expecting to see someone walking along the terrace, Robbie Silver with her stick, tapping the stone, but the only thing I see is my own startled face reflected in the dining-room window. 'Did you hear it?'

'What?'

'That noise? I've been hearing it everywhere. Ever since we arrived here. Like someone striking a stick on the ground. Tap, tap, tap, just like that.'

Jess stares at me blankly, and the sun burns fiercer, the colours of the cosmos making my head even worse. 'I don't know what you're talking about. I thought I heard something in the wardrobe, but . . .'

I rub my forehead, berating myself. Why did I let my guard down like that? The last thing I need is Jess worrying again. 'It's my tinnitus,' I say, making a deliberate show of rubbing my ears.

'Your tinnitus?'

'Yeah, I know. I haven't had it in ages.'

She smiles sympathetically and gives me a hug, leaning over the deckchair, her long hair stroking my cheeks. And like that, I could tell her everything. It's on the tip of my tongue. Not just about the dreams and the feeling in the house. Not just about the money. But all of it. Right from the very beginning. Right from the moment I looked up and saw my mother in the tabard, clutching her feather duster. From the moment I collapsed on the floor. From the moment I stood with Dad on the ridge. But I can't. Because it's not as straightforward as just spilling a story. It's been locked inside me for so long, I'm no longer sure I have the key.

37

SUMMER

—∞∞∞—

I feel self-conscious, adjusting the straps of my vest-top, pulling my shorts down at the back. My feet slap in their flipflops, announcing my presence. Aaron glances over his shoulder and grins.

'Hey.' He rolls on to his back and I see the grass creases criss-crossing his bare chest. I guess he's been out here on the lawn for a while. He waves the paper in his hand. 'Guess what?' he says. 'I was right.'

'Right?' I sit down beside him, trying to act like all the stuff yesterday didn't happen. But I can't. I'm too aware of him. Too aware of myself. I pluck at the grass, wondering whether I should bend down and kiss him, or just stay where I am, wait for him to make a move. It really doesn't help that he's topless. I stare at the tanned perfection of his skin, the definition of his muscles. Not for the first time, I wonder if he runs, or works out in the gym, or swims, or . . .

'Latin. Those words you heard were definitely Latin. What's more, I'm pretty sure I know what they mean.'

I feel a jolt of excitement. 'Oh?'

'It's the Hippocratic oath.'

'What?'

'You know? The oath the doctors have to swear by. At least in the old days. About, refraining from doing harm, practising to their best ability and, basically, not murdering their patients.'

'I know what it is, stupid,' I lie, feeling my cheeks flush. 'What I mean is, how do you know that this,' I point at my scribbled handwriting, 'is what you think it is?'

He grins again, looking pleased with himself. 'I translated it.' He flips back on to his front, and points at the various sheets of paper pinned to the lawn with stones. 'Not that it was exactly easy. Your spelling is way off. Most of it is just an educated guess.' He points at his own scrawled handwriting. '"Apollinem" means Apollo. "Dea" is something to do with gods. "Judicioque meo" means my judgement. But, this was the giveaway.' He points at the words at the bottom of the page. 'The phrase you wrote several times. You even got the spelling right, or almost right. "Primum non nocere" – First, do no harm.'

'Do no harm,' I repeat the words.

'Not part of the original oath, but a later addition.'

I shake my head. It seems incredible I came up with Latin phrases that actually make sense, that relate to something tangible.

'So,' I say, excited by the discovery, 'what does it all mean? I mean, I know *what* it means. But why did I hear it?'

Aaron shrugs. 'I guess it means, St Cross is haunted by a doctor with a moral conscience.' He mimics someone far older, far more serious than himself: *'Do no harm.'*

'A doctor.' I let the word linger. 'Or a surgeon. Charles Keller. Except didn't Lucie say Keller's family were from Germany? Why would he speak to us in Latin, and not German or English?'

'Latin is the language of medicine, maybe?' He rolls towards me, almost touching. 'Whoever talked to you in the mirror is still there in the house. He hasn't passed over to the spirit world yet. Or if he has passed over, he's taken the trouble to come back. Not once. But twice. There must be a reason for that.'

'Except the first time I heard him, I was here.'

Aaron looks up at the cottage. 'Perhaps he used to come here. It's not exactly far, and I think this has always been the gardener's cottage. Perhaps he came here for a reason.'

'What do we do next?'

Aaron fingers his chin. 'We need to find out more details of his death. There must be records. I've been doing some googling.' He pulls his phone from his pocket, taps words into the search engine.

They need to die.

The words bolt into my head. 'No,' I say, clutching my brow. I can't do this, not now. Despite the discovery, despite Aaron's impressive detective work, I need a break. I lay a hand on his, stopping him from typing. He looks at me puzzled. 'This has all been way too intense. Can we do something else?'

'But, I thought you wanted . . .'

THEY NEED TO DIE.

I panic. It's that voice again, trying to get inside me. Only this time, it's different. It's not a memory of the voice, it's happening right now, except there is no mirror, just flower-beds and grass. Which means ... I swallow hard ... which means there are other ways too. 'I just want to do something normal,' I say, hoping I don't sound too odd. 'This whole thing – the voice, the Latin – it's weird, okay? Maybe this is normal for you, but it's not for me, it's freaky. I just need to do something ordinary, something unconnected to the house, just for today.'

'Okay.'

He sounds disappointed, and I grapple for ideas. 'What about the beach? We could go swimming. Or, we could just chill out in your bedroom. Listen to music. Or, I dunno. Do stuff.'

'Stuff?' He stretches his eyebrows.

'Yeah, stuff. Normal everyday stuff.'

'Like what?'

'Like not talking to dead people for a start.'

He jumps to his feet and grabs his top from the lawn. 'Wait here.'

He walks into the cottage and returns a minute later, carrying something wrapped in his T-shirt. He parts the T-shirt, revealing a bottle of vodka. 'Stuff,' he announces. I look up at him in astonishment. He beams. 'Picked it up the other day while Nan was in the bookshop. Come on.' He pulls me to my feet, then keeps his hand firmly wrapped around mine. 'The beach it is.'

The vodka goes straight to my head. I wish I'd eaten a decent breakfast, not just the thin slice of toast I'd spread with mar-garine. I strip to my underwear, telling myself it's no more revealing than my bikini. Anyway, there's hardly anyone else here, just an old couple walking their dog near the rocks at the far end. It's not a popular beach because there's nowhere to park and the path down isn't exactly easy. I splash after Aaron through the waves, then throw myself under, feeling the weight of the water above, then surprising him when I resurface close by. Grabbing hold of his arms, I drag him with me under the next big wave.

'Are you trying to kill me?' he says, gasping and wiping water from his eyes.

I swing back my dripping hair. I'll admit it: I'm enjoying showing off, knowing I'm a better swimmer than he is. 'Race you to the cliff.' I indicate the point where the cove ends and another begins, then swim hard, relishing the movement of the waves beneath me and the beat of the sun above. When I look over my shoulder, I find Aaron's close behind. I slow deliberately, allowing myself to be caught, his strong hands brushing my ankles, his body eventually coming alongside mine. I forget the race as he circles around me, pulling me into him. He kisses me, our bodies touching beneath the waves. The sun blazes. The water sparkles like crystals.

'Do you know what that is up there?' I say, pointing at the rocks over his shoulder when we stop for breath.

He turns and shades his eyes. 'The rocks?' he says puzzled. 'Or do you mean the chalets?'

'The rocks.'

He shrugs. 'They're just rocks.' He circles my neck with kisses. 'But they have a sad story.'

'Oh yeah?'

He lifts my bra straps and runs his fingers beneath them.

'Tell me the story.'

'Some children were messing around on the beach. There was a storm and they weren't fast enough to find shelter. They drowned.'

'Drowned?'

'Their bodies were found, washed up on the rocks.'

I gasp, remembering the way I'd been drawn to that part of the beach, the way I'd lain down and the rocks had seemed to cry.

Aaron nods. 'It was a long time ago. Victorian times, I think. Nan told me the story when I was little.' He windmills his arms, spraying me with water, and I've a feeling he doesn't want to talk about the rocks. He wants to have fun.

I wade after him to the shore, shivering as I emerge from the sea, but I can't shift the story just like that. I purposely keep my gaze from that side of the beach; I don't want to look at the rocks; I don't want to imagine those lifeless bodies. We lie on the sand together, seawater glistening on our skin, taking turns to sip from the bottle of vodka. I run my fingers over Aaron's chest, feeling reckless. Unstoppable. I feel I could do anything.

'You must work out,' I say dreamily, admiring the clear absence of fat across his abdomen.

Aaron sucks his stomach beneath his ribs. 'They don't feed us in school. That's all it is.'

'What?'

'Stale bread on a good day. You should count yourself lucky.'

'I am lucky,' I say, resting my head on his chest. 'But I don't believe you.'

'Don't believe me about what?'

'About boarding school.' Something flickers behind his eyes. 'I bet it's all four-course meals and parties. I bet you eat caviar for breakfast.'

He pushes me back on to the sand and rolls on top of me, supporting his weight with his arms, then he kisses me deeply, parting my mouth with his tongue. I grab hold of him, kissing him back, tasting vodka and toothpaste.

Charles Keller's diary:

<u>2 July 1848</u>

Clara came to me in my dream last night, more vivid, more beautiful than ever. She held my hand and led me into a garden bursting with vibrant flowers. There, we lay together, our clothes discarded, her body unrestricted, warm against mine. Her hair was splayed gold upon the grass, her discarded corset like a pile of ivory ribs. 'Go back to London,' she whispered when we had sated our desire. 'This place is killing you.'

I awoke to yet another fine morning, the clock showing the hour of ten, my breakfast long grown cold upon my plate, and my absence at the morning service no doubt noted. My headache was worse than ever and my hands shook a great deal, but my spirit did not weaken, for had I not seen my love?

38

SUMMER

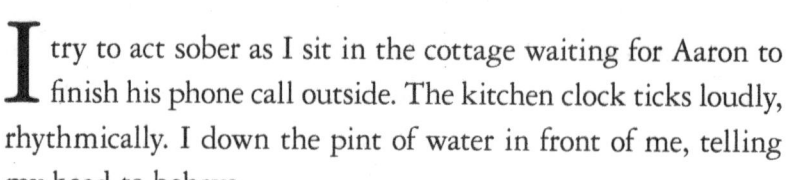

I try to act sober as I sit in the cottage waiting for Aaron to finish his phone call outside. The kitchen clock ticks loudly, rhythmically. I down the pint of water in front of me, telling my head to behave.

'Did you have a nice time at the beach?' Mrs Harrison prises the lid from the cake tin.

My stomach tightens. I've drunk far too much and I'm feeling a bit queasy. 'Lovely, thanks.' I try my best to sound sober. 'We went swimming.'

Mrs Harrison hands me a knife and a plate. 'Help yourself. You look famished.'

'Thanks.' I cut myself the smallest slice possible. 'We met that old lady again, yesterday,' I say. 'The one who lives in the gatehouse.'

'Robbie Silver? Poor dear. I'm afraid she's rather beyond help, that one.'

'She said you two used to be friends.'

Mrs Harrison takes the knife, cuts a thicker slice of cake, then swaps it for mine. 'I said, you look famished, you need to eat. As for Robbie and I, that was a long time ago.' She dishes out cake forks. 'We hardly speak these days. She's rather taken against me.'

'Oh?' I pretend to be surprised.

'Years ago, she was in love with Peter, and when we married, she became spiteful and jealous. She convinced herself he was in love with her too and that I was spreading rumours about her. She was deluded, of course. Fifty years we've been neighbours and we've barely spoken in all that time, and not for the want of trying on my part.' She shakes her head. 'When I first moved into the area, Robbie was kind to me. We were both interested in the spirit life, which, I guess, was pretty unusual in a tiny place like St Cross. A kid who lived in one of the chalets had recently died and death was very much on our minds. Robbie and I used to go to seances together. Of course, our parents didn't know. They were heavily involved in the church and anything to do with channelling the dead would have seemed deeply improper. They thought we were going to dances in the town and meeting boys.' She smiles wistfully. 'Then, for reasons I never understood, Robbie became convinced that the manor house was a bad place. She was obsessed with the idea just like she later became obsessed with Peter. She was, and still is, a very unstable person. One night, hippies arrived and camped out in the old ruins. Three days later, there was a fire.'

'The fire that destroyed the place?'

'It was more or less a shell by then anyway, but yes, it brought the manor house to the ground. You could see the flames for miles. The heat was incredible, even from a distance. Everyone thought it was the hippies, but it wasn't.' There's a pause filled only by the ticking of the clock. Mrs Harrison folds a strip of icing into her mouth, then licks her fork. 'That's the real reason Robbie and I fell out, not because of Peter. I rather think the thing with Peter was just a distraction. Robbie set fire to the manor. I saw her do it.'

I gasp. 'But why would she do something like that?'

'The hippies left a lot of rubbish behind. Robbie made a bonfire, saying it would clean the air, get rid of the negative energy. She was into that sort of thing, always making potions, and using different herbs to protect herself. I don't think she meant for the entire house to burn.'

'You never said anything to the police?'

'I wasn't about to betray my best friend. It was an accident, at least that's what she said, and no one was hurt. What point would it have served?'

'Did she tell anyone else?'

'No one. Not even her parents as far as I'm aware. But we argued about it. Badly. I probably said some things I shouldn't have done, and then she started the obsession with Peter and accused me of all sorts of things. But as I said, she's deluded. Deluded and lonely.' Mrs Harrison gazes at Aaron through the window, talking on the phone to his mum. 'And that's another lonely one. I'm glad you two are friends. St Cross is hardly the place for a young person to spend the entire summer holidays. It hasn't been an easy time for him with all the stuff going on at home.'

'At home?' I blink. 'You mean, at school?'

Mrs Harrison looks confused. 'He hasn't told you? I thought

he would have said. You two seemed close. His parents – my daughter and son-in-law – are going through a divorce. A rather messy one, I'm afraid. That's why he's here. His mum thought he'd be best out of the way while they sort things out, find a new place for them to live. He stayed with Clarissa for a while, but that didn't work out.'

I push the plate away, feeling even worse than before. 'He told me he was here because he was grounded. He told me he got into trouble at school.'

Mrs Harrison laughs. 'Dear me, no. That's a new one on me.'

'But he does go to school, right?'

Mrs Harrison frowns.

'I mean, he does go to boarding school?'

She lays down her fork. 'I think he's been pulling your leg. My grandson goes to a regular school.'

'Who's Clarissa?'

'His girlfriend.' Mrs Harrison falters. 'Don't tell me, he didn't tell you about Clarissa either?'

I shake my head. The nausea rises, forcing me to swallow. *His girlfriend.*

'Oh dear. Let me make you a cuppa.' Mrs Harrison stands and hunts for a tea mug in the stack of drying up. I glance at Aaron through the window, my head pounding. 'They've been together for years.' Mrs Harrison says. 'Grew up on the same estate. But it didn't work out, him staying like that. Aaron's got a lot of anger inside him to do with his parents. It's all been rather unsettling.'

'I didn't know. I didn't know any of it.' I slide on my flipflops. 'I'm sorry, Mrs Harrison. I don't think I'll stay for a cup of tea. I need to get back.'

'Yes, of course. Let me wrap up some cake to take with you.'

But I don't give her a chance. I run out of the cottage, across the little garden to the front of the house. Aaron's still on the lawn, speaking into the phone. But I can't look at him. I don't even wave goodbye. My head burns with a fierce, unsatiable anger. I run to the gate at the top of the road, then into the wood, towards the garden. Tears blur my vision, brambles snag my skin. 'Primum non nocere.' I recite the words over and over like a mantra, feeling their energy.

Eventually, I stop to catch my breath, staring up at the house. St Cross. For the first time, the building makes sense to me. Everything forlorn. Everything decaying. I think of Harry and his videocall. I think of Aaron and his stories about school. I feel it all like fire in my veins as I twist and twist the strands of hair between my fingers.

39

⊸≪⊸

Xanthe

Xanthe ducks behind a tree and waits for her sister to pass. She hasn't much time. Daddy's fallen asleep again and Mummy's upstairs, taking a bath. But Mummy will soon go looking for her, searching the house, the garden, the wood.

She thinks of the mist that is everywhere now, the same green mist she sees in her dreams, not just in the bedroom, but out on the landing and in the bathroom and down the stairs, floating into the hallway, filling the rooms on either side. She knows where it's coming from too. Not their room, but the room next door. The locked room. 'Mummy,' she said earlier when they were alone in the kitchen, when Summer was out with the boy and Daddy was outside. 'The mist. I'm scared of it. Do you see it too?'

Mummy had looked at her strangely, those big glassy eyes the same shape as Grandma's had been. 'What mist, darling?'

'The green one. It's following us. It's following Daddy. I saw it following him into the garden.'

Mummy had hugged her and said it was just her imagination, but she knew that wasn't true. It was more than that. She'd pushed her face against the soft pillowy scent of her mother's sundress, digging her fingers hard into her palm, squeezing in the place where she'd held the little fairy in the gatehouse garden.

Now, when the way is clear and her sister has taken the main path back into the garden, she steps out again, keeping her gaze fixed ahead. She runs through the wood, twigs snapping beneath her, brambles tearing her arms, but she doesn't cry, she doesn't slow. When she reaches the road, the grumble of a car stalls her, turning out of the cottage driveway, choking the air with unburned petrol. She stands as still as she can, just beyond the shadow of the trees, holding her breath, praying Mr Harrison won't see her. She can't be stopped now. Not when she's so near to escaping. All it would take is for Mr Harrison to turn his head. The car rattles its way up the hill, the engine fading to a distant burble, then she runs past the cottage, past Mrs Harrison bent over the flowerbeds, past Aaron on his phone, all the way to the gatehouse.

Robbie Silver is in the garden, pegging out washing. 'You came back,' she says, putting down her basket of pegs. She smiles as if she's been expecting Xanthe all along. 'I knew you would. I'll make us some tea.'

Xanthe tells herself to be brave as she walks up the path, eyeing the front-room window and remembering the little skeletons. 'I won't touch your fairies,' she says, wondering if, after all, this is a really bad plan. 'I promise I won't.'

Robbie's face cracks into a smile. 'You're a good girl,' she says.

'The fairies are scared of humans, that's all. You can look, but don't touch. How would you like it if a giant picked you up and carted you away?'

'I didn't mean to frighten them.'

'I know you didn't.'

She takes a deep breath. *Hold the fear.* 'Why do you collect skeletons?'

'Why not? I didn't kill them, if that's what you're thinking. And I don't turn little girls into skeletons either. They are mice, and rabbits, and blackbirds, and starlings, and even a hawk. They're beautiful, don't you think? Even in death.'

Xanthe doesn't say anything because she doesn't think they're beautiful. They make her want to cry. Instead, she follows Robbie along the rough path to the back of the house, trailing in the flap of her dressing gown. She sits at the garden table while Robbie sorts the tea things. Angel sits in the seat opposite, ears standing to attention, and she's a funny feeling he's guarding her, making sure she doesn't run away.

Robbie returns with a tray and a plate of biscuits.

'Why do you drink funny tea?'

'It's good for me, that's why.' Robbie hands her a cup and she wrinkles her nose. 'The word "sage" is taken from the Latin word "salvia", which means to save or to heal. I pick only the brightest, youngest leaves, then I dry them and steep them in boiling water. You should ask your mother to do the same.'

'But why is it good for you?'

'Sage is a traditional remedy for warding off negative spirits.'

Xanthe takes a tiny sip. It doesn't taste as bad this time, even without honey. Maybe she could even get used to it. 'What are negative spirits?'

Robbie leans back in her chair, teacup in her lap. She stares straight ahead. 'Evil things. Things that walk in the dead of night.'

'You mean, things that walk in dreams?'

'Sometimes in dreams. Sometimes not. You need to learn how to control the spirits. How to control your emotions, so the spirits won't attach themselves like they attached themselves to Verity. The tea helps.'

'Who was Verity?'

'The lady who lived in St Cross, before Marianne Clarence. Verity had a child, she called him Elijah.' Robbie smiles at the memory. 'I can see him clearly. Such a bonnie little thing. Verity's husband, Mr Laurence, didn't like me very much, but I saw Elijah anyway. I made a point of it, whenever Mr Laurence was out of the house.'

Xanthe takes another sip of tea, scalding the top of her mouth.

'Verity turned one of the rooms upstairs into a nursery and Mr Laurence put a cot in there. But even though the child seemed to thrive, Verity was frightened. She was convinced that the house was trying to get her baby, trying to harm it. She told me she could hear whispering in the house. Other children's voices. Of course, her husband, Mr Laurence, thought she was being irrational, that it was just the child, Elijah, talking to himself.'

'Irrational?' She's not sure she knows what the word means.

'Stupid. But I knew she was telling the truth, I could see it in her eyes. A real fear. So I tried to help her.'

'What did you do?'

'I made spells.'

'So you really are a witch?'

Robbie laughs. 'If I'm a witch, then I'm a good one.'

'Is that why you have fairies and skeletons? Is that why you wear a dressing gown?' The questions are flying like darts, all the things she's been wondering.

'The fairies protect me and my house from the outside world. The skeletons are pretty and the bones, if placed correctly, prevent evil from entering. And it's not a dressing gown, it's a house coat.'

'Why is your name Silver?' *Silver like water, or shining glass, or knives.*

'Because that's my name. Just like your name is Kennedy.'

Xanthe chews her lip; she'd thought it was more than that. 'And what happened to Verity's baby?'

'He died when he was just three years old. Verity died too, soon after. She cut herself in the kitchen. A wound that should have healed quickly but turned septic. She didn't use the spells, you see? The bones and bags of salt I'd given her for laying at doors. She should have used them. She died of a fever, a horrible, frightening, lonely death. No one knew about it until her husband returned from a business trip. At that point, I hadn't seen Verity for days. Mr Laurence was a cruel man. He kept her away from me, said I was bad news. There were no more children after that. Mr Laurence married again, Verity's older sister, Marianne, but the new Mrs Laurence didn't want to have babies. Perhaps she sensed the house wouldn't be kind to a child, or perhaps Verity had told her something about the house. When Mr Laurence died, she married Mr Clarence who already had a child by his previous marriage, a child who never lived at St Cross.'

'But why didn't Mr Laurence want you talking to Verity? That's not fair when you were only trying to help.'

'Adults can be crueller than children, that's why. He thought the spells were nonsense. He thought they'd done more harm than good. And he thought I'd planted the ideas about the house in Verity's head. But it wasn't me – although I could sense it – that was Verity herself. She was terrified of the house, of the old infirmary. She'd found a diary from the Victorian days and it convinced her the house was bad. And then she found a letter hidden behind the wallpaper in the attic. A letter written in German.'

'What did the letter say?'

'I don't know. I never saw it myself. Verity told me it was written by someone who used to live there in the old days. A surgeon called Charles Keller. Verity translated the letter – it took her weeks – but she wouldn't show it to me. All she would say was that the letter was bad, just like the house.'

They sit in silence for a while, just the sounds of the garden, the hum of insects and the tinkling of the windchime.

'I think the thing that killed Verity and Elijah is trying to kill my daddy.' Xanthe's voice is small and fearful but she has to tell Robbie. She has to tell someone. 'I think the evil things are trying to get him and I don't know what to do.'

Robbie sets her teacup down on the tray. 'Yes, you do.' She reaches out and touches Xanthe's hand, her skin soft and cold as if the blood no longer runs there. 'Have you seen the snake skin in the window, along with the bones?'

Xanthe nods. She has an image of coiling, paper-thin skin, dry and yellowed.

'The snake is the symbol of medicine. It's a Greek symbol, associated with Asclepius, the god of healing. Asclepius had a rod entwined with a snake. The snake sheds it skin and is reborn. New life. Everyone thinks the snake is evil, but it isn't.'

A pause while Xanthe tries to make sense of this information but all she can think about are the snakes on the gates at St Cross.

'I know what you did.' Robbie says it so quietly, Xanthe can barely hear the words. 'I knew it from the moment I set eyes on you. That first night you were here. You may have fooled everyone else, but not me.'

Xanthe fights the urge to cry. How does Robbie know? She hasn't told Summer. She hasn't even told Mummy. She hugs herself tight, remembering the hush of the night. The midnight air. The key in her hand. *No one knows.* 'I don't know what you mean,' she says, thinking it's impossible.

'I think you do. Just like you know that the snake is good.'

She stands up and the dog's eyes fly open. 'Can I go now, please?'

'Take the dog.'

'I'm sorry?'

'Take Angel. He won't hurt you. He'll look after you.'

'But,' Xanthe hunts for an excuse, 'what about the cats?'

'He won't bother the cats. Not if I tell him not to. You two can be friends if you try. Remember what I taught you?'

Hold the fear.

'Stretch your hand out, like this.' Robbie stretches out the back of her hand, and Angel lifts his head and sniffs before gently nibbling the end of her fingers. 'You see? He's not biting, just playing. Now, you do the same. Tell him to behave if he tries to nip.'

She edges away from the dog, away from Robbie.

'Call him. Go on. Offer him a biscuit.'

'I want to go home.'

'You can't keep running away.' Spit flecks Robbie's lips, and Xanthe remembers the time with Titania, the way she'd screamed at her. 'He won't bite. I promise.'

Hold the fear. She takes a step forward, takes one of the pink wafer biscuits and holds it out at arm's length. 'Angel?'

Angel jumps off his chair and runs towards her, tail wagging. *Hold the fear.* She closes her eyes, hardly daring to breathe, feeling the wet warmth of dog on her fingers.

'See?' Robbie claps her hands together. 'You've made a friend.'

When she opens her eyes again, Robbie is beaming down at her and Angel is sitting at her feet, waiting patiently for another biscuit.

'Now offer him your hand.'

She bends down and holds out her fingers. Angel sniffs but doesn't bite.

'That's right.' Robbie dusts the flaps of her house coat. 'Give him a stroke. He won't harm you. You see? I knew you two would become friends eventually. You need to trust him. Just like you need to trust yourself.'

40

Jess

I hear something or someone in the kitchen and open the door, expecting to find Xanthe raiding the biscuit tin or concocting something impossible from our meagre supplies. But it's not, it's Summer. I hide my surprise that she's back so soon. I'd presumed she'd spend the rest of the day in the cottage. And then I notice the knife in Summer's hand. A sharp metal blade, the same one I've been using to slice vegetables and bone fish for Liam and the girls. Summer must have clambered up on the dresser to find it, which explains the noise.

'What are you doing?' I say. My voice trembles, though I don't know why.

Summer looks up. She's pale and her hair is dishevelled, falling into her eyes. 'Project for school,' she says with a disorientating smile. 'I had to dig deep for the worms. Seems when you actually want to find them, they hide.'

'Worms?' I look down at the plate. It's one of the blue and white ones I found yesterday and cleaned up for the meal with Aaron. I see it now: two worms lying side by side, curled into themselves, their tiny bodies clumpy with soil. 'What project? It's the holidays.' It's the only thing I can think of to say. I stare at my daughter. Her hands are black with soil. Her nails, which she usually takes pride in, are smudged with dirt. 'What are you doing exactly?'

'An experiment.' Summer stretches out one of the worms with her fingers, takes the knife, and cuts it in half.

'Summer, no!'

'Theory goes, the two halves keep living.' Summer's voice is a dead calm, like she's talking about the weather or a dull afternoon. 'Only, it isn't true. Only the part connected to the head survives, the other part dies. See.' She points her knife at the severed worm, one half wriggling, the other half still. 'It's like when you amputate a limb. The limb dies. But the person, if they're lucky, keeps on living.'

'Summer. Please. It's disgusting. I can't believe you just did that!'

Summer stares at the worms on the plate as if she's fascinated by what she's just done. 'Actually, Mum, I've made a decision.' She cuts the second worm in half, tosses the knife on the table, then stands up and reaches for the jar of coffee.

I feel the blood drain from my face.

'I've decided I'm going to study medicine when I go to university. I'm going to change my A levels.'

'Okay.' I try to process this new information; Summer's always seemed dead set on drama and art. 'It's just I thought—'

'See?' Summer spins around, coffee jar in hand, and glares. 'I knew you'd be like this. I knew you'd try and stop me. You're just as bad as Dad.' She drops the jar, just like she dropped the jam jar, and I realise, with horror, it's cold and deliberate. Glass smashes on the tiles. Coffee granules cascade beneath the table. Suddenly, tears are streaming down her face. She wipes them angrily, smearing muck and mascara.

'I didn't say anything,' I gasp, staring at the mess on the floor. 'It's just a surprise, that's all. I didn't even know you were thinking about university. Not now. Not on holiday.' I feel a wave of giddiness as I reach out and hold on to the dresser. I breathe deeply, trying to regain a sense of control, of the person I am. Summer's mother. A *good* mother. A person my daughters look up to. The sort of person who can sit down with them, discuss things rationally and find solutions. But maybe I've got that wrong? Maybe I've been fooling myself? After all, this. What the hell is *this*?

Summer pushes past me, slamming the door as she runs into the hallway, leaving me in the mess. The coffee. The severed worms. I run to the sink and dry heave, my stomach clenching but not releasing. Oh God.

Extract from The New Surgeon's Handbook, *1832:*

The location of the operating theatre should be given careful consideration. Ideally, the room should contain a source of natural light. A surgeon forced to operate by candlelight alone is likely to inflict unnecessary pain either through bringing the candle perilously close to his patient, or through errors made due to inadequate illumination. The room should be within easy reach of the wards, but not so near that the cries of the patient can be heard. A well-lit attic room is thus ideal for the purpose.

41

Liam

I shiver in my sleep, wincing at the sound of the knives in my dream.

'Good evening, Mr Kennedy.' The voice stills my twitching muscles, and fear twists up my spine. I look up and see the same man as before, sharpening knives, one against the other, like he's about to carve a Sunday joint. His jacket is open, and his shirt beneath is stained red like a butcher's.

The man smiles a cold thin smile. 'I am the surgeon here,' he says. 'We *have* met before but you were a little,' he coughs delicately into his fist, the knife glinting wickedly, 'delirious.'

I twist again, kicking the air, but I'm held fast. Two burly captors tighten their grip on my arms.

'Now, now, Mr Kennedy,' says the surgeon as though he's

talking to a small child. 'There's no need to struggle. I won't keep you long. It's for the best.'

'Will it hurt?' My voice comes out as a croak.

'No worse than a scratch.'

The surgeon points at the table behind him with one of the knives, and I feel myself being hoisted up and laid in place. The table feels hard and unrelenting beneath my head and there's a complex smell – metallic and rotten – seeping from the wood. A strap is placed around my chest and the same rough hands belonging to my captors anchor my legs to the table.

The surgeon puts down his knives, and selects another from a little velvet case, blood encrusted like everything else. He wipes the knife against his jacket. It's only now that I'm aware the room is full of spectators: young men, standing on either side of the table, craning their necks for the best view.

'And now, gentlemen,' the surgeon addresses the audience solemnly, 'observe the speed at which I perform the operation.' He takes his watch out of his jacket pocket and lays it on the table next to my leg. *My bloody leg.* The room is suddenly so silent, I can hear the watch tick.

The first cut sets me screaming. A sharp hot pain like my insides are on fire. Something's shoved into my mouth, something hard for me to bite into. The surgeon's stick. I gag, choking on my own saliva, before gripping the stick with my teeth.

I think my heart might give out when the knife cuts again, my forehead and chest dripping with perspiration. I bite down into the stick, tasting the leather, feeling the grooves left behind by hundreds of other sets of teeth. I can't think beyond the stick, beyond my terror, beyond the tremendous clanging of my heart.

Then, somewhere in the blur of my agony, I hear the knife

being laid down and replaced by another. But no, not a knife. What I see in the surgeon's hand is more like a small saw.

Oh please, God, no!

The saw rests just below my knee. The hands tighten on my thigh, and one of the captors turns to me with a smile like a grimacing pig. A moment later I hear a deep clunk as my leg lands in a bucket.

The surgeon raises his pocket watch. 'Thirty-one seconds. You see, Mr Kennedy. We didn't use the machine, not this time. We didn't let you sleep. Because you didn't want it, did you? You rebelled, you disobeyed the rules, and so ...' the surgeon's laughter echoes around the room and I realise we're alone again, no spectators, no men pinning me down, ' ... and so, this time, you got what you deserved.'

I think of Dad, the ridge, the buckle of Dad's backpack gleaming in the sunshine, and I know that everything the surgeon is saying is the truth.

The surgeon grins. 'You got to feel it all.'

Charles Keller's diary:

<u>4 July 1848</u>

The machine must have wheels and the nozzle adjusted for increased volume of anaesthesia – Massingham is insistent upon these matters and has ordered the revisions to be made at once. Meanwhile, I am too busy to think. My work is ever pressing, the patients brought to me from the workhouse with all manner of disease and ailment. I am in want of rest but cannot sleep.

<u>6 July 1848</u>

Today, two deaths occurred upon the operating table. Massingham appeared very unwell but was determined to assist me. It is his duty, he exclaimed, his calling in life. If he cannot help others, his life will have been in vain.

<u>10 July 1848</u>

A day spent in the operating theatre. Three patients – young children of ages unknown – were brought to me directly from the workhouse with various complaints: one badly scalded and two with broken limbs resulting from a scuffle. Massingham insisted that they be operated upon at once, and, for a moment, I doubted my judgement. Surely, surgery is not always needed? There is a restlessness about him that I have seen in other such syphilitic cases before. He takes a heady delight in the knowledge that he is dying and his energy, though spent early in the day, is, in its flush, infectious.

20 July 1848

More revisions to the machine have been made. More children are being brought to my attention, many orphans from the workhouse. My work is tireless. This morning my body purged itself of the poison I have ingested. I am feeling weak and shaky, but lighter in spirit. I will not ingest chloroform again.

24 July 1848

A bad night. Despite my good intentions, I took an ounce of chloroform to bed with me, inhaled directly from the green bottle and fell into a stupor before I had the sense to cork it again. The bottle was empty on awakening this morning. My head is pounding and I am in no fit state to work. I have pleaded with Mrs Harker that I am ill and in need of rest.

26 July 1848

Dr Marne attended to me this morning, this being my third day in bed. He insists on strict bed rest and laudanum for my pains.

27 July 1848

I arose early, berating myself. What good is a surgeon who lies ill upon his bed? What would Clara say if she saw me thus?

I dressed quickly, washed and inspected myself in the mirror. My hair is greasy, my beard untrimmed, my skin sallow. When I pulled down my eyelids, I saw that my eyes were yellow beneath. But I could not let these physical signs prevent me from my work. I picked up my instruments case from where it had lain idle upon my desk, opened the lid, ran my hands over the fine ebony-handled knives and the tiny saws.

Out on the landing, the light from the roof window hurt my eyes, blinding me momentarily. As I looked down at the silent house, I thought how easy it would be to fall, to tumble to oblivion. But then, as if surfacing from underwater, the house returned to me: the clatter of pans from the kitchen, a bell ringing, a child crying for his mother, a woman screaming for want of peace.

Suddenly, I could not stand it. I could not bear to hear the patients' cries. George Reynolds is right: this place has infected me and I cannot stay here. I must return to London. I stumbled backwards into my room, dropping my instruments case, hearing the clatter of knives across the floor.

42

SUMMER

I wrap myself tightly in the quilt, not wanting to wake up, not wanting to face the day. But I'm awake anyway, despite my attempts to block out the noise of the house, the sound of doors being opened and closed, voices reaching up to me from the hallway. I think I recognise Mum and Dad, but there are others. Other people in the house, I'm sure of it.

I roll over, dragging the quilt with me. My stomach groans. I remember I didn't eat last night, not after the cake I forced myself to swallow in the cottage. When I'd got back to St Cross, after I'd spoken to Mum in the kitchen, I'd made an excuse about not feeling well – period pains – and gone to bed early, pretending to sleep every time Mum checked in on me. But I hadn't slept at all. I'd sat up for hours, composing messages to Aaron and not sending any of them.

I pull my phone from beneath my pillow and stare at the screen, half-hoping, half-dreading he's messaged me instead. But there's only one message waiting for me in my WhatsApp, a message from Harry. Even after everything, a familiar warmth spreads across my chest just seeing his name on my screen. I open the message.

Sorry about the other day.

I groan. *Sorry.* Is that all he can say? I think of the way he demanded I take off my T-shirt and bra, the way he abruptly ended the call. But despite myself, I find myself typing back, Apology accepted, and tug at my hair, feeling the welcome sting of release as I wait for his reply.

There's something you should know. His response sets my heart racing all over again. I was taking photos the other day when we video called.

Photographs? I feel physically sick. It goes against every un-written rule, everything we've been warned about at school, every irritating but well-meaning lecture Mum's attempted to give me since I turned fifteen. He types some more: They were just for me, honestly. I would never have shown them to anyone else.

I stare at the screen in disbelief. First Aaron, and then this.

But then the phone went weird.

Another pause while he types.

I realised it wasn't you I was taking pictures of. It was someone else.

A jolt of fear displaces the anger I feel. I glance around the room, expecting to find someone there, someone watching my reactions. But of course, there's no one, just Xanthe fast asleep, a mess of clothes and books and Xanthe's drawing stuff. Still, the sounds in the house are louder now, the voices, the tapping. I turn back to the screen. Harry's sent me a succession of screenshots. In the first, I can see the edges of the bath, my hair, the taps, but that's all. The rest is blurred, thank God, a fog of darkness. In the second, the darkness covers the entire screen, but when I zoom in, there are distinct shades and contours. In the third, I can clearly see a man's face. The features thin and drawn. And the eyes. God. I can barely look at them. They reach into the screen.

I drop the phone, remembering the feeling I had when I grabbed my clothes and stumbled out of the bathroom: the need to escape coupled with the knowledge that I couldn't. That there was nowhere to hide. That I could run to the end of the world and this thing in the house would follow me there.

Tap ... tap ... tap ...

I breathe through my fingers, telling myself there's a perfectly rational explanation. When I pick up the phone again, there are three other photos waiting in my inbox, all showing the same thing. I tell myself it's just Harry trying to mess with my mind, a sick joke because he's bored or pissed off with me for some unfathomable reason. But I know I'm kidding myself. It's not Harry, it's the house.

The tapping is louder now, somewhere on the landing. 'Shut up,' I shout. 'Just shut the fuck up.' I throw off the quilt and grab yesterday's clothes from the floor. It's way too early to be up despite the racket in the house, but I know what I need to do. Now isn't the time for arguments. I need to get out before Mum and Dad question me. I need to speak to Aaron.

43

⎯⎯⦙⦙⦙⎯⎯

Jess

**FRONT DOOR ‖ PARLOUR
DINING ROOM ‖ WOMEN'S WARD
MEN'S WARD ‖ ISOLATION WARD
CHILDREN'S WARD ‖ OPERATING THEATRE
MORGUE**

I feel a breath of air against my neck, lifting the tiny hairs beneath my ponytail as I read the labels beneath the servant bells. The words are clearly visible today. There's no mistaking it: the letters are bright, as if they've just been painted.

I turn away to make breakfast, distracting myself. I can't think about that. I can't think about the letters. Today, we'll eat in the dining room. I'll clear a space on the huge mahogany table, serve eggs and mushrooms and tomatoes and whatever else I can find in the fridge. Today — I'm firm in my mind – we're leaving, whatever happens, we won't stay another night in St Cross. I'll ask Peter Harrison to feed the cats until Mrs Clarence returns. I'll insist Liam contacts the house-sitting company.

I take plates from the drying rack, select the best cutlery from the drawer, carry them through to the dining room. I draw back the curtains and sunlight strikes through the windows, dancing between the dust motes. I stare out at the sunbathed terrace, my heart feeling heavy as I hear someone moving about upstairs, footsteps tapping on the floorboards above. It's Liam, I tell myself. Then I make my decision: I'll tell him before breakfast, catch him before the girls come down. I'll tell him we're leaving today.

'Hey.'

And then I'm startled by Liam behind me. How has he done that? How has he appeared already, crept up without my noticing, when you can hear *everything* in this house? But that's the thing about St Cross, it's deceptive – you think you know it until you find the next hidden layer.

'Hey,' I reply, leaning back as he wraps his arms around me, resting my head on his shoulder. 'You're up early.'

'I couldn't sleep.'

'I know what you mean. This house . . .' The unspoken stuff stirs between us. The way the house breathes. The pregnant silences. 'I've been thinking,' I say, reminding myself it's no big deal, cutting a holiday short. 'I think we ought to go home. I don't mean at the end of the week. I mean, go home now.'

I feel him stiffen. Silence. Then I hear it above, that sound of someone walking. It must be Summer or Xanthe.

'We can't. The cats.' He loosens his hold on me. 'We have to look after the cats.'

'No, Liam.' I swivel in his arms, prepared to fight if need be. 'We need to look after ourselves. We need to look after our family.'

'We *are* looking after our family.'

'Not here we aren't. Everything feels different here, unsafe, and just ...' I hunt for the word, feeling my control slipping away – just like when Liam announced he'd found this place, organised the holiday without me knowing ' ... wrong.'

He groans and presses his hands to his forehead. 'Not this again. Not this thing with the house. We can't leave now. You don't understand. We have to stay.'

'What do you mean I don't understand? What don't I understand? That there's something not right with this house? That everything here feels fractured? That this house is trying to kill us?' The words fly from my mouth before I realise what I've said. *This house is trying to kill us.* Do I really believe that? I take a step backwards. 'Why can't we just leave?' I say, softening my tone. 'Please, Liam, just tell me why. Why can't you just telephone the house-sitting company? Explain it's not working out. Or make an excuse? Say there's an emergency back home.'

Liam sighs and stares at the floor. Times stretches between us. A few seconds. A whole lifetime. 'Because there is no house-sitting company.'

'*What?*'

The footsteps mutate to a regular tapping, and I remember what Liam told me in the garden, about the tapping sound that was driving him crazy. Cold shivers down my spine.

'I made it up. Oh God.' He cradles his head in his hands. 'Oh God.'

'Liam?' I search his face for reassurance, but he doesn't lift his eyes to mine. 'Liam.' It's a plea this time, not a question.

'I fucked up,' he says. 'I fucked up big time.'

'I don't understand.' I feel sick. It's almost as if I knew all this time, the holiday was a lie.

'This house belongs to Marianne Clarence.'

'I know that—'

He holds up a finger to silence me. 'The mother of an acquaintance of mine.'

'An acquaintance?'

'Yes.' He shakes his head. 'I'm so sorry.' He takes a deep breath. 'I met him last year in France. It was the last night of the holiday and everyone stayed up late drinking. Except I was sober. You'd been drinking wine, and I more or less had to carry you to bed. When I got back to the bar, the guy we'd got friendly with in the chalet next door was talking to a friend of his. A friend who was also holidaying on the Riviera. He'd bumped into him by chance. His name was Callum Clarence.'

Callum. The name I'd seen on the slip of paper.

'Half an hour later, it was just me and Callum left. We got talking about the stock market.'

'The stock market?' I frown.

'Yeah. Bloke stuff, you know. We realised we both had an interest. I told him about the success I'd had day trading, how I'd quadrupled the money I'd made from the book sales.'

I look at him incredulously. 'You'd quadrupled the money? You never said anything.'

'I wasn't going to tell you either. I wanted it to be a big surprise. I wanted to wake you up one morning and tell you we were millionaires.'

I take a step backwards, jamming my thigh against the dining-room table. I wince in pain. 'I still don't understand. What do you mean by day trading?'

'A trading account. IG trading. That's where I put the money. I made bets as to whether the stock market would rise or fall. Turns out, I was rather good at it and Callum was doing the same. After France, we kept in touch. It was good to have a friend to chat with about the market. I knew you wouldn't understand if I told you, you'd think I was wasting my time, not being true to myself, neglecting my muse.' He laughs without joy. 'But it's hard to listen to your muse when you're making ten thousand pounds an hour.'

'Ten thousand pounds?'

'When you gave me that money, the inheritance from your mum, twenty thousand pounds, it seemed comical. I was making that in my sleep.'

I reach for the cool mahogany table top behind me. Something to make me feel steady. In control. Like my whole life isn't slipping away from me. I grapple to make sense of it. 'You said you'd put Mum's money in investments. Blue-chip British companies. We sat down and chose them together.' I stare at the man I thought I knew. 'Please tell me, that's what you did.'

He holds up his hands. 'I just threw it in the pot with everything else. I was so confident I was doing the right thing. I didn't even question it. By that point I was four hundred and fifty thousand pounds up. Think of it, Jess, almost half a million pounds. Then, one day, the stock market crashed. Callum was safe, he pulled out just in time, whereas I wasn't so lucky. He lent me some money, just to keep me afloat. But then, the stock marked dived again.'

I close my eyes, breathing audibly. One, two, three . . .

'In the space of a single day, I was almost wiped out. It was all my fault. I should have kept a closer eye on the market. But I was busy that day, doing stuff with you and the girls.'

Suddenly, I'm bristling with anger, my breathing forgotten. 'So it's *our* fault?'

'No. I didn't say that.'

'But that's what you implied.' I grip the table harder, counting to three again. 'How much money did Callum give you?'

'Twenty thousand pounds. It sounds a lot, but it wasn't a big deal at the time.'

'Not a big deal?' I swallow hard. The same amount as my inheritance. The money we were saving for a rainy day. The money, if there was any left over, we'd hoped to split between the girls when they went to university.

'I know it sounds bad,' he says. 'It must sound terrible to someone who doesn't understand. But it made sense at the time. I promise I'll make it up to you. This house – St Cross – well, you see why we can't just leave? I promised Callum I'd look after the cats, it's the least I can do. And it's not just that.' He stares at his shoes. 'Callum got angry. Threatening. I was afraid—'

'God, Liam.' I can't look at him. I can't get my head around any of it. This whole year when I'd thought he'd been writing, when I'd been dealing with Summer and Xanthe almost single-handedly, dealing with Summer's issues at school and Xanthe's crisis over Mia, he'd been, well, what exactly? Throwing our money away on a whim. Borrowing more than he could ever pay back.

'Say something,' he says, taking a tentative step towards me. 'Say something. Anything. I can't bear it, Jess. I can't bear the silence. I can't bear to lose you as well. I'm so, so sorry.'

'What do you expect me to say?' I stare straight at him, at his downcast eyes, daring him to raise them to mine, but he doesn't.

'I'm clawing it all back. Little by little. We're not completely broke. There's still two thousand pounds. At least, there was the last time I looked. But then I lost my phone.'

'It's not about the money,' I scream, and the house screams with me, an echo like the bricks are shifting, the windows bulging from their frames, threatening to break. 'It's about the lies.'

'I didn't lie. I just didn't tell you. There's a difference.' He looks so small. Shrivelled. Half the man I thought he was.

'You lied to me, Liam. Lied by omission. Lied when you told me where you'd placed the money. Lied about this house. Do you really think . . .' Tears slide down my cheeks. 'Do you really think we'd be happier if we were millionaires? The girls needed you, Liam. They needed their father. I needed you. It's been a fucking tough year. But I let you off because I thought – stupidly presumed – you were writing your book.'

He holds out his hands in submission or shame, I'm not sure which. An invitation for me to forgive him. But I can't. Not yet. Perhaps, not ever.

I turn away from him and stalk across the room towards the door. When I pull it wide, I find Xanthe standing behind it, watching, listening. 'Mummy?'

'It's okay, love. Daddy and I were just talking.'

'Mummy,' Xanthe tugs my sleeve. 'I have to tell you something. It's about this house. I'm scared.' She peers around me into the gloom, sees her father silhouetted in the light from the dining-room window. Then she turns and runs into the hallway.

I take a deep breath.

'Let her go,' Liam says quietly.

'What?'

'Let her go. She's upset. She must have heard us arguing. She'll calm down.'

'No, Liam.' I swing towards him. This time my anger is unstoppable. I want to scratch him, tear at him, hurt him in some physical way so that he can begin to understand the pain I'm feeling inside. 'You might not care. But I do. I care about our daughters. I care about how they're feeling. I care that our seven-year-old daughter's upset.'

'And you think I don't care?'

'Do you?' I dare him to answer me truthfully for a change.

'Of course, I bloody care. Who the hell do you think I am? I did everything for us. For you and the girls. It wasn't easy you know? I had to hold my nerve. While you were making dinner or ferrying the girls from A to B, I was shitting myself, hoping I'd made the right decisions, placed the right bets, ready to act quickly if I needed to. I did it for us, Jess. I did it so we would have a future. You have to believe that. We were hardly going to make it, make a decent life for the girls, with your shitty job and my one-off bestseller. But the book gave me an idea of what it might be like to be something. To have people look up to me. To see me, to see *us*, as a success.'

'Fuck off.' It comes out as a whisper, but the words bounce of the walls. *Fuck off. Fuck off.*

I slam the door behind me as I run into the kitchen, looking for Xanthe. The back door is wide open, the warm weather breezing through. I run into the garden and down into the wood, my hair falling loose, my feet slipping in their sandals, only stopping when I reach the road. I look from left to right, follow the snake of empty tarmac with my eyes. But there's no sign of Xanthe anywhere.

Charles Keller's diary:

<u>30 July 1848</u>

Today, after the morning service, I walked alone to the coast and sat a while on the rocks, watching the gentle movement of the waves, the sun sparkling upon the water like precious stones. My malaise of several weeks, nay months, seemed to pass. I felt at once blessed and redeemed. Have I not a path and purpose in life? Is this not what God has called me to do? I cannot, <u>will</u> not, give up now. I returned to the infirmary with a lightness of spirit I cannot recall since before Clara fell ill.

<u>I August 1848</u>

This afternoon Harrison brought me the machine. There is much improvement. The box now runs on a set of four wheels so that the machine can be hauled towards the patient quickly if the need for further sedation arises. The nozzle has been cleaned and the hose extended for better reach.

<u>4 August 1848</u>

I awoke suddenly, the light falling upon my pillow, reminding me that I had forgotten to close the shutters. My head throbbed and I rose quickly, spilling a glass of water upon the floor. Last night – what happened? I remember rising in the moonlight, inhaling more of the sweet-smelling liquid, slumping to the floor, picking myself up again, crawling into my bed. And now, I am worse than ever. My hands shake. My heart beats too rapidly. My stomach clenches painfully. But I must attend my duties. Massingham will be here soon. I can hear him already. I can hear him tapping his cane upon the floor.

44

Liam

I need a drink. To hell with being virtuous.

I scan the study for the bottle of whisky I'm sure I left here. Left on the bookcase. But there's no sign of it anywhere. I throw papers off the desk, my scrawled notes for the book, pull dusty volumes from the bookshelf, hear them thump on the floor, their ancient spines splitting. There's no way the bottle could be hidden beneath the papers or behind the books, but my frustration overrides my reason. *Jess.* She must have found the bottle. Found the bottle and hidden it.

Or maybe I took it upstairs? I scratch my chin. Is it possible, that night when I'd drunk far too much, I'd carried the bottle up to our bedroom? It's worth a try.

Leaving the mess in the study, I take the stairs two at a time.

The bedroom window is open a crack, and there's an incongruous sound of birdsong from outside. I look beneath piles of clothes, inside the wardrobes, beneath the bed and the chaise longue. Nothing. I sink to my knees, digging my hands into my scalp, then scratching my nails down my face, catching a scab where I've cut myself shaving, drawing blood. I stare at the tiny speck of red on my forefinger, then lift it to my lips, tasting the dull tang of metal.

It's just a scratch. Dad's voice, loud and clear in the room. *Pull yourself together, son.*

I draw my hand back, and see that it's covered. Bright red blood. *My* blood. My gaze darts to my arms, my T-shirt, my jeans. Everything is splashed with it. My pulse races, but even as terror riots through my body, I know it's just an illusion. My mind is working overtime. When I blink, it's gone, and I'm staring at my pale hands and my clean clothes, and everything is exactly as it was. I look up and see one of the fox-fur stoles peeking at me from between the wardrobe doors. Seeing me with dead eyes. I feel the death in the house. I feel the certainty of my own mortality. I'm going to die. How did I ever think I was going to escape it?

I don't know what's got into you, son. Pull yourself together. Be a man.

For a moment, I'm that schoolkid again, standing in the yard, watching all the other kids play football while I'm frozen to the spot, paralysed by pure terror, by a threat that no one else can see . . .

I'm that twenty-something-year-old, sitting in some backstreet therapy centre, staring at the brick wall through the dirty window, too damned terrified to go ahead with the hypnotherapy session I'd planned and paid for . . .

I'm that scared thirty-two-year-old who's listening to my wife scream from the blow-up home birthing pool in the room next door, unable to race to her assistance even though I desperately want to, even though she's calling, *screaming*, my name.

Dad was right. I'm a failure. An utter failure. I don't deserve Jess, I don't deserve the girls. There's only one thing that will make me feel better right now. I dig my hand in my shorts pocket and pull out my car keys.

Charles Keller's diary:

<u>8 August 1848</u>

More deaths. My hands are caked in filth. The blood. I cannot get rid of it though I scrub and scrub and bathe myself in scalding hot water.

Massingham brought a child to me today, a child with wandering eyes who complained of stomach pains. He ordered me to cut into the abdomen immediately, but I resisted – the child needs bedrest, I said, not surgery. I went to my books, to the notes I had made as a student, to the anatomical drawings I had sketched with such care, seeking an answer but finding none. I turned back to the child and prodded the sunken mass of the stomach, the liver, the pancreas, finding nothing obvious. What good would it do to operate without purpose? Without hope of effecting a cure?

But Massingham raged against my decision. We must perfect the machine! More patients are needed. This is the great invention that will make our names known. Sacrifices are necessary for the greater good. And I saw in his eyes something else: a thirst for blood, for a suffering to match his own.

45

SUMMER

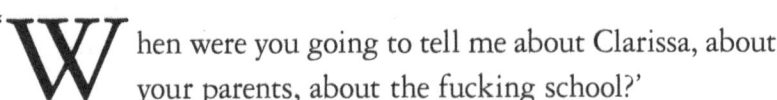

'When were you going to tell me about Clarissa, about your parents, about the fucking school?'

Aaron looks up at me from the flowerbed, startled. I'd purposely slipped off my flipflops and tiptoed across the lawn and I smile inwardly at the shock on his face. Bastard, I think, even as I run my eyes over his naked chest. He jabs his trowel into the ground and stands up.

'Summer. I—'

'Don't fuck with me, Aaron. Don't you dare fuck with me.'

'It was a joke about the school. Okay? I was going to tell you I was just kidding, but you seemed taken with it all. So, I just went with the flow.'

I scowl. Not good enough. 'What about Clarissa?'

'Nan told you about Clarry?' He swears beneath his breath.

I don't answer. He doesn't deserve to know how I know, only that I do.

He sighs. 'We split up. At the start of the holidays. It's a non-issue.'

I groan loudly. 'A non-issue for you, maybe. But what about me? I'm not in the habit of stealing other people's boyfriends.' I shove aside the memory of last year, the stolen kiss with the boy who got me drunk.

'I'm not Clarry's boyfriend any more. We lived together for a bit. At least, I stayed with her and her parents, but it didn't work out.'

'What about the Latin?'

'What?'

'The Latin lessons? The posh school? How much of it was a lie?'

He digs a hand in his pocket and pulls out his vape. 'If you really want to know, I go to a regular shitty comp. I got Ds in my GCSEs. I've never studied Latin in my life. My mum's a personal trainer. My dad's a mechanic. We live in a crappy part of town.' He draws on his vape, releases the smoke from his lungs. 'Happy now?'

'No.' I furrow my brow. 'How did you know about the Hippocratic oath? How did you know it was in Latin?'

He looks at me flatly. 'I googled it. I googled the words you heard, and it came up with Latin. Look, I'm sorry. I was bored. Mum's going through a rough time and I'm out here going crazy. It was fun to pretend I was someone else, to make up a story about school, about getting grounded. Me and my mates did mess around with Ouija boards and mirrors and stuff – that bit wasn't a lie – but no one ever found out. And we don't sleep in dorms, we sleep in regular beds in regular rundown homes.'

'Then, why—'

'It seemed easier, okay? Easier and way more fun making up stories rather than talking about my parents' divorce.'

I tug at my hair. Despite myself, I get it. It's what I'd wanted to do myself, be someone different, pretend I wasn't the social failure I am. 'What about the kiss?' My cheeks flame with the word.

'What?'

'Was that a lie too when you kissed me?'

'No. I swear. I liked you Summer. I still like you. You're the best thing that's happened all holiday.'

'Spare me the crap.'

'I mean it.' He shoves the vape back in his pocket and grabs hold of my hand. 'I like hanging out with you. I like kissing you.'

I push his hand away. 'I didn't come here for that.' I take my phone from my pocket, flick to Harry's messages, show Aaron the screen. 'It's a photo a friend took. We were chatting on the phone. A videocall, and he was taking screenshots.'

'Screenshots?'

I wave a hand dismissively. I'm not about to go into all that. 'He was taking photos of me, all right? And this came up. I was in the bathroom. We were just messing around. The photo should have been of me, but it wasn't.'

He takes the phone and stares at the screen. 'But . . . what the fuck?'

'Exactly.'

'Who is it?'

'There was no one else in the house. I was completely alone. The bathroom door was closed. It's impossible.'

'Maybe your mate's messing with your mind? This could be anything. Something from the internet.'

'No.' I remember the look in Harry's eyes, the way he'd quickly made his excuses to end the videocall. 'He was completely freaked out. There's another photo, almost the same, and it clearly shows the bathroom at St Cross in the background. It's like this person, this man, whoever he is, was trying to block me out. Was trying to send my friend a message.'

I take the phone and flip back to the first photo.

Aaron leans over me, and I feel his heat, the warmth of his chest against my back. 'Those eyes, they're . . . horrible.'

'What if it's him? The surgeon?'

'Keller?'

I nod, swallow hard.

'So, what now?'

I stare at the detritus on the lawn: the gloves, the upturned plant pots, the straggly pile of weeds. It touches me that Aaron's obviously been helping out in the garden. 'All I know is that there's something in St Cross. Not just something in my imagination. Not just words I could have picked up from a TV show. But something real. Something threatening.'

Aaron reaches out a hand. 'Come inside.'

'I can't—'

'Please. There's something I need to show you. Yesterday, after you left me, I was upset. Pissed off. You just ran off and I didn't know why.'

'I—'

He holds up his hands. 'I know. I know. You had every right to be angry, but I didn't know you knew that at the time, not until I'd spoken to Nan and found out you knew I'd been lying about the school. I caught a lift with Granddad into town. I was just going to hang out. Go to the pub. Get drunk. But then I bumped into the girl from the museum again. Lucie. She said she'd been doing some more digging around. She'd found some old plans of the infirmary, thought I might want to see them.'

'And?'

He tilts his head on one side. 'I've got photocopies. They're in my room.' He glances up at the cottage windows.

I hesitate, toying with the idea. 'No mirrors, okay? And no more lies. Promise me, no more lies.'

He reaches again for my hand, but I shake my head. It's too soon for that.

He looks solemn. 'Okay, no more lies.'

There's no sign of anyone else in the cottage; the kitchen is minus its usual baking material, the lounge has been cleared of magazines and newspapers.

'They're out for the day,' Aaron explains, answering the question I haven't asked. 'We've got the place to ourselves.'

I follow him upstairs, feeling the thrill of being alone with him despite everything that's happened. On the desk in his bedroom are a couple of sheets of A4 paper: plans dated to 1848, showing the ground and first floors of St Cross. I study the map of the ground floor first, the men's and women's wards, the various kitchens and offices. Then I turn to the second drawing, making out the words 'children's ward', 'isolation ward', 'linen cupboard', 'storage room'. My parents' room, I note, was reserved for storage, and the locked room – Mrs Clarence's room – contains an inner staircase, presumably leading to the attic, to the room with the internal window. Next to it is the smaller room I share with Xanthe.

'Lucie also found some letters,' Aaron says, interrupting me. 'Published letters from Charles Keller to a physician in London, George Reynolds. Seems Keller was a bit of an inventor.'

'An inventor?'

'He wanted Reynolds's advice. He was inventing a machine to administer chloroform. According to Lucie, anaesthetics were very unpredictable at the time. His machine was meant to regulate the dose, only his ideas fizzled out. Or Keller died. Either way the machine never took off.'

'The machine.' I say the words mechanically as I trace the tiny stencilled letters in the space where I sleep, picturing the floor-to-ceiling cupboards. I feel the blood drain from my face. Not linen cupboards at all.

Aaron's still talking about Charles Keller's machine but I don't hear the words.

'Oh God,' I lift my gaze to his and reach for his hand. Despite everything – the lies, the half-truths – I need him. I swallow hard. 'The room we're sleeping in. The room I share with Xanthe . . .'

He nods as though he already knows.

' . . . it's a morgue.'

Charles Keller's diary:

<u>10 August 1848</u>

I am tired, so very tired. My sleep is dreamless though I inhale more chloroform than I know is good for me. Those brilliant, vivid dreams in which Clara appeared to me are now elusive. My dreams are blank, empty spaces that haunt my waking hours.

46

Jess

I survey the empty hallway, feeling waves of panic at the doors propped open on all four sides. The way I hadn't left them. There's no sign of Liam or either of my daughters.

'Xanthe, please come out,' I call. 'I know you're hiding. This isn't funny any more.'

There's movement beyond the window in the study and I dart towards it. It's our Ford Fiesta turning on the driveway. I spurt to the front door, twisting the key in its lock, but it's stiff, determinedly resisting my efforts, trapping me in. I twist harder until the key reluctantly clunks into place, then I yank the door open just in time to see the tail end of the car disappear down the driveway.

'Liam!' I scream, knowing he won't hear me. I haven't spoken to him since breakfast, haven't known what to say. I listen to the putter of the tyres, gradually dimming to a groan, followed by silence. Not even the buzz of insects or the twitter of birds. An unnerving deadly stillness. Just like the fountain in the centre of the turning circle that no longer works.

The air feels muggy, thick, like it might break any moment, clinging to me as I turn back inside. I've a horrible sense that everything's crumbling – my family, my marriage, this house. I cross the empty hall, climb the stairs, taking them in threes, counting the rhythm – one, two, three – then peer into the girls' room. Xanthe's cardigan is dropped near the window. Her diary is open next to it: a drawing of Angel. I rub my temples, trying to think, trying to imagine where our youngest daughter might be hiding. Then, I walk back to the landing and look down. There's a key balanced on top of the painting in the hallway. The painting of Mary at the foot of the cross. The key Xanthe was trying to reach when she fell from the table, only visible from this angle. A key, I think – I *know* – to the locked room.

I run, my hand gliding down the banister. *This key is the answer to everything.*

'Mummy.'

I stop where I am and listen. 'Xanthe?' I call back, daring to hope.

The silence is palpable. The house rings with it. And then a scream, 'MUMMY.'

I dart in the direction of the sound, tripping down the last few steps, racing across the hallway, pulling wide the kitchen door. And there, thank God, is Xanthe's standing at the table. But my relief is short lived. There's blood. So much blood. I feel faint at the sight of it. I grab Xanthe's hand. Grab a tea towel. There's a deep gash in the centre of her palm, and my rational brain, the one that isn't panicking like crazy, tells me it probably needs stitches. I wipe Xanthe's hand with the towel, my mind racing, thinking how there's no way to get her to the hospital from here, not without a car. We'll have to wait until Liam returns from wherever he's gone. Either that or call a taxi.

'What happened?' My voice sounds strangled. 'Oh God, what happened?'

'I was cutting ...' Her words are jerky with tears. 'I was cutting meat.'

'Meat?' I frown at the lump of ham on the table. The ham from the fridge. 'You know you're not allowed to use knives.'

'But I was hungry. Please, Mummy, it hurts.'

'We have to wash it,' I say, forcing myself to act calm. Looking down, I see splashes of blood on the floor. *Don't look.* I've never been good with blood, but it always has to be me, the fearless one, who looks after the girls when they injure themselves. Not Liam. Never Liam. I lead Xanthe to the sink and run the cold water. As I clean her palm, I thank God it's not as bad as I thought.

'We just need to get rid of the dirt. We don't want to risk infection.' *Xanthe in the bath. Xanthe catapulting from the table. Verity's child falling from the tree.* I hold Xanthe's hand steady beneath the tap, the blood running freely, splashing pink against the white ceramic, then I lean over the sink. It's then that I feel it. An unmistakable presence in the room behind us, filling the space.

'Mummy?' Xanthe's voice is barely a whisper, but it's filled with fear. *She can feel it too.* The knowledge makes it so much worse. It's here. This thing in the house, this thing I've felt right from the beginning. Only now, I realise what it is: *a man.* He's standing right behind us in the kitchen.

'Xanthe,' I whisper back. 'We have to leave the house now.'

Xanthe grips my arm with her good hand. 'Where will we go?' The water splashes harder, faster in the sink. Above the sound of it, I hear a solid, rhythmic tapping.

'The beach. We'll go to the beach. We'll wait for Daddy and Summer there. We just need to grab a few things to take with us. You wait in the garden.'

I turn off the tap, grab a fresh tea towel, wrap it around Xanthe's hand, knot it clumsily. Good enough. Strong enough to stem the flow of blood. The light darkens. I push Xanthe through the back door and tell her to wait, then I swing around, but the room is just as empty as it was.

I scrawl a note to Liam, telling him to meet us at the beach, grab my phone to text Summer, then slice rough chunks of bread and cucumber and throw them in a Tupperware box. I grab the tube of suncream sitting on the table, an ancient-looking first-aid kit, a bottle of water; thrust it all in a carrier bag. The table is a mess. The ham. The blood. But there's no time to sort it.

I take one last look at the kitchen. The knife glints from the centre of the table. The knife I've been keeping high up in the dresser, too high for Xanthe to reach. The servant bells sway almost imperceptibly. The inner door stands wide open, though I'm sure I closed it firmly behind me, exposing the dappled tiles in the hallway. And the sunlight streams in through the cupola, not bright and welcoming like it should be, but stark and revealing.

47

Liam

I know I'm driving erratically. I know I ought to slow down. Whatever trouble I'm in, it's not going to be helped by me crashing the car. I slam it into fourth in an attempt to gain a semblance of control. The engine groans. I look at the gearstick and realise I've thrust it into second by mistake. I throw the car into neutral, taking a corner at the same time.

There's a tractor coming in the opposite direction. I jerk the gearstick back into second, then put my foot down to straighten up out of the bend. The other driver blares his horn.

A near miss. A low burbling sound rises in my throat until tears are streaking my cheeks.

I pull up at the nearest country pub. It's not yet eleven. I'll need to sit in the car park until it is. But that's okay. I'll sit here and read the news or watch YouTube videos to pass the time. I wipe the tears from my face, dig my hand in my back pocket, pull out my phone and press the on button. Dead. Completely out of battery.

I laugh this time. Laugh until my sides ache. My phone. The phone I've been searching for everywhere, in the house, in the garden. Even in the old greenhouse. I hadn't thought to look in the most obvious place, in the pocket of the jeans I'd discarded a few days ago, the ones Jess had folded and placed on the chaise longue. Is it really possible that my phone's been there all this time?

48

SUMMER

───◦∞◦───

I sit cross legged on Aaron's bed, drinking vodka and lemonade. We've studied the floor plans several times and almost exhausted references on Google. There are a couple of mentions of Charles Keller's death, one comment on his close relationship with the Massingham family, but that's all. No suggestion of murder or any other foul play. It feels like a dead end. And then I stumble across this on a history website:

> Charles Keller was a renowned London surgeon who wrote several articles for the British Medical Journal on the advancement of surgical practices in the 1840s. Although English by birth, his family originated from Rothenburg ob der Tauber in Bavaria, Germany, and Keller himself was fluent in both English and German as well as a scholar of

Latin and Greek. In his last years, he set up a practice in Blythe, Suffolk, fulfilling his philanthropic mission of helping the poor. He died at the age of thirty-four in the infirmary where he worked.

But it's not the text that grabs me – I've read that or similar before – it's the portrait below. A portrait of a Victorian gentleman in a dull grey jacket. The same man as in Harry's photos? I fish out my phone, go back to Harry's messages, zoom in and out, trying to make sense of what I see, but I can't. Apart from the eyes, everything else is too blurry. I show Aaron the photos again. 'Is it the same man?'

Aaron turns the phone around for a better view. 'I don't know. Maybe. It's hard to say. The drawing is so, I don't know, generic. It could be anyone from that era. The eyes in the photo are different.'

'Exactly. That's exactly what I was thinking.' I shudder. 'The eyes are evil. Whereas these eyes just look, I dunno, dead.'

'So now what?' he says.

I feel drunk. The vodka. The closeness of Aaron. The scent of his skin in the muggy heat of the bedroom.

He moves towards me and kisses me deeply. My body responds without hesitation. I feel momentarily bad, but then, what the hell? Is it such a crime to be wanted? Don't we all have our secrets? Just as Aaron didn't tell me about his parents, I haven't told him everything about Harry, about the girls in school, about the boy I kissed.

'I think we need tea,' he says, pulling away from me.

'Tea? Right.' I try not to feel deflated. 'A cup of tea, yeah sure. Why not?'

He leaves me alone, and I scroll through my phone for what

seems like ages. There's a text from Mum telling me not to go back to the house, to meet them at the beach. I frown. The message seems odd, there are typos for a start. Mum always checks her messages before sending. But I'll deal with Mum later. I can hardly turn up to the beach drunk like this.

Aaron returns, handing me a mug.

'You took your time. One of your granddad's special recipes?'

He smiles mischievously. 'Something like that.' He sits beside me on the bed. 'So, what else? Tell me something about yourself. What music are you into?'

'What?'

'Music, you know?' He waves his phone. 'Maybe we can listen to something.'

Music. Normal stuff. I smile. Maybe tea isn't such a bad idea after all. I take a sip. It tastes weird, earthy. I frown at the light brown liquid.

'Shrooms,' he says, grinning.

'What?'

'Magic mushrooms. Thought we could do with some better entertainment.' I stare at him in horror. 'Don't tell me you haven't done shrooms before?'

'No.' I feel a clawing sense of panic.

'Go, on. Drink it. It will be fun, I promise.'

I take a tentative sip, wrinkling my nose at the taste, then another and another.

He leans over and kisses me, wrapping a hand around my neck, drawing me into him. I forget everything, the lies he told me, the mushrooms in my tea. His lips feel urgent against mine, his hand moves up my T-shirt, and he moans softly. We stay like that for a while, stroking, kissing. When he pulls away to top up our glasses with vodka, I feel exactly the same as I did before. Perhaps I haven't drunk enough of the tea to make a difference?

'Your turn,' he says.

'What?' The room shimmies.

'Your turn to choose the music.'

'Right.' I reach over for my phone and open Spotify, but the screen doesn't work right, the buttons not responding. I giggle and try again. 'Where shall I start?'

Time is working in strange leaps.

Aaron is shimmering, green and yellow. He's so beautiful, so incredibly beautiful. I reach through the green, but somehow miss him, landing face down on the duvet instead.

'Whoa. Steady yourself.'

I look over my shoulder and smile. Lights. The bedroom is full of them. Yellow. Blue. Green.

'Keller,' I say. The name feels like chocolate on my lips. It sticks to my teeth. I can't get rid of it. 'Charles Keller. Charles Keller.' Then I try something else, the family Aaron told me about before, who built the infirmary. 'Massingham.'

'That's right.' Aaron is stroking my back and it feels incredible. His hand reaches beneath my T-shirt, tickling my spine, seeming to creep through my skin. I flip over. The outline of him is fuzzy, but the inside is all lines and shading. I see him as a diagram, an anatomical diagram, as I touch his warm skin, my fingers lingering on his chest, tracing his ribcage. I giggle as I lift his ribs out one by one and carefully lay them beside me on the duvet.

'What are you doing?'

'I'm dissecting you.'

'Summer.' His voice is thick with lust. He pushes me backwards when I try to rise, his mouth on mine, pinning me down. His mouth tastes of peaches and blood. I want to devour him.

'The mirror.' His voice is breathy as he detaches his lips from mine. 'We should do the mirror again.'

'What?'

'The mirror. We should look in the mirror. It's stronger like this, with the mushrooms.'

'What?'

'The mirror. It works better like this. I googled it.'

'Ra . . . ai . . . ght.' My voice comes out funny. I reach around him and pull off his arms, first one then the other, laying them next to the pile of ribs. I frown when they reattach themselves. 'Naughty arms,' I say, taking them off again.

He leans over and cradles my face, his fingers melting into my skin. 'You're tripping,' he says, then kisses me deeply. 'I like you when you're tripping. You're funny.' He moves his mouth to my throat then down to the skin above my chest. 'The mirror.' He repeats the word softly between kisses. 'Let's do the mirror. It's more powerful like this. *He's* more powerful.'

'He?'

'I'm a Harrison, remember? I know what I'm doing. I've been told what to do.'

There's movement. Colours dart across the room like strobes. Aaron seems to be dancing. I don't know how I get there, but I'm sitting on the floor with the lighted candle. The flame throws specks of green across the room. The smoke is a green vapour.

'Look in the mirror,' he says, wrapping his arms around me as the lights waltz on the wall opposite. He's sitting behind me now, kissing, kissing, kissing. Our roles are reversed and he's the one doing the dissecting. My skin is so pliable, it wants to be stretched, moulded by his fingers.

I look in the mirror, for how long I'm not sure but it seems only seconds before it starts to change. The mist is thick. A green mist emanating from the depths of the glass. It wraps around me, making me feel safe. It's safe to look in the mirror, I tell myself. I know there's no harm.

Primum non nocere.

The Latin words come fast, binding themselves tightly around my head, squeezing just like Aaron's arms. Tightly, tightly, pinning me to the spot. I realise I want to be dissected. I want him to take me.

Primum non nocere. Primum non nocere.

'Do no harm,' I repeat out loud.

'You can hear him?' Aaron leans into me, leans *through* me, our bodies becoming one. 'He's more powerful with the mushrooms, isn't he?'

'Yes.'

'What else does he say?'

I struggle to concentrate. The words are too fast, Latin words. *Somnum. Mortuus. Chloroformium.* The space is changing too. Aaron's body is hot on mine, but the room is too small. Cloying, like earth on a grave. The mist in the mirror swirls, taking shape, and the words morph from Latin to English.

LIAM KENNEDY DIED THE NINETEENTH DAY OF AUGUST IN THE YEAR OF OUR LORD 2023 . . .

JESSICA KENNEDY DIED THE NINETEENTH DAY OF AUGUST IN THE YEAR OF OUR LORD 2023 . . .

SUMMER KENNEDY DIED THE NINETEENTH DAY
OF AUGUST IN THE YEAR OF OUR LORD 2023 . . .

XANTHE KENNEDY DIED—

I scream, toppling the candle with my foot. It catches the edge of one of the photocopied maps.

'Fuck.' Aaron's on the floor, batting the flame with his hand, then reaches for the dregs of lemonade and dowses the fire. 'What did you do that for?'

'What's the date?'

'What?'

'The date. You know?' For a flicker of a second, I'm perfectly sober. 'The calendar date.'

'I dunno. The nineteenth, I think.'

'The man. I saw him.' I jump to my feet. 'He spoke to me. Did you see him? Did you see him in the mirror?'

'No. I can't see anything. It's you, not me. You're the one who connects.'

'He's in the house. He's in the house, looking for my little sister. He said . . .' But I can't repeat it. I can't repeat those words. 'I saw the room. I saw the wallpaper. The green wallpaper.' I run to the door and try to open it, but the handle won't turn. I try again. A bolt of panic that he's locked me in. When I turn, Aaron is grinning, and I don't know if the danger is him or something else.

'Which man?' he says, amused.

'Keller.' That name again. It binds my teeth together like glue. But it's not Keller I see in my mind, it's someone else. We got it wrong. We got it so wrong . . . 'It's not Keller,' I say, though I can't explain it. I see the face in the shadows. The man in the portrait in the hallway at St Cross. I've barely glanced at the portrait, but the words leap in my mind: *Lord James Alexander Massingham.*

'I think you need to lie down.' Aaron takes hold of my hand and leads me to the bed.

'No.' I try to pull away, but I can't. I don't have the strength. 'The house. Xanthe.'

'Xanthe's fine. It's just the mushrooms. They're strong. I shouldn't have given you so many.'

A shadow creeps across the wall behind the desk. Fear tingles down my body, thousands of tiny pinpricks. *Massingham.* 'He's here. He's in the room with us.'

'Well, that's good then, isn't it? If he's here he can't be with your sister.'

I'm better lying down, feeling Aaron's semi-naked body next to mine, feeling the stroke of his hands, watching the lights shimmer across the ceiling. It was just the mushrooms, I tell myself. Didn't I drink the rest of the tea when he told me to? My mind loops: colour, light, Aaron. I can't remember why I was so terrified a moment ago. If I lie here as still as I can, I'll be okay. I melt into the bed. Melt into Aaron. Melt into the lights gliding across the ceiling.

Charles Keller's diary:

14 August 1848

I have received another letter from George Reynolds imploring me to leave for London at once; the infirmary has become a poison in my mind, and no further good can come from my being here.

How true these words, spoken by my dear friend who can only guess my suffering!

I am sitting at my desk, paper in hand, ready to pen my resignation. The infirmary is quiet tonight. A hush has settled on the wards. Only a moth flickers near the candle flame, perilously close to burning its wings. Sometimes I wonder if these walls can hear my thoughts. If the windows see all that happens within. If the furniture has eyes that follow me around.

49

Jess

The heat sticks to me, even as I paddle in the sea with Xanthe, trying to keep my mind off the house. Xanthe's wound is deep but the yellowing bandage from the first-aid kit is doing its job and the bleeding has more or less stopped. I wonder how long we can stay here waiting for Summer and Liam, at what point we'll be forced to return to the house.

I wade through the surf, sinking into the silty sand, feeling the waves rush over my feet, cleansing my skin. But, despite my efforts, I'm unable to shake the house from my mind.

'Mummy.' Xanthe tugs on my arm and I'm grateful for the distraction. 'I need a wee.'

'What?'

'I need a wee *now*.'

I scan the empty stretch of beach, before bending down to Xanthe's height. 'There's no one here. No one to see.'

'I can't have a wee here!' Xanthe does an exaggerated dance, indicating the urgency.

'Up on the dunes, then. I'll come with you, keep a look out, and then we'll have lunch. It's late. I'm starving.'

We splash our way out of the water and head towards the costal path, the wind picking up as we climb, no longer the autumnal breeze of a few days ago, but warm and heavy.

'What about that dip over there?' I suggest as we crest the first sand dune and look down towards the road.

Xanthe nods and releases my hand. 'Don't look.'

I smile to myself at Xanthe's newfound need for privacy, staring out to sea as I wait, the water a brush of perfect blue, calming my mind. But even on the higher ground, the air feels thick, like I could cut it with a knife. I swing the carrier bag in my hand. The carrier bag with our lunch. The hunk of bread. The cheese. The cucumber. And then right at the bottom, something else. It catches my eye, has me reaching into the bag and pulling it out: a faded red note book. *Charles Keller's diary.* My hand trembles on the hard cloth cover. How did it get in the bag? How did I not notice it before? I must have taken it by mistake when I hurriedly grabbed our lunch, though I can't remember doing it. I let the bag fall as I turn the pages, the blurred ink, the wafer-thin paper, the writing more chaotic – a scrawl rather than the neat if elaborate writing of the earlier entries – as the diary progresses.

'Have you finished?' I call to Xanthe over my shoulder.

Xanthe doesn't reply so I give her a minute longer, distractedly scanning the diary, trying to make sense of the faded scrawl. *The operating theatre ... Massingham ... the machine ... the great machine* ... Overhead, I feel the tension, the need for rain. I lift my eyes from the page, drawn by the movement of the sea, the never-ending rhythm. 'Xanthe?' I say. I turn around but don't see her. I scan the dunes and the coastal path, telling myself Xanthe's just lower than I thought. I take the nearest winding path, looking left and right, expecting to see Xanthe at any moment, crouched between the dunes. But there's nothing. No scuffed footprints in the sand. No sign of Xanthe.

'Xanthe?' I call again, my words muted by the wind and the first heavy spots of rain. I think I hear something and spin around, but it's just the wind, the thrash of waves, foamy white marring the blue. Still no sign of Xanthe in any direction. But I know the dunes are deceptive; there are hidden crevices and paths I can't see. I shove the diary back in the bag, dump the bag where it is, and follow first one track and then another, scanning the landscape, knowing Xanthe must be here somewhere. It's impossible for her to just disappear like that. Probably, she's gone exploring. I turn to the right, and run along the higher-most ridge, surveying the dips beneath me until I reach the steep rise of cliff ahead. I turn back towards the village, chest tight with panic. Have I been searching in the wrong direction? Maybe Xanthe's back on the beach already, sheltering behind the rocks? I half-run half-stumble on to the beach, my footfall slowed by the softness of the sand, the emptiness ebbing around me like the huge expanse of water.

'Xanthe,' I call into the wind and rain. 'Where are you? Please come back. This isn't funny any more.'

Something catches my eye. A long wrap of bandage, tangled in the coarse grass. A bloodstained bandage. I pull it free and spin in all directions. But there's only the emptiness of the landscape and the pulse of the storm and the warning cry of a gull overhead.

I run along the coastal path to the nearest chalet, knock on the door, battering my fists into the peeling painted wood. No answer. I run to the next, and the next, but there's no one in, and the holiday homes look deserted. The railings are broken and there are clear gaps in the decking where you could easily break an ankle. I peer through the windows, through murky glass, between drab curtains. The chalets are completely empty.

The isolation sweeps around me. I'm completely alone. Even Summer isn't answering her phone. I've failed my daughters, and everything is wrong. I run back to the road, back in the direction of the house, the bloodied bandage bunched in my hands, calling their names.

50

S U M M E R

I'm not sure how long I lie on the bed next to Aaron. The lights are gone. The room is still. My head feels almost normal apart from a faint drilling sound. I turn to Aaron and find he's fallen asleep on top of the duvet. Fallen asleep, how is that even possible? Maybe his tea wasn't as strong as mine, or maybe there was nothing in his tea at all. Maybe he tricked me. *Bastard.* I draw back the curtains and see that the drilling sound is actually the rain pattering against the window. It feels cleansing, like something that had to happen.

I stand up, finding my trainers among the mess on the floor. The candle is still upturned, wax splashed across the carpet. The mirror next to it is broken. I can't remember how that happened. I've no recollection of the glass smashing.

I look for my phone and find it beneath the bed. There are

three garbled messages from Mum telling me to meet her at the beach, not to go back to the house. But I need to go back. I need to wash and change my clothes. I need something to eat and about a gallon of water to drink. I tiptoe out of the bedroom, the door opening easily this time, the handle obeying the laws of physics. My mouth is dry, my eyes hurt. I have a headache, but everything else, thank God, feels normal. I stare at Aaron face down on the bed, his back bare, his boxers showing above his shorts, and I feel . . . what? Nothing, except a sense there was something else. Something he said when I was tripping. Something about the man being more powerful like this, about the fact he's a Harrison.

I sigh with relief when I realise his grandparents haven't returned in the four hours – has it really been four hours? – I've been upstairs, that I can leave unobserved. As I open the back door and step into the cottage garden, I'm grateful for the rain, the way it breaks through the heat.

I walk through the wood towards St Cross, my gaze drawn to its depth. A dart of movement registers something in my mind, but it's gone in a breath, and I'm too slow to chase it. By the time I reach the garden I'm soaked. The lawn sparkles with rain and everything seems vivid. Greener. So much greener.

I cross the terrace and open the back door. Immediately, I know the place is empty, just as I'd hoped – I don't want to have to explain myself to Mum and Dad. It's nothing palpable, just a feeling. A feeling similar to entering a cave. There's only the cats helping themselves to something on the table. I take a step forward and frown at the mauled hunk of ham. Then, I walk into the hallway and climb the stairs, drawn by the light and the sound of the rain on the cupola, soothing, dulling the pulse in my brain. I pass Mum and Dad's room and the room

I share with Xanthe, all the way to the room with the locked door. I don't even know why I go there, or who's calling me, only that I *am* being called, just like the times when I looked in the mirror, when I felt the anger, when I cut the worms.

'I'm coming,' I say out loud, my voice echoing.

But the room isn't locked. The door stands wide open. I see the floorboards and the grey light cast by the narrow, arched window. To the left, I see the little steps and the opening to the attic stairwell.

Here, I think. *It's been here all along.*

I take a deep breath and walk inside.

51

Liam

I shouldn't drive. I *know* I shouldn't drive. Over the space of several hours, I've drunk five pints of beer. But I need to find Jess. I need to talk to her, explain that I'll try harder. I've been an arse, but I won't make the same mistakes again. I've got a plan with the day trading, one I'll explain to her in full. Slowly and steadily, I'll claw the money back. No silly moves. No rash decisions. No more lies.

But first, I need to get back to the house. Stupid of me to run away in the first place, thinking a drink would solve my problems. A drink solves nothing, I know that now. Funny, it took me five pints to realise it. I sweep up my car keys, ignoring the concerned frown of the publican behind the bar, and step into the rain and the saturating heat.

In the car, I tear my phone from its charging lead and check my emails. No reply to the message I sent Callum calling him a bully, so I dial his number. The first two calls go through to voicemail, but, on the third, he answers.

'Hi—'

'Fuck you.' I'm slurring my words, but I don't care. 'You knew,' I said. 'You knew about the house.'

I hear a jumble of voices on the other end. Callum talking to someone else. Then he's back on the line, quieter but insistent. 'Look, I've got people here. You sound ... I dunno ... You sound a bit drunk.'

I don't grace him with an answer. Instead I think about the men who turned up at the house when Jess was at work, the men who threatened me about the money. Callum might deny it, but I know it wasn't a mistake, a friendly reminder gone too far. 'Tell me about the house,' I say. 'Tell me everything. Don't you dare lie. My daughter, Xanthe, she had an accident. But it wasn't an accident was it?' My drunken brain is finally making connections. 'They all link, don't they? The strange noises, the accident, the vivid dreams?'

There's a long pause on the other end. When he finally speaks, Callum's voice has lost its usual composure. 'Oh God. So it's true.'

Sweat trickles down my neck. 'What do you mean?' I pull at my collar, feeling the familiar surge of anxiety.

There's a pause. The sound changes as if Callum's walking to another room. A door slams. 'I thought it was all bollocks, all the stuff my stepmum said about the house. I thought she was finally losing the plot.'

'I don't understand—'

Callum laughs but there's no humour in his voice. 'My step-mum's not well, she's not going to be with us for much longer.

No point denying the facts. I'm about to inherit St Cross, and I've got plans. A five-star hotel. A luxury conference centre. I'm going to renovate the entire estate, clean the stonework, modernise the interior, landscape the gardens. Only my stepmum won't let it go that the place is haunted.'

The word whispers down the phone line, wrapping itself around me.

'She's become obsessed with the idea, something planted long ago by her sister. My stepmum didn't believe it at first – Verity was, by all accounts, mad – but recently, she's been talking. I put it down to the stroke, or a touch of dementia, but I had to be sure.'

Realisation hits me like a gush of cold water. 'You utter bastard.'

'*Sorry?*'

'You were using us.' I'm so angry, it's an effort to speak.

Callum clears his throat. I sense him stiffen on the other end. 'I'd rather call it making the most of a bad situation.'

But I've no time for his crap. 'We were guinea pigs, weren't we, testing out the house? Testing out your grand idea?'

'I needed an objective opinion, that's all.' Callum's voice is hard. 'Someone who knew nothing about its history. It was just meant to be a bit of fun. And I thought you'd be grateful for the holiday.'

'*Grateful?*' I almost choke on the word. 'You've no fucking idea. My daughter almost died. Jess is barely speaking to me. I've had flashbacks to things I'd rather forget. I've seen things that aren't there. My imagination has gone into overdrive. And all because,' I pause, gathering my thoughts, 'because you – a man who already has everything, who doesn't know what it means to count every penny that goes in and out – wanted to be sure nothing was going to wreck your precious plans.'

'You're overreacting—'

I cut him off, pressing the end-call button, then toss the phone on to the passenger seat and start the engine. The car jolts forward – I'd forgotten I'd left it in first – the bonnet grazing the car-park wall.

I feel clear headed as I drive, as if seeing things properly for the first time in years. Callum's words mush about in my brain, but everything else is crystal clear. I think about all the things I've told myself – that I'm better, that I'm coping, that my past has no bearing on my present – and realise it for what it is: lies. The past never goes away, not really. It just creeps up on you, catches you out when you're least expecting it. When you're vulnerable and feeling down. But I couldn't have gone on lying to Jess for ever. As I negotiate the winding roads with the windows open as far as they'll go and the windscreen wipers flashing through my vision, I decide I'm going to tell Jess everything.

I turn up the radio until its blaring, trying to block out my other thoughts. All I need to think about is Jess, about getting back to the house, about saving my daughters. But it doesn't work.

You don't have to pretend you're all right just so that other people feel okay. The voice of the school counsellor is as clear as the DJ. *Tell me what you're feeling, Liam. It doesn't have to go beyond these four walls if you don't want it to.*

I grip the steering wheel harder, my shoulders hunching, my muscles clamping up. An old habit, one I'm not sure how to break. I see my dad in my mind. Not the old man in the wheelchair who I hardly ever see, but the young man he'd been, who wore his disappointment as blatantly as the colours of his rugby shirt. *You fucked up, son. You really fucked up.* And then, before I know it, I'm on that ridge, staring down at the rock face, Dad egging me on. *Come on, son. Show me you're a man.*

I put my foot down hard on the accelerator.

I'm not standing on a ridge. I'm not standing on anything. And the school counsellor is just an illusion, my mind playing tricks. Just like the last sixteen years or so have been an illusion – the sobriety, the pretence of being normal, the pretence of being a stable human being. Whatever happens now, I promise myself, I'll tell Jess. I'll find a way to tell her why I'm so afraid, the reason I don't drink – or do drink, I'm not sure which – the reason I check myself daily for symptoms.

The road bends into Blythe. The white church swims into view like a colossal gravestone. I slam the brakes, clipping the grass kerb near the churchyard gate. Then I straighten up, knowing the entrance to St Cross is just around the corner. Almost there. Time to set things right.

Rain splatters the windscreen and dusts the inside of the car through the open window. A welcome coolness. I press my foot firmly on the accelerator, impatient to get back, to start over again. The hedge on the next bend glides into focus. I swerve to the left, overcompensating, the backend of the car swinging out.

A bang as the suspension breaks.

I jolt forwards, my head smashing into the airbag as the car wing crumples. I stare at the iron gates of St Cross, tasting blood in my mouth, my vision holding on for just a moment – just long enough to see that the metal snakes are moving, slithering impossibly between the bars.

And then everything darkens.

Charles Keller's diary:

<u>18 August 1848</u>

Terrible things have happened here. Terrible things that must be written down. A record of sorts, though I can barely bring my pen to the paper, my hand to the pen. Dear God, give me strength!

It was an hour ago that I awoke to sounds above me. Not rats or some other creature, but footsteps sounding clearly from the attic. I hastened to my feet, grabbed my shirt and dressing gown. I knew there was danger although I could not fathom what that danger could be. I ran from my room and threw wide the door to the attic stairwell. Even from the foot of the stairs, I could smell chloroform – that sweet, unmistakable scent of flowers. I consulted my pocket watch – five o'clock in the morning. No one should be in the operating theatre at all!

I climbed the stairs, steeling myself for what I would find, for this was surely not a servant come to clean. Whatever scene awaited me, it would not be good.

I was not mistaken! In all my nightmares I could not have imagined anything like this.

Lord Massingham stood in the centre of the room, his hair uncombed, his shirt unbuttoned. He looked wild – a creature rather than a man – a grin spread wide across his face, his eyes gleaming. He was wearing my surgeon's jacket, the shoulders loose, the wool caked from the many years of my labour, yet somehow suiting him perfectly. In his hand, he held a knife, it's ebony handle as black as his eyes, and he was reciting those words – words I know so well from my youth – words in Latin spoken mechanically, spoken by one who is neither a physician nor a surgeon, but one who is playing God.

Juro Apollinem Medicum, et Aesculapium,

Hygejamque, ac Panaceam, et Deos omnes,

itemque Deas testes adhibens, me ratum pro viribus,

judicioque meo jusjurandum hoc,

hancque contestationem effecturum.

Upon the operating table, a child was sleeping peacefully, a child I had attended only the day before and proclaimed no surgery was necessary for the child is an epileptic, more suited to an asylum. 'No!' I ran towards Massingham and pulled him backwards, but he laughed and struck my cheek. I fell, slamming hard against the operating table – how weak I have grown from my addiction. I clutched my head in pain, the room spinning, as Massingham stepped forwards and waved a letter penned in my own hand, outlining my resignation.

If I will not do my job, he said, then he will do it for me.

I had no choice – dear God, believe me – but to take the knife from his hand and do his bidding, acting exactly as he instructed. At least in my hands, there would be a chance that the child lived. So, I incised the boy's head, cut deep into the brain tissue, and as I did so, Massingham spoke in Latin, chanting his perverse refrain, justifying his own terrible actions with words.

Primum non nocere. First, do no harm.

At last, when the ordeal was over, I staggered to the ward with the child limp in my arms, my shirt soaked red, the body growing heavier with each painful step. But heavier still was the burden upon my soul, the burden that weighs upon me even now. Mrs Harker hurried across the room and took the child without question, folding him into her arms. She whispered to me, her voice hoarse and cracked: three children had escaped in the night. They had slipped from their beds and escaped through the kitchen door into the garden. The servants have already searched the grounds, but there is no trace. Harrison had roused his lordship with the news, and his lordship had appeared at the infirmary in an insatiable rage.

52

—⊶⊰⊱⊷—

Jess

'Have you seen my daughter?' I gabble my words, clutching my side, breathing through the pain from running. My hair sticks to my cheeks, my clothes are sodden. I must look a mess but I don't care.

'Come inside.' Robbie beckons to me from where she's standing beneath the gatehouse porch.

'I can't stop,' I shout. 'I haven't time. I just need to know, is she here? Have you seen her?'

'Your daughter's safe.' Robbie turns into the house, leaving the door wide open in invitation.

I feel a rush of relief as I lift the latch of the garden gate and run towards the gatehouse. Xanthe must have got lost on the sand dunes, wandered off in the wrong direction, and Robbie must have found her. Robbie, the lady I've doubted until now. I almost laugh at how stupid I've been.

A minute later, I find myself in a small sitting room that smells of herbs and wet linen, a sitting room where the furniture is all made out of cardboard. There's only one proper armchair, stacked with old cushions.

'I was taking in the washing,' Robbie explains. 'The weather's so unpredictable. Sit down and I'll fetch you a cuppa.'

'But, I—'

'Just sit.'

It takes all my willpower to do what she says. Is Xanthe here? I look around for Angel, but there's no sign of him either. My eyes dart to the two doors at the back. The kitchen and presumably a bedroom or bathroom. I'm about to investigate when Robbie returns with the tea – black tea that smells smoky.

'Xanthe and I are the same,' she says, taking a seat in the opposite chair. 'I knew it from the first time I met her. The time she came to find me. I knew *someone* would find me. I could feel their energy, whoever it was, coming from St Cross. And I knew things were changing. I saw the black cat escape from the house into the garden. Animals know, don't they? They know when there's danger. The cat ran from the house to hide. And then your daughter came knocking on my door. She looked so small, so innocent. It made me smile.'

'I don't understand.' I scan the room for what feels like the hundredth time, the boxes, the coffee table, the doors at the back. I've an urge to run over and yank them open. 'Please, tell me where she is. Is she here?'

'I knew it would happen with the change in the weather. It's been brewing for days. The energy was so strong, I could feel it tingling in the tips of my fingers. And then I found your other daughter at the manor, meddling with that boyfriend of hers. She shouldn't have been there. No one should go there. She didn't know how careless she was being, messing with things that ought not to be messed with. The manor is a dead place. It was me who saw to that. The energy there was bad. I knew I had to burn it. I wanted to burn the infirmary too, but there was never a chance, there were always people living there or the place was shut up. Then, after all these years, Xanthe came to see me.'

'Here? Xanthe's here? She came here today?'

'Yesterday. She was so scared, poor love. I gave her the dog for company. I taught her how to control Angel, just as she needs to learn to control her gift. I learned to control it myself when I was a little girl. I was reckless at first. I thought the only way was to destroy it, but I was wrong.' She closes her eyes, her eyelids fluttering with memories. 'After Verity died, I was so very frightened.'

'*Verity?*' I'm struggling to follow the old lady's rambling.

'The lady who used to live in the house before Mrs Clarence. She said she could hear voices in the house. Children's voices whispering to her, asking her to let them out. To help them escape. They'd tried to hide from him on the beach, but there was a storm and the tide came in.'

I lean forwards, the box creaking beneath me. 'Please, Robbie, I'm begging you. Tell me where Xanthe is. I'm frightened too.'

The old lady opens her eyes. 'She's with him. With Angel.' Her face crumples. Suddenly, she looks incredibly tired. 'I gave her Angel to keep her safe. The house, you see, it takes children away.'

I frown. None of it makes any sense.

'Every twenty years or so, a child dies at or near the house. A little girl got into the grounds, into one of the old glasshouses before they pulled them down. She was killed by falling debris. Before that, Verity lost her child. And then, there were the accidents. Deaths that shouldn't have happened, despite the house being an infirmary. A child with polio got locked in the attic and no one heard him screaming. A young soldier, only seventeen, fell through the window of one of the bedrooms. A child got killed when a bookcase slammed to the floor.'

I think about the graves in the churchyard, the names of all those children. *Emily, George, Anne, Elijah, Sophie.* A cold sweat creeps across my forehead. 'Where's my daughter? Please. I need to know.'

'I told you, she's with Angel. She's learning to control her gift.'

'Gift?' I set the teacup down, the tea untouched. 'I don't know what you're talking about. What gift?'

'Her gift of speaking to *them*, of course. Of speaking to the children. Of speaking to the dead.'

I jump to my feet, grab hold of Robbie's hands. How cold and frail they are. 'Please. She's only a little girl. She's only seven. If you know where she is, then tell me.'

Robbie blinks in confusion. 'She's with Angel. I told you that. The doctors have only given me a couple of months. They say I have cancer, but I don't want anyone meddling. When I'm gone, what will happen to Angel then?'

'I'm so sorry. I had no idea . . .'

Robbie shakes her head dismissively. 'Your daughter's look-ing after my dog. She took him away with her yesterday.'

53

Liam

'It's okay, Daddy. You're going to be okay. I'll look after you.' Xanthe's voice is soft and reassuring. I lift my head from the airbag, feeling stunned. Everything hurts, my head, my jaw, my back.

'Xanthe?' I reach out, my hand falling on the gearstick, then the empty passenger seat. I slump back against the airbag, realising I'm alone. Xanthe's not here, her voice was just an echo in my head: the words she'd spoken to me the night she'd called out from her sleep. I remember stumbling across the bedroom, hitting my foot on the chaise longue, everything still feeling strange and new, and at the same time peculiarly familiar; feeling my way along the landing, guided by the cool touch of the banister and the shimmery moonlight through the cupola, to the room next door.

I hated the way Xanthe had chosen to sleep in the cot. She was far too big for it and had to curl her legs up. She'd smelled of sleep and musty linen.

'I was dreaming about you,' she'd said. 'You were lying down . . . And there was a man standing over you. He was going to hurt you. He was holding a knife. But it's okay, Daddy,' Xanthe had reached up to me, our roles reversing. 'You're going to be okay. I'll look after you.'

Her words had followed me as I'd crept back to Jess.

'What was all that about?' she'd said, turning beneath the quilt.

I'd mumbled something about Xanthe having a nightmare about spiders and told her to go back to sleep. Then, I'd spent the rest of the night, tossing and turning. Spiders – if only it had been that innocent, that benign. The next day, I'd glimpsed a drawing in Xanthe's diary, a drawing creased by my own footfall, so lifelike it sent shivers down my spine: a drawing of me lying on a table. Leaning over me, was a man with a knife.

After that, the memories had come back in nauseating waves: my mother standing on the landing with her feather duster, the agonising pain that had sent me crashing to the floor, the blur of movement and voices and well-meaning smiles.

'Xanthe,' I mumble again as I peel myself away from the airbag, my mouth filling with saliva. I shove open the driver's side door, step out into the drenching rain, puke until my stomach hurts. Wiping my face, I survey the damage. The bonnet is smashed. The passenger side door and the front wing are caved in. There's a crack running the length of the windscreen. Despite my pulsing headache and aching belly, I know I'm lucky. It could have been far worse. It could have been fatal.

I hold on to that thought as I stumble up the driveway, my

legs not quite coordinating with each other, more than once tripping over stones or other debris. A snake startles me on the path – an adder – and I'm taken back to the night we arrived, the snake in the darkness, the oppressive weight of the house as I'd climbed out of the car. And then I realise it's not a snake at all, just a twisted length of shrivelled skin. A snake skin. I step over it and round the corner. The house lunges towards me, a shadow pulling me inwards. The grey arches, the domed roof, the opaque windows. I reach the porch and stand beneath the swinging lantern, soaked through from the rain, catching my breath.

I dig in my pocket and, like a miracle, pull out the key, then I open the front door. A sound. A whisper of welcome. I feel the energy emanating from the walls, the windows, the furniture, the paintings, and I know I'm expected. I know I'm exactly where I'm meant to be.

'Good afternoon, Mr Kennedy.' The voice calls to me from above, drawing my gaze to the cupola, then down to the blocked-up window. Was the voice inside my head, or coming from elsewhere? Does it even matter? Perhaps it was just the distorted sound of the wind and the rain.

I take the stairs slowly, my head heavy, the infernal chatter inside – the waves of self-criticism – dulled if not muted.

Tap . . . tap . . . tap . . .

The sound of a stick striking the floor is a welcome interruption. Not a regular stick, but a cane. A walking cane.

'You don't need to struggle,' says the voice as I reach the landing. 'Someone else is performing the operation today. Our surgeon, Mr Keller, is somewhat unwell.'

Tap . . . tap . . . tap . . .

I pass the room I share with Jess, pass the girls' room, reach the room with the locked door. Except the door isn't locked at all. It's standing wide open and there are wet footprints leading to the open stairwell. Someone has been here already. Recently by the look of things.

'Come in, Mr Kennedy, there's no need to be afraid.'

It's easy to obey the order. To obey the tapping stick. I don't need to be bound or gagged like in my dream.

Tap . . . tap . . . tap . . .

I turn into the stairwell. It's lined with the green wallpaper I've seen before. Peels of wallpaper that look like scratch marks, and here and there, the vibrancy of its original colour. I climb the stairs methodically, one foot then the next. Ahead of me, the flicker of a candle flame disappears to the left, into the attic room. I follow, turning the corner. In front of me is a wooden door with a brass doorknob, embossed with the sign of the snake. I push the door wide: a long low creak. The tapping stops. The silence is accompanied by a cool chill against my face.

'Welcome, Mr Kennedy. Or may I call you, Liam?'

The voice is coming from somewhere inside the room. But although I don't see anyone, I don't panic. I'm a kid again, twelve years old, obeying the rules.

'Lie upon the table if you will.'

Unlike my dreams, there's no one to force me. No one to silence me if I choose to protest. I step inside of my own accord, knowing I have to do this; I have to face the truth. The room is the size of the bare room below. A single arched window casts a mottled light across the floorboards stained with age-old dirt. In the centre of the room is a narrow wooden table, a headrest at one end.

'Take off your shirt, there's a good boy.'

My fingers obey, pulling my T-shirt over my head. I drop it to the floor, to the place where the floorboards are stained darker, redder. Then I climb on to the table, feeling the worn wood beneath me, my neck uncomfortably crooked upon the headrest.

'You sure I won't feel anything?' I say, sensing the surgeon smiling. 'I won't wake up?'

The room shimmers and distorts. I'm in a different space, a different time. A white room in a modern-day hospital. The man who smiles down at me has kind but tired eyes. 'Don't you worry about a thing. See here? See this badge?' He points to a label on his tunic. 'I'm a trained anaesthetist. I do this every day, several times a day. Removing a burst appendix is no big deal. No one ever wakes up. You trust me, don't you?'

'I want my mum.'

'Your mum's going to wait outside while we do the operation. Then she'll be straight back in to see you.'

I nod and close my eyes, not wanting to look, not wanting to know what the consultant and the anaesthetist and the nurses are doing, just waiting for the sting of the cannula and the darkness I know must follow.

I wait. People talk softly around me. The anaesthetist rubs the back of my hand and tells me a story about a dog. There's a cold sharp prick . . .

The next time I open my eyes, I find myself in hell.

I'm staring at the ceiling, at the dirty polystyrene tile that's flapping free, trying to roll my head, trying to flick a finger, trying to scream. But I can't do anything. My lungs can't suck in enough air. My heart can't pump fast enough. My limbs won't move. And the person at my side isn't my mum at all, but a man in a blue gown. Not the anaesthetist but someone else. The doctor, I think. It's the doctor who spoke to me earlier. *The surgeon.* The man leans over me and prods my abdomen, and I want to scream even more, alert the man to the fact I'm awake. Awake and terrified and feeling absolutely everything.

The surgeon clears his throat, adjusts his cap. His eyes are narrow slits. 'Pass me the scalpel.'

No! I scream, but I make no sound. My mouth doesn't work, I can't even move my tongue. *No!*

The pain that follows is so bad I want to die.

I jolt back into the present, into the room in St Cross. The sense of calm and inevitability I'd felt earlier is replaced by a drenching all-consuming fear.

Tap ... tap ... tap ...

The sound is louder than before, heading from the window to where I'm lying, to what I know now is an operating table. My heart gallops. My chest is slick with sweat. I want to get up, but I can't. My legs aren't working. My arms won't move. It's just like the time when I was twelve, my mind working, my nerves feeling everything, but nothing else. *Fuck.*

'Liam, darling.' I'm back in my parents' house, my mother regarding me sternly from the kitchen, hand on a loaf of bread, a knife poised above the crust, ready to cut. 'This has to stop. It's not doing you, or me, or your father any good. We've spoken to the hospital. You know they deny everything. No one wakes up during an operation, not these days. There's no point even fighting it. It's your word against theirs. You were just dreaming, that's all, and it's driving us crazy. It's driving your father crazy.'

Itemque Deas testes adhibens.

I'm back in the sickroom at school, the school counsellor leaning into my space. 'Why won't you talk to me, Liam?' I shrug, clamping up just like my mother told me to do. No matter that I've just had the biggest panic attack of my life, boom out of nowhere. It's all in my head, that's what I keep telling myself. That's what my parents *want* me to believe. They want their twelve-year-old son back, their *normal* twelve-year-old son who plays football and rugby and hangs out with his mates. Not the shell I've become. The disappointment.

Me ratum pro viribus.

It's two years since the operation and I'm standing on a ridge, looking down at the rocks. *Go on, son,* my dad says from behind. *Prove you're a man.* I clamber down, my heart hammering, the height dizzying below. How has a family walk got so out of control? I feel Dad's eyes on my back, willing me to continue as I sink to my hands and knees. *Don't give up, son, whatever you do.* The threat is there in his voice. I take another step, knees scraping the earth, hands grasping the rock face, but I haven't enough grip. I fall, sliding on the sandy rock, screwing my eyes tight shut. When I open them again, I'm stranded, feet wedged against a root, breaking my descent. But I can't go any further. I can't move a muscle. The panic overwhelms me. My ears clang. My heart thuds. *Move it, son.* But I can't. I remain there for what seems like ages, clinging to the root, thinking of my mum and aunty safely on the other path, completely unaware of my predicament. Then Dad throws off his backpack and calls me a wuss. He starts to head downwards, sweat glistening on his forehead, T-shirt stinking. The next thing I see is his sliding bulk, racing past me, his hands reaching out, gripping the empty air.

Judicioque meo jusjurandum hoc . . .

I'm an eighteen-year-old with no prospects, leaping from one shitty job to the next. Drinking is my only escape from the boredom, escape from the fear, escape from the thought of Dad in his wheelchair, paralysed from the waist down after his fall on the rocks. I've convinced myself I'm seriously ill so many times, suffering from various life-threatening diseases, moments away from dropping down dead. But I can't bring myself to see a doctor. I can't even bring myself to open the door of the GP surgery let alone make an appointment. Even the thought of an examination spirals me into panic. And, anyway, I wouldn't deserve help even if I did go asking.

... hancque contestationem effecturum.

So, I drink and drink, until ten years later, I meet Jess and swap the drinking for symptom checking. I tell myself I'm in control, no need to tell my new girlfriend the truth – about the operation, about Dad. The truth is so distorted anyway, so woven into the layers of my character, I don't even know what it is any more.

Tap, tap, tap ... TAP.

I stare at the peeling green wallpaper, fear racing through my veins.

'We won't be using the stick today,' the surgeon says. In my mind, I see a leatherbound cane, marked by thousands of teeth, some small, some large. Men, women and children alike.

'Today, I will be demonstrating my great machine. A machine that pumps just the right amount of anaesthesia to ensure optimum sedation. Gentlemen ...' I look around me and realise I'm not alone after all; the room is crowded with eager young faces, all staring down at me – an interesting medical specimen, something to be prodded and poked and remarked over, '... observe my great invention.'

A machine is rolled forwards. A machine with a long hose and bellows. A machine with a vial of green floral-smelling liquid and a label: *Chloroformium*.

Somewhere at the back of my mind, I remember the brace-let. The bracelet with the silver snake charm. I'd found it one night after I'd awoken from a nightmare. I'd gone into the girls' room to check on Summer and Xanthe, unable to shake the irrational fear that something was wrong. I'd bent over Xanthe and touched her forehead, feeling her warmth. When I'd drawn my hand away, I'd found the little bracelet beside her pillow. I'd known I shouldn't take it, but it had felt comforting in my hand. Comforting, just like those words: *It's okay, Daddy. You're going to be okay.*

Now, I fumble in my pocket until I find it, drawing it out, threading it between my fingers. I tell myself nothing bad can happen, not with the bracelet in my hand. Then, I squeeze my eyes closed, listening to the sounds of the operating theatre. The men chattering. The rustle of a cloth mask pressed over my face. The surgeon sharpening his knives. But, no, not the surgeon, because the surgeon is ill, isn't he? This is someone else. Someone playing a game. A game of life or death.

I listen to the men babbling away, sensing their impatience, their curiosity, their judgement, waiting for the man with the knife to act.

But something puzzles me. Something familiar cutting through the cloying smell of flowers. I open my eyes. 'What did you say your name was again?' The room is almost empty now. The men are gone. There's only the person standing next to me, standing beside the table, looking down. I smell the scent of her – stronger even than the rancid smell of the jacket she's wearing, stronger even than the floral notes of chloroform – the scent of suncream and shampoo.

Summer.

But the voice that sounds from Summer's lips isn't her own,

and the knife in her hand is far too deadly to be one of the ones from the kitchen. 'Massingham,' she says. Her eyes glint as black as the knife's ebony handle. 'My name is James Alexander Massingham. I am the surgeon operating today.'

Extract from a letter by Lord James Alexander Massingham to the Medical and Chirurgical Society of London, August 1848:

The Keller-Massingham Machine

This deceptively simple-looking device, consisting of hose and mask, is far more sophisticated than the inhaler currently making the rounds, and will undoubtedly transform the modern practice of surgery. The optimum dose of chloroform is administered by means of bellows that can be operated by a bystander. The dose can be set according to the recipient – man, woman or child – and is quickly administered resulting in the required heavy sleep.

54

***

Jess

I run through the wood, across the garden, playing over Robbie's words in my mind, how the house takes children away, all the deaths and accidents that shouldn't have happened. Out of breath, I pause for a heartbeat on the terrace. A black cat arches its back, it's fur gleaming with rain, before skittering away. The missing third cat? *Animals know, don't they?* But I don't have the time to investigate. Instead, I throw wide the back door and step into the kitchen.

It's deserted. The knife Xanthe cut herself with is still on the table. The floor is still dotted with blood. The debris from the hurried lunch I'd shoved in a carrier bag is still scattered on the workstation. But nothing moves, no cats, no children. The stillness is almost eerie.

I make for the hall, catching sight of my reflection in the

glass panels of the kitchen door. For a heartbeat, I stare at the dishevelled woman before me – the bags under my eyes, the worry lines across my forehead.

There's a movement high up. One of the servant bells sways gently, then faster until the clapper hits the bell with a deafening ring. I stumble backwards, hitting the table. The bells don't work. I know they don't work. But this one is ringing: the bell to the operating theatre. I run to the door and yank it open, calling for Xanthe, then run into the hall and up the stairs, counting in threes. One, two, three . . . one, two, three . . . one, two, three. Reaching the landing, I turn left towards the locked room. But it's no longer locked. The door stands wide open and the light from the window is cool and grey. The room is as bare as I'd seen through the keyhole. Not a bedroom at all, but a vacant space with a single wooden chair. To the left is a short flight of steps, leading to another open doorway. I tiptoe across the room, as if afraid to wake whatever is in here, and peer inside. It's a stairwell devoid of natural light, and the smell of it makes me gag. A thick smell of dust and mice.

I cover my nose with my hand, breathing into my palm, and climb, tracing the green wallpaper with my fingertips, using the light from the room below to see my way. The smell grows stronger as I near the door at the top of the stairs, the door leading left into the attic room. I twist the doorknob, expecting resistance, but the door swings open easily, as if it wants me to walk inside, as if I'm meant to be there. I find myself in an almost empty space, dimly lit by the arched window on the left. The other window – the window overlooking the hall – is bricked up. The air is thick with oppression, but it's not the smell that bothers me now, it's what I see.

It takes me a moment to take in the scene, the drawing in

Xanthe's diary flashing through my mind: *the room, the table, the man*.

Liam is lying in the middle of the room, stretched out on a simple wooden table. Behind him, standing motionless with one hand raised, is Summer.

'Summer,' I gasp, but she doesn't respond, doesn't even lift her head. She's wearing the light-grey jacket with the brass buttons over her T-shirt and shorts, and suddenly I realise where I've seen the jacket before, where I've seen the gleaming buttons. The portrait in the hall. The Victorian gentleman with the walking cane. And then another image spins through my mind: the cold stone in the church, the intricate carved letters. *Lord James Alexander Massingham.*

I dart forwards, grasping my daughter around her waist, pulling her backwards. Something drops from her hand – the one that was raised – and clatters to the floor. I stare at it in horror: a glinting silver blade with an ebony handle.

55

SUMMER

———— ❧ ————

I fall backwards, coming to, aware of Mum shouting at me, shaking me. 'Summer. Wake up. WAKE UP. You're sleep-walking.'

'What?' I blink in confusion, taking note of my surroundings. I'm in a room I don't recognise. An almost bare room with pale green wallpaper, lit only by the sunlight that trickles through the window, struggling to reach us through the rain. I look down and see a knife at my feet. A knife I've never seen before, but which reminds me of the knives in the surgeon's medical case in the museum. A knife with an ebony handle.

I kick it to one side, hearing it slide and then thud against the leg of the table.

'Mum?' I struggle to speak, releasing myself from her grasp, shrugging off the jacket. Outside, lightning cracks through the sky. 'What happened?'

'You must have fallen asleep.'

'No, not asleep. I—'

'You were asleep.' Mum's voice is determined. 'You must have sleepwalked here. Your father. We,' Mum's voice breaks, 'we have to wake him up.'

It's then that I see Dad lying on the table before me, lying in some sort of stupor. His chest is bare and gleaming with sweat. His feet dropped over the edge make him look lifeless.

'We have to get him out,' Mum says. 'We have to move him. Now.'

I nod. Yes. We have to get Dad out. Whatever happens, we need to leave this room. I can feel it. I can feel the danger, though I don't understand it. There's no physical threat apart from the knife – the knife I was holding when Mum grabbed hold of me. I remember it now like a nightmare returning. I know I wasn't sleepwalking, just something like it. I remember climbing the stairs. I remember looking out of the window. I'd seen my reflection in the glass. Except it hadn't been my face looking back. It had been the man's. The *other* man. Not the man in the portrait on the internet, but the man in Harry's photographs, the man who talked to me in the mirror. *James Alexander Massingham.* I'd known it by the eyes. I'd also known I couldn't fight him. I'd not had the strength.

Dad shifts on the table, knocking the headrest to the floor.

'Dad!' I try lifting him up, tugging at his arm, but he resists, too heavy. *Gravibus somnum* – heavy sleep. 'Please, Dad. Try.'

He opens his eyes and groans. Mum grabs both arms and drags him from the table. He stumbles forward, finding his feet. He looks a mess. His hair is stuck with blood. A bruise has formed over one eye.

Suddenly, the walls are flickering with light. A warm, yellow glow: oil lanterns. I can smell them, the air thick and suffocating.

'We have to hurry. Now,' I scream.

Behind us, I hear a noise, faint at first, then louder, louder. The squeak of wheels rolling across the floor. I help Mum to pull Dad to the top of the stairwell, too scared to turn around. It is slow, exhausting work, and we pause to catch our breath, looking down the narrow flight of steps. There are more lights flickering against the walls, the wallpaper now a vibrant, toxic green. It would be so easy to fall, I think, fear racing through my veins, to go tumbling to our deaths. 'Move your legs, Dad. *Please* move your legs.'

He buckles, catching his foot on the edge of the topmost step, falling sideways, slumping against the wall. The wallpaper rips, a strip curling around him.

'Liam.' Mum's voice rings with fear. Can she see the lights too? Can she hear the wheels on the floor, the rolling thud-thud of something being dragged towards the stairs? 'You have to walk. We can't hold you any more.'

He lunges forwards, one step in front of the other, finding his rhythm to the room below. 'Nearly there,' Mum says, encouraging him as we half-run, half-lurch out on to the landing. The landing is ice-cold. I'm shivering uncontrollably. I can still hear the squeak and thud of the thing behind us – the machine – but it's muffled, fading. But I know it can't be this easy. The house will try to stop us. *Openings.* My eyes swivel to the rooms below, the front door, the kitchen – the only ways out. *Openings.* Yet, I've a horrible feeling there are no openings.

Just traps. 'Come on,' I shout, taking the stairs, one hand on the banister, the other on Dad.

Tap ... tap ... tap ... The noise fills the house. An explosive, sonorous beat.

Mum's eyes dart upwards as we reach the hallway. I'm suddenly aware of the eyes in the paintings, the eyes of the sculptured saints on the newel posts. Looking, judging. I see the portrait of the man I've only glanced at before. The man with the same eyes as the photos on Harry's screen.

Tap ... tap ... tap ...

'Where's Xanthe?' Mum suddenly stops in her tracks, her expression clouding over. 'I was looking for Xanthe. I've lost her, haven't I?' She starts to cry and I realise I've never seen Mum cry before. Mum's always so strong, so sensible; she holds the rest of us together. I see her reach for her neck, feeling around her collarbone, and I know what she's looking for: the St Anthony that isn't there. 'I've lost my little girl.' She darts to the foot of the stairs.

'No,' I scream. 'Don't go back up. Whatever you do, don't go back up there. The house is trying to trick you. Xanthe's in the wood.'

'What?'

Mum swivels, one hand on the banister, her eyes shining with hope.

It all comes back to me: leaving the cottage, taking the path through the wood. I'd seen a dart of movement between the trees, the familiar outline of someone running. Only my head hadn't been working right thanks to the mushrooms. I'd been still coming round.

'The wood. Xanthe's in the wood. She's sheltering from the rain. She's in the Wendy house. I saw her earlier. I saw her with the little dog.' I let Dad fall and grab hold of Mum instead, pulling her towards the kitchen, towards the safety of the back door. A rumble of thunder and the hallway darkens. A moment later, the lights are everywhere. I can feel the heat of them cutting through the cold. The glow of oil lanterns lighting the way, but not towards the door. *Upwards.* They're drawing us back upstairs.

TAP ... TAP ... TAP ...

There's a shrill cry. I stop where I am near the kitchen door, heart pounding, eyes drawn to the roof. Breaking glass. Splintering wood. And then I see it, as if in slow motion, a cascade like a waterfall: thousands of glass shards, deadly as knives, raining down from the domed roof into the hall.

Letter translated from German into English by Verity Laurence, the day before her death, 18 August 1974:

<u>To whomever finds this letter,</u>

This is the testament of Charles Keller, surgeon, written Sunday, 19 August, in the year of Our Lord, 1848. As God is my witness, these words are the truth.

Since my youth I have attended to my work with the utmost diligence, spending hours in the dissecting room, studying the mechanisms of the body and the modern methods of surgery. My thirst for medical knowledge remains insatiable, my desire to help my fellow men unwaning. Like a musician who places his bow precisely upon the strings, so have my hands held the knife with the greatest care. For is not that the task of the surgeon? To do no harm.

In my thirty-second year, I suffered a terrible setback. My wife died leaving me bereft and unable to focus in my usual manner. It was also at this time that I was offered the position of resident surgeon at St Cross in Suffolk. The invitation came from one Lord Massingham, an old acquaintance who had, for many years, sought my counsel in London for his own poor health.

How the weeks and then months seemed to fly at St Cross. The needs of the poor who came from all over the county were many. A surgeon, I soon devised, had been sorely needed. Tooth pullings, cauterising of wounds, amputations, the removal of tumours, bloodletting – such was my work. His lordship encouraged me in my endeavours, taking a keen interest in the new advances in surgical practice. He was, as I have intimated, not a well man himself, suffering from a moral affliction sustained in his youth, and one he took great pains to disguise. But the signs of syphilis were increasingly obvious. I came to understand that his care of the poor was his way of atoning for the sin so aggressively manifest in his body.

Over time, his interest in my work intensified to the point of obsession. He pressed me to perform greater and deadlier procedures, his own hands often bloodied as he assisted me with ever-growing fascination. Together we cut deep into the stomach, or removed eyes, or drilled into heads. For a while, I was taken with his fever myself. Surgery, it seemed, had come of age, and perhaps, at last, I was doing some good. But the deaths were many, indeed they were increasing not decreasing. Chloroform was deadly if administered in too large a quantity. In too small a quantity, the patient would wake upon the table, screaming. If only a machine could be designed to administer just the right amount, thus freeing the surgeon to focus fully on the task at hand.

His lordship was taken with the idea. Could this not be the great invention that would make our names known, our lasting legacy? It was a simple design, constructed by his aid, John Harrison: a wooden box on wheels, bellows, a pump, a nozzle, a mask that would be fitted to the patient's face. But alas, the machine proved more deadly than human hands. Many succumbed to its effects, for the pump would fail without warning as if it had a mind of its own.

I began to see Massingham in the machine itself. It was as if the two had become one, his obsession entwined in the many revisions. What matter that he was an ill man, a sullied man? With Harrison's help, he would live for ever through his great machine!

He brought to me more and more patients – the weakest, the most vulnerable. Children, many motherless or from the workhouse, whom he knew would not resist. He encouraged me to perform operations that were previously impossible, his desire to prove himself a righteous man greater than his reason. And all the time, the sickness of Massingham grew inside me as if the man himself was a pox of the mind.

But today I awoke and saw sense for the first time since arriving in Suffolk. The matron, Mrs Harker, knocked upon my door, and informed me that the children who had escaped from the house yesterday had now been found. They had drowned on the beach where they were hiding, their little bodies washed up on the rocks. Had Massingham pursued them there? Had they tried to escape him when the tide rolled in? Had they paid for their disobedience?

The truth may never be known, and yet, I know this in my heart: there is blood upon my hands, for what Christian man can excuse himself because of another? Just as I failed Clara in her final days, I have failed in my task as surgeon and must pay the price. There is only one path left for me, one path that draws me fearfully and yet joyfully to the window of the operating theatre, a path of brightness and everlasting light.

Clara, my dear Clara, is that not what you believed? That light awaits us all?

God forgive me,
Charles Keller

56

APRIL 2024

⸻ ∞ ⸻

Jess

I watch my daughters walk away from the semi-detached house on the outskirts of the city, Summer trailing her book bag, Xanthe clutching her latest artwork. It's my new routine, watching them walk to school rather than accompanying them to the end of the road, another step towards allowing them freedom. But I know I'll wait here until Xanthe turns into the primary school gates at the bottom of the road, and Summer's safely on the bus to the high school in the middle of town.

Out of the corner of my eye, I see Angel cocking his leg against one of the shrubs on the edge of the lawn.

'No, Angel,' I say, trying not to mind the mess as he digs a hole, spraying muck with his back legs. I look up at the house, a regular town house, the smallest on the street. Something catches my eye in the window of Xanthe's room and my heart freezes.

It hasn't been an easy few months, but every day we're making small steps towards a semblance of normality. Summer is self-conscious about the scar on her left cheek, the result of the falling glass from the roof at St Cross. In hospital, she'd confided in me about the bullying at school, the bullying that seems to have stopped since the start of the new school year, perhaps out of sympathy. The scar will fade and is far less obvious than Summer thinks it is, but it will take time to build back her confidence and self-esteem. The scar, I have long suspected, is just the tip of the iceberg.

Liam's injuries were more challenging. The glass shards had buried themselves deep in his leg, severing several tendons and requiring significant surgery. But far worse than the physical injuries was the mental anguish triggered by going into hospital, and the problems revealed there I'd known nothing about. Post-traumatic stress disorder or PTSD. It sounds simple put like that, a label to explain why Liam is the way he is, but beneath the label, it's complex and messy. It's going to be a slow recovery, facing the childhood trauma he's suppressed for so long, accepting what his parents wouldn't allow him to accept, the way they'd convinced him that *he* was in the wrong, the way he'd blamed himself for what happened later to his dad, but the counselling is helping and Liam's even started writing again.

Yesterday, he told me he'd had news from Callum. I'd hoped we'd never hear from Callum again, not now Liam's paid him back what he owed, topping up what little he had left with a bank loan. The gist of Callum's email was this: the infirmary has been condemned. The domed roof was rotten through and through, and it was only a matter of time before it collapsed – the storm in August last year had finally seen to that. On closer inspection the house wasn't fit to live in. The mould was extensive, a result of the underground stream that ran beneath the house to the lake in the wood, and could potentially have proved fatal to whoever was living there. The green wallpaper was laced with arsenic, a popular but deadly dye from the nineteenth century, the vibrancy of the colour lost over time. The very air we were breathing was poisonous, even hallucinogenic. Liam had laughed as he'd said it, but I'd read between the lines. *It was more than bad air, wasn't it?*

I think of Mrs Clarence, gone to live in a residential home in Scotland. I hadn't realised she was Verity's older sister – a half-sister much older than herself – not until Callum let that slip in his email too. I often wonder how much she knew about the house, whether there was a reason she kept the attic door locked. How much she told Callum we'll probably never know. Liam's hinted that Callum told him something on that fateful day – apparently, they spoke on the phone – but he can't really remember, and I haven't pressed him either. Some memories are better left buried after all.

Now, I stare at Xanthe's bedroom window, the words *bad air* running through my mind. Is there bad air here too?

There's a child standing behind the glass, looking out at the street. A child about the same age as Xanthe dressed in what looks like an old-fashioned nightgown. A girl with long hair and a pale, jaundiced face. I take a step forwards. What on earth is a child doing in Xanthe's room? There's no one in the house apart from Liam, who's asleep after another restless night. What I'm seeing is impossible.

A chill wraps itself beneath my coat and for the first time in a long time, I feel watched. I used to hate that feeling in the house, the feeling that someone was always following me, that I couldn't escape. Now I feel it again, singled out, as if it's just me and the child and no one else around.

Someone honks a horn at the bottom of street. Angel looks up and barks. I count to three in my mind. *One, two, three*, and then as if to test myself, a solitary *four*. When I look back again at the window, to my relief there's nothing there. The window is empty, just the reflection of the house on the other side of the road.

I drag a hand through my hair, pulling knots with my fingers. I need to take care of myself too. I'm always so busy looking after everyone else. How long was it since I went shopping for myself? Treated myself to coffee and cake? Went for a decent walk? Not since August, I think. Not since we left the house.

Sometimes I awake in the dead of night and remember the attic room, the knife in Summer's hand, the blade so bright it was almost translucent. Those nights are the worst. I can't get back to sleep after that. I've given up trying. Instead, I tiptoe across the landing and sit in Summer's room until the dawn, watching my daughter sleeping peacefully, knowing there's no harm while she remains there. Sometimes I think I see a light dancing on one or other of Summer's shoulders, protective and safe. I know deep down its just my eyes playing tricks, but it's comforting seeing it there, a tiny, dancing guardian angel, as I play and play with the St Anthony around my neck – the St Anthony necklace I'd found tangled at the bottom of our suitcase. I must have dropped it there by mistake when I'd unpacked our things that first day in St Cross, the day, I reflect, I'd started to lose my daughters. But they're back now. We're all back together, even if the restless nights are leaving me empty and exhausted. Even if I'm so busy being a mum I can't remember who else I am.

I bend down, ruffle Angel's fur, feeling the familiar nips of excitement as he circles my fingers.

It's time to start again.

THE OPERATING THEATRE
NOTICE FOR PATIENTS

No one must enter the operating theatre
unless summoned by the surgeon.

57

AUGUST 2023

—⦿⦿⦿—

Xanthe

Xanthe wakes up in the ice-cold room on the first night of the holiday. Even in the darkness, the room looks green, a green mist rising and falling, whispering to her between the bars of the cot. It takes her a moment for her eyes to work right, to look through the mist to the bed by the window where Summer is sleeping.

She doesn't want to get out of the cot, but she knows she has to. She can hear the children calling to her from the walls. It's the reason she chose this room. She'd known the other children were here as soon as she'd stepped inside and seen the cot and the huge cupboards. The other children wanted to play with her, at least that's what she'd thought. But now, she realises they don't want to play at all. Or rather, they don't want to play *here*. The children want her to let them out.

Xanthe, help us.

Their whispers are so loud, she's scared they'll wake Summer. But Summer doesn't stir. She climbs out of the cot and pads about until she finds her sandals and cardigan, then she tiptoes to the bedroom door and opens it. The whispers rush out, grateful murmurs floating down the stairs, congregating in the hallway. She feels so very cold; it's even worse here on the landing. The moon is shining through the roof window, pale and indistinct, brightening the walls and the dark, dark paintings. She knows the children want her to follow, to let them escape completely, but, she's too frightened to move. Because it's not just the children in the house. There's someone else.

A man.

She can feel him, just as she can feel, rather than see, the children. The man is in the room next door to theirs, the one Mummy said was Mrs Clarence's bedroom.

Xanthe, Xanthe, Xanthe.

But it's not the man who calls out to her, it's a child. She sounds so frightened, so desperate, and Xanthe immediately works out why: the man has trapped her.

She presses her hands to her ears, her mind flitting to Easter last year, to Mia Williams in the old school. The old town before Mummy and Daddy decided to move. She'd known Mia was ill. She could *feel* the illness floating towards her in waves across the classroom, making her head tingle. Eventually, unable to keep it to herself any longer, she'd told Joe and Megan about Mia, and they'd told the teachers. After that, it had all gone horribly wrong. The teachers had told Mia's mummy, and

Mia's mummy had told the doctors and the doctors had made Mia take all sorts of medicines, which had just made her sicker.

The last time she'd seen Mia, they'd sat in their old garden and eaten jam sandwiches together. It was clear that Mia didn't need the doctors any more. She hadn't been to school in ages, but she wasn't as small as she had been, and although they weren't best friends, Mia had made herself at home and eaten more jam sandwiches even than Xanthe.

But, that evening, Mummy had sat her down and told her Mia Williams had died in the hospice the night before. Xanthe hadn't said anything. In a strange way, she already knew. She'd stared out the window and watched the wasps hovering over the plate of uneaten jam sandwiches, and when she'd gone outside to fetch the plate in, she'd found Mia's silver snake bracelet on the lawn.

And that's why she knows she has to open the door. She knows that the child inside is dead like Mia, but she needs her help anyway. Just like Mia had tried to give her a message with the bracelet, to tell her she was okay, that she knew Xanthe was sorry for telling Joe and Megan, that she forgave her; that the doctors didn't make her sicker, they were only trying to help.

She tries the doorknob and finds the room is locked, and it's too dark to see where a key might be hiding. So, instead she creeps to their parents' room and feels for Daddy's phone on the floor where he always leaves it, beneath the bed. She punches in his passcode – her date of birth – and switches the phone to torch mode. Then, she creeps back on to the landing, the torchlight falling on the cabinet.

It doesn't take Xanthe long to find the key pushed beneath the sheets in the topmost drawer. Later, she'll put the key back somewhere safe, not the cabinet but on top of one of the dark paintings in the hallway. Later, she'll also follow the children to the Wendy house in the wood. It's the same place where she'll drop Daddy's phone – the one she'll eventually return and push into the back pocket of his jeans; where she'll hide the dog; where she'll run to when Mummy has turned her eye on the sand dunes, scared that Angel will be frightened alone by himself with the ghost children.

But now, she puts the key in the lock. The whispering is louder. The whispering from the hallway. The terrified whispering from the child inside the room.

Xanthe, Xanthe, Xanthe.

'I'm coming,' she calls back, her head tingling. The mist is so thick she can barely see, just the torchlight picking out the door and the shiny brass knob.

She uses two hands to turn the key. The door swings wide.

ACKNOWLEDGEMENTS

Books don't get any easier to write and this one, written in a particularly chaotic and challenging year, required a lot of tea and encouragement.

Many thanks to my three children, Wilfred, Ebah and Taliesin, and husband, Steve, for always believing in me. I no longer know what it is to write in silence, but I wouldn't have it any other way. Thanks also to the two waggy tails in my life, Digit and Ben, who made me walk for hours across the Welsh countryside, providing much-needed breaks.

I struck lucky with my editor, Rosanna Forte at Sphere, and my agent, Cathryn Summerhayes at Curtis Brown. Rosanna is absolutely brilliant at what she does and my books are always better because of it. Cathryn is my tireless champion, keeps me going when I need a boost, and gives the best hugs. Thank you both. Thanks also to the teams at Sphere and Curtis Brown for the many things you do to bring books into life. And thanks to my copy-editor, Howard Watson, for once again being spot on with suggestions to improve the text.

Whilst this is first and foremost a work of fiction and any historical errors are my own, I owe much to the Old Operating Theatre Museum and Herb Garrett in London for inspiring me to delve into the murky world of Victorian surgery. Thanks also to Dr Pete for helping me brainstorm ideas over a pint or two in Lincoln.

Thanks to my writing group, Asha Hick, Sarah Daniels, Emma Clark Lam and Joanne Clague. We've been together for eight years which is crazy. Books, wine and writing are obviously a winning combination. Thanks to my parents, Sue and Darrol, for your continued love and support, and to my sister and fellow author, Heather Davey, who helped me through my writing wobbles. I am *so* excited to be publishing this book in your debut year.

Thanks to all my readers. If you've enjoyed this book, please take a moment to review it. Reviews really make a big difference.

Finally, a note about myself. I have suffered from health anxiety and a fear of medical places for over twenty years. It's one of the reasons why I wrote this book. If this is also you, know you are not alone. After all, we are all haunted by something.